"I promised I' She's carr, Backing out wasn't an option."

Ian, in decisive mode, usually turned Sophie's legs to Jell-O and her mind to mush, but just now her brand-new groom sounded like a man who'd looked the executioner in the eye and gone under a blunt blade.

He'd lied to convince her to marry him.

She was nearly sick right there on the floor. As she slammed her hand over her mouth, Ian and Jock came around the corner. Unlike most of his overly buff colleagues, Ian was lean and long, agile and—right now—furious.

As if she'd lied to him. As if *she'd* married *him* under false pretenses.

"What are you doing?" Shock made his voice too harsh to recognize.

Swallowing, she said, "Hiding behind a marble column, listening to you end our twenty-minute marriage."

Dear Reader,

Welcome back to Bardill's Ridge, Tennessee, and to the Calvert family, whom you met in September's *The Secret Father*. Are you ready to meet Sophie and her new husband, Ian?

Sophie's not so sure she's ready for Ian. She marries him because she believes they both want to create a family for their unborn child, but seconds after the wedding she hears him telling his best friend he *had* to marry her because she was carrying his child.

She confronts him. He admits "forever" sounds impossible to a bodyguard who's never been home long enough to own a pet, but he's determined to try. He's so determined he follows Sophie to Tennessee, where he uses her family against her. They remind her how unhappy she was because of her own parents' divorce, and Ian convinces her he cares enough to make their marriage real. But can she see forever now that he's broken her trust?

I'd love to hear what you think. You can reach me at anna@annaadams.net. Come back to Bardill's Ridge in March when Sophie's cousin Molly Calvert falls in love with a man who couldn't be more wrong for her.

Best wishes,

Anna

The Bride Ran Away

Anna Adams

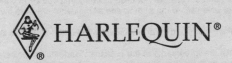

HARLEQUIN®

TORONTO • NEW YORK • LONDON
AMSTERDAM • PARIS • SYDNEY • HAMBURG
STOCKHOLM • ATHENS • TOKYO • MILAN • MADRID
PRAGUE • WARSAW • BUDAPEST • AUCKLAND

ISBN 0-373-71168-9

THE BRIDE RAN AWAY

Visit us at www.eHarlequin.com

Printed in U.S.A.

To Steve, again, always—the sweetest love I've known

Books by Anna Adams

HARLEQUIN SUPERROMANCE

Coming Soon: THE PRODIGAL COUSIN*—
Harlequin Superromance #1188 (Available March 2004)

*The Calvert Cousins

Don't miss any of our special offers. Write to us at the
following address for information on our newest releases.

Harlequin Reader Service
U.S.: 3010 Walden Ave., P.O. Box 1325, Buffalo, NY 14269
Canadian: P.O. Box 609, Fort Erie, Ont. L2A 5X3

CHAPTER ONE

ICE TAPPED AT THE stained-glass windows like a million small fingers begging to come in as Ian Ridley fought an unfamiliar compulsion to run. On an unseasonably frigid Tuesday night in April, on the outskirts of Washington, D.C., he waited at the altar with his best man and a minister he hardly knew.

He licked his lips. They dried again immediately, despite the damp that seeped from the cold stone floor into his shoes and slowly climbed his body. This wedding was all wrong, a church even Sophie didn't know and a minister who'd agreed to perform their hasty ceremony because the bride-to-be was pregnant.

Ian could have asked the minister he'd guarded a few years ago to marry them, but he'd been ashamed to admit he'd gotten Sophie pregnant. In a world where he made life-or-death decisions every working day, he hated to lose a friend's respect.

His whole life had been an effort to prove he was tough enough, good enough. Even smart enough.

A professional bodyguard, he'd once been barely able to protect himself. As an eight-year-old, he'd been bullied at boarding school, where his parents had sent him to free up their time. Strength was a front he'd willed into existence the first time one of the older, bigger boys, had shoved his head in a toilet.

Sophie knew nothing of his past. They didn't know each other well enough to commit to a regular dinner date, much less marriage.

Take their ceremony. He'd wanted to stand before a justice of the peace. She'd wanted the wedding to "feel real." One of her friends had suggested this church, and Ian had gone along with the idea. A formal service in unfamiliar surroundings, performed by a minister who'd be grateful they were doing the right thing.

He'd asked Jock, his colleague on several jobs, to be his best man. Sophie had planned to have a maid of honor, but she'd uninvited her friend at the last minute as if she, too, was ashamed of their quick wedding. Ashamed she was marrying him?

Shame was no way to start a marriage, even if marrying Sophie Calvert was the worst mistake he'd made with her yet.

From the moment he'd first seen her, he'd wanted her, pure and simple. Maybe not so pure. He'd wanted her, knowing he was the wrong man for her. She believed in big, protective families like hers. He knew no such animal.

His folks had not only kept him away at boarding school, they'd lived a life quite separate from his. For him family meant Christmas break or brief summer holidays. Not every-day-in-the-same-house contact.

He'd wanted a different kind of family for himself. He'd even been engaged once. That woman—who'd wisely jilted him—was now the wife of an insurance salesman in Reading, Pennsylvania, and, last Ian heard, the proud mother of three. After she'd suggested he eat his engagement ring, he'd stopped pretending to be a man who could stay home long enough to own a cat.

His work required him to live on the fringes of other people's lives. A bodyguard since the age of twenty, when he'd been assigned to drive a Supreme Court Justice's nanny to and from work, Ian had fought for fourteen years—with weapons and his bare hands. He'd avoided fights when walking away better served the people he protected, and he'd willingly stepped in front of almost every weapon smaller than a rocket launcher. To keep his clients safe, he'd shoved fear to the back of his mind where it couldn't hurt anyone.

Tonight, the prospect of marriage to Sophie froze the blood in his veins.

She'd helped him forget who he was. Unable to resist the mutual, blinding desire, he still distrusted its staying power. He'd met Sophie in Bardill's Ridge, Tennessee, when he'd accompanied a client, publishing tycoon James Kendall, to the town to visit his daughter, Olivia. When Ian had left with Kendall, Sophie had seemed almost relieved.

Back in Chicago, he hadn't anticipated the hunger he felt—for the scent of Sophie's hair, for the endearing curve of her joyful smile, for the need of him that glittered in her green eyes and made him feel as if he mattered to her more than anyone else.

He'd resisted that hunger for a month. On his first free weekend, he'd located Sophie at her town house in D.C. Two months after that, he'd shown up at her office, and they hadn't gone very far before she'd parked her car on the side of a dark road.

Another month later, she'd come to Chicago, and they'd eaten, slept and made frantic love in his bedroom for the first three days of her weeklong stay. Two more months and he was waiting in front of an altar, trying to become a father to the baby he'd created with Sophie.

He cared for her. Whatever raged between them wasn't just sex, but Sophie and he had changed too quickly from strangers to lovers to parents.

Jock nudged his arm. "Here she comes."

Candlelight brought her out of the shadows at the back of the church. Ian's gut tightened.

Her dress caressed each curve of a body that nearly brought him to tears. Her stomach already rounded by their baby's growth, she made him want to be better than he was, capable of promising to be with her when their baby came. He wanted to give his family what he'd gone without all those lonely boarding-school nights—love that went deeper than providing practical necessities.

She met his gaze, her eyes anxious, and he felt again the emotional coil of desire. He'd wanted Sophie in her grandparents' apple orchard. He'd wanted her in the reception area of her OB/GYN office, surrounded by at least six women in different uncomfortable stages of pregnancy. He wanted her now, as urgently as he needed his next breath.

"Ready?" Jock asked.

Hell no. As if she could hear Jock and sense her husband-to-be's less-than-heroic response, she lowered her head. Ian nodded.

Love was supposed to last. Lust burned itself out. How could he tell which had him in its grip?

Sophie carried no flowers and, staring at her hands, clamped together yet shaking, she moved down the gray flagstone aisle without music. They'd skipped all the usual trimmings except her dress and his black suit. As he watched Sophie approach, Ian could almost taste her skin. He tilted his head to catch the memory of her nighttime whispers. What secrets curved her mouth now even as doubt shadowed her eyes?

They hadn't discussed what would happen after they left this church. He couldn't just quit the only job he'd ever known and take up knitting. They hadn't talked about her medical practice either. He slid moist palms down his thighs.

Tonight's wedding had been their only goal, another sign that two people who'd planned each step of their lives until they'd met were bad for each other. His mind ought to be on the vows he was seconds away from making, and that summed up his problem in a nutshell.

Sophie had robbed him of his ability to distinguish priorities. With her practice in D.C. and his job in Chicago, they'd lived too far apart to get serious. They'd both known it. Neither had said so out loud. He hadn't explained that he'd learned to protect other people because he'd once been unable to protect himself. She needed roots. He had none.

He didn't want to hurt her. The salient facts all ran through his head, months too late, as she stopped at his side.

"Take each other's left hands," the minister said.

Ian silently forced Sophie to meet his gaze again. As she stared at him, her eyes filled with a strange conflict of trust and reservation. Her warmth seduced him as he rubbed his thumb over the fragile bones of her hand. Lifeblood pulsed beneath her skin.

He was wrong for her, but he wasn't capable of walking away. Even if they were about to ruin their lives, he'd make Sophie Calvert his wife.

"Shall we begin?" The minister searched Sophie's pale face and then Ian's. "I assume you've both soberly considered what you're about to do."

Ian nodded again.

SOPHIE HAD SEEN almost six hundred patients through pregnancies both easy and difficult, deliveries both simple and dangerously complicated. Not one of those women had prepared her for the horror of experiencing morning sickness in a silk wedding dress that had looked alluring three weeks ago. With her twentieth week of pregnancy straining the seams, she felt like a huge white balloon on the verge of exploding.

The ceremony had passed in a blur. She still couldn't think as she made her way into the bride's room.

Three weeks earlier she'd anticipated Ian's lustful appreciation as he watched her float up the aisle. Instead, she'd avoided looking at him, half-fearful of his dismay as he contemplated marrying such a bloated pregnant woman. Her snug dress foretold a load of responsibility for both of them.

She'd glanced at him as the minister asked them to take each other's hands. After one peek at his flat blue gaze, she'd avoided him until he'd tilted her chin to kiss her.

That chaste kiss continued to confuse her as she struggled out of the dress. Nothing about their short relationship had been chaste. He was a fever that constantly burned in her.

Bending over, she undulated to work the dress over her head. And nearly passed out.

Grabbing the nearest chair, she caught her breath and gripped handfuls of material to slowly inch the dress over her shoulders. This wasn't the wedding she'd dreamed of.

She'd imagined arguments with her mom, who would have become uncharacteristically maternal and tried to control everything—the wedding dress, the catering, even the setting—Bardill's Ridge where her father lived, instead of D.C., where her mother had moved after the divorce. None of these would have mattered to her dad and her grandparents, her aunts and the cousins who'd stood in as brothers and sisters all Sophie's life. They'd only want the opportunity to surround her with the unconditional love she craved tonight.

She hadn't invited any of them, even though she'd wanted her cousin Molly to be a bridesmaid.

She'd been concerned that her family's presence would make Ian feel bad about his parents' absence. Rachel and Alex Ridley had turned down their son's invitation, claiming they couldn't get home from Ireland—where they'd retired for the golf—on such short notice.

Sophie would pay for the slight to her own family. Her mother would assume she'd planned her "elopement" just to get back at her parents for their divorce. The Calvert side, her father's family, just plain expected invitations to all big events.

She smiled to herself, remembering the day she'd met Ian at one of those occasions. She'd been home to celebrate her grandparents' anniversary, and he was there as a bodyguard to her cousin Zach's father-in-law.

The moment she'd met Ian, she'd wanted him. He'd felt the same. Their undeniable attraction frightened her, but it was all they had. Passion and good intentions and a marriage certificate now duly signed and witnessed.

Initially, she'd been reluctant to tell Ian about the baby, but he had a right to know, and when she couldn't avoid telling him any longer, he'd immediately wanted their child. He'd assumed they'd make a life together, a family. Everything he'd said had persuaded her he'd live or die for the child, whose only outward signs of life were her thickening waistline and her inability to digest anything with more taste or aroma than water.

He'd understood she wanted commitment that might lead to real love. She had no interest in simply being rescued. They'd been honest. No one could get hurt.

She yanked her dress. With the sound of a tearing seam, it flew over her head and fell into her open hands. She peeled off her hose and turned to stuff them into her bag. Taking stock of her green face in the tiny mirror the church provided for its brides, she blamed the harsh lighting for her horror-movie pallor.

No amount of crackers, no wishing morning sickness was all in her head, ever slowed the spin cycle in her stomach. "Damn," she said and then prayed she wouldn't burn in hell for swearing in church.

She pulled on jeans she hadn't worn in two months and stared down at the parted zipper that refused to fasten. Her sweatshirt covered the problem and made her decent enough to go hunt for a washroom—which would have made a handy accoutrement for the bride's dressing room.

Shivering in the damp cold, she tried each door along the corridor. At the sanctuary's arched entrance, the eerie silence made her feel as if she was trespassing. Feeling sicker by the second, she tiptoed inside and crossed in front of the altar. They'd put the groom's room over here somewhere, and Ian probably hadn't needed extra time to wrestle out of his suit. He'd be in street clothes by now, and she'd just as soon he not get another glimpse of his perennially sick bride.

Nothing a palette full of makeup couldn't repair once her stomach settled.

She eased around a cool marble column, still fighting waves of nausea. She was a strong woman. She just had to be stronger than morning sickness.

"Man, you're sweating like a marathon runner. You shouldn't have gone through with the ceremony. Sophie's going to kill you."

Brought up short, she recognized the voice. Jock, who judging from that statement knew her better than Ian.

"I promised I'd marry her. She's carrying *our* baby. Backing out wasn't an option."

Ian, in decisive mode, usually turned her legs to Jell-O and her mind to mush, but just now her brand-new groom sounded like a man who'd looked the executioner in the eye and gone under a blunt blade.

He'd lied to her to convince her to marry him.

She was nearly sick right there on the floor. As she slammed her hand over her mouth, Ian came around the corner, his expression wary. He knew he'd screwed up. Unlike most of his overly buff, iron-pumping colleagues, Ian was lean and long, agile and—right now—furious.

As if she'd lied to him. As if she'd married him under false pretenses.

"What are you doing?" Shock made his voice too harsh to recognize.

She eased her hand just beneath her lips. "Hiding behind a marble column, listening to you end our twenty-minute marriage."

"I don't want to end—"

"I need a bathroom. I'm gonna be sick."

He pointed down the hall, and she ran, her feet smacking the marble. Just in time, she flung open the door and bolted into a stall. Thank God Ian wasn't chivalrous enough to follow.

At last, with her stomach as empty as her heart, she braced her hands on the stall and stared at the tile through watery eyes. Longing to sink to the floor, she plucked up enough pride to stay on her feet.

Her idiotic tears were a side effect of being ill and pregnant and hormone ridden. Nothing more. It wasn't as if she loved Ian.

She stumbled to the pedestal sink and twirled a squeaking handle imprinted with an old-fashioned *H* for hot. Nothing happened, but *C* for cold worked.

The hinges on the washroom door squeaked in a long, low protest as someone slowly entered. *Someone*. Who was she kidding? Ian couldn't pass up a chance to lope to the rescue.

Bending farther into the sink, she splashed cold water on her face. Long legs in black gabardine appeared in her peripheral vision. Straightening, she turned off the water and met his I-dare-you-to-face-the-truth stare.

"This is the women's room."

"Men's, actually." He jerked a thumb toward the far wall where three urinals hung in a row. "I'll bet the faucets work in the women's room."

His dry sense of humor had seduced her from day one. Not tonight.

She grabbed a paper towel that protruded from a black plastic holder, jumping as she glimpsed her mascara-streaked face in the mirror. "Where's Jock?" She wiped her hands and concentrated on sounding as if she didn't care, as if nothing too terrible had happened.

"He went home."

She took refuge in patting water off her cheeks. "Ian, I won't stay with you."

"You heard something I never would have said to you."

She considered pulling the sink off its pedestal and throwing it at him.

He licked his lips as if he couldn't get enough saliva and went on, "I have to protect you and my child, and I agreed to something I actually didn't believe in, but I am committed."

"You don't get it." She had believed they might come to love each other, and she'd only married him because she'd thought he'd felt the same.

Turning away from him, she ended up in front of the mirror, facing their reflections. Neither of them looked familiar.

He was clearly scared. She was too furious to think straight. And whacking him with a bathroom sink might not help.

She held on to the anger, a nourishing, healthy rage that would keep her on her feet and make her a strong mother for her child. Since her own mother had left home, Sophie had vowed never to need anyone. "I didn't ask you to marry me. I don't want your pity, and I despise your sense of duty."

He reached for her, his long fingers curling into nothing as she moved away. "I protect people. Why wouldn't I protect you?"

She grabbed the edge of the sink. Unfortunately, it didn't budge. Misunderstanding her urge to brain him, he moved closer and pressed his palm against the small of her back.

"Are you still sick?" he asked.

She shook her head, unable to speak over a lump in the back of her throat. Who knew the truth could hurt this much? She wanted—no, she needed to be far away from Ian Ridley. She danced out of his reach again.

"You only had to admit you didn't want the baby. I'm twenty-nine years old, and I'll take care of myself and my child."

"*We'll* take care of our baby," Ian said. A sound from outside the rest room turned his head toward the door. On the alert, twenty-four hours a day.

Even so, she had a nasty surprise for him. "We're not staying together," she said as she wadded the paper towel into a ball and shoved it through the flap of the waste container. "If you'd told me the truth an hour ago, instead of telling Jock after we were married, we wouldn't be in this mess. Now we're going to have to find a way to annul our marriage when I look pretty damn consummated."

"Sophie, don't swear in church." He smiled, no doubt to persuade her he was teasing, but the twist of his mouth looked more like a bloodless threat.

"I'd like to commit murder in a church. I'm only holding back on the off chance that killing you here would make you eligible for sainthood."

She had to run before she started to reconsider. Start saying things like. *We can try to make the best of this. We care about each other. Our child matters most. We can be parents. We can make marriage work.*

Claptrap. He'd only married her because she was pregnant. She refused to be rescued. "I'll never thank you for doing the right thing."

He looked confused, but that was because he knew next to nothing about her. She'd caused her own parents' divorce because she'd come home early from school one day and walked in on her mom making love with a stranger, and then she'd asked her father who her mother had been wrestling. When he'd confronted her mom, Nita had tried to lie. She'd accused Sophie of making up a story, and her father had tried to believe his wife. Wanting to believe lies was her family's flaw.

They'd failed, of course, and her parents' split had been unbearable for Sophie. She'd felt abandoned.

She'd never been vulnerable in another relationship until she'd let herself care for Ian. If he'd only married her because she was pregnant, he didn't care as deeply, and she couldn't allow herself to be the one with the most to lose. Better to leave Ian before he left her.

She clasped the mound of her belly with both hands. God help her, she was willing to sacrifice her child's chance at a family to save her own soul.

"My feet are cold." She pointed at her cranberry toenails as if she had no deeper care. She pulled open the door. "Get in touch if you want to know about the baby," she said over her shoulder. "E-mail me, or call my office."

She reached the hall before he caught a handful of her sweatshirt. "Wait a minute. I made a mistake, okay?"

"Several." She tugged, but he held on tighter.

"Tell me you're more sure than I am," he said. "You only looked twice at me because your aunt wanted time to talk to James Kendall alone. Otherwise, I was, probably still am, just a big dumb ox to you."

"I don't care about your job." Now she was stretching the truth. She had assumed bodyguards were all brawn, no brains. She freed herself from his grip and shook her shirt back into place. "It's true. At the anniversary party Aunt Beth wanted me to occupy you for an hour, so she could talk to James Kendall alone, but I've wasted a lot longer than an hour on you." What more did he want from her? She'd reshuffled her life and her patient schedules to see him in Chicago. "I meant what we said in that ceremony." Honesty forced her to expand. "Maybe I thought for a second that I didn't know you well enough to marry you, but I planned to work at our marriage. It wasn't some temporary penance."

"Like it was for me?" He tried to catch her hand, but once more she slipped away. He obviously didn't know how to handle an antagonist he couldn't drop like a bag of fertilizer. "I don't care what you heard me tell Jock. I'm serious about our marriage, too. I wish we'd done things the right way, but—''

''You mean with a string of dates and a proposal and a virginal wedding and eventually a baby? You can't have that with me. I don't know what happened between us, and I must have been in a daze until tonight, but I'm not binding myself to a man who's doing me a favor.''

He curved his hands around her shoulders, his grip tight but not painful—as if he knew just how much strength to use. ''What you overheard was panic. I want you and our baby.''

She shrugged, and he tightened his fingers instinctively to hold her. She gripped his wrists and pushed him away. ''I—don't—need—you.''

Something shattered behind his eyes. She'd managed to hurt him, but she couldn't afford to care and she didn't look back.

The rest room door swished closed behind her and this time Ian stayed put. She made straight for the bride's room and finished dressing, though her arms and legs seemed to refuse input from her brain.

She gritted her teeth, determined not to cry. Weeping over a bodyguard who'd simply done his job would be ludicrous and humiliating.

Yanking the zipper on her jeans as high as it would go, she wrapped herself in her coat, wadded her wedding dress underneath her arm and fled through the nearest marked exit. The frigid night reminded her of Tennessee. The mountains that held Bardill's

Ridge in their safe embrace would be full of mist in the morning.

She yearned to be there.

Because she was sliding on the icy sidewalk, she crunched through the frozen grass, hurrying around the church to her car. She opened the door, tossed in her dress, hitched up her jeans and climbed in.

How many times had Gran asked her to work at the "baby farm," a clinic and spa for pregnant women who wanted time out and pampering before they delivered their babies? Sophie had always resisted. Though she loved her family, she'd wanted to be the only Calvert she knew, not a minor member of the teeming crowd.

What had she been trying to prove? She shivered, planting one frozen hand between her thighs as she used the other to insert the key in the car's ignition. Her baby needed family—not a dutiful father, but a family whose special gift was unstinting love.

She stared at the church doors as her car shuddered to life and her breath hung in the icy air. She could deliver a baby one-handed in the middle of a typhoon. She always carried a well-stocked medical bag in her car, but she knew nothing about raising a child. Maybe she needed family, too.

Time to see if Gran still wanted an OB/GYN who had no idea how she'd managed to get herself pregnant.

CHAPTER TWO

IN THE MORNING Sophie forced herself to stop and rethink her next move. Getting pregnant had taught her everything she needed to know about following impulses.

Two weeks passed while she considered the consequences of staying and of going home to her family.

She used her caller ID to screen Ian's calls. He showed up at her office one cool evening, and she brushed past him. He waited on the porch at her town house that same night for twenty minutes before he gave up. He'd broken her trust, and she refused to forgive him.

She wasn't proud of her own behavior. One slip, a lie that even she could see he'd meant for the best, and she felt justified in taking their baby far away. Maybe a more trusting woman would be able to meet Ian halfway, but she had to assume that lying for a good reason might be something he did as a habit.

Her longing for the people she could depend on grew with each hour.

She'd felt safe in Bardill's Ridge. Her family interfered, but they knew when to back off and when to race to the rescue. And they understood moderation. No one threw away their own lives and freedom—as Ian had been so damn anxious to do.

Still, she made no effort to see a lawyer to end her marriage. She blamed her lethargy on total exhaustion. A pregnant woman couldn't deliver a patient's baby at three in the morning and then rush out to arrange a divorce before her office hours began.

Another lie. If she really wanted the divorce, she'd find the energy.

She hardly felt married. When the certificate arrived in her mailbox, she tossed it into the rubbish bin before she remembered she might need it to break her legal bond to Ian.

At the beginning of her third week of married life, the baby moved. That first little flutter gave her plenty of energy and a reminder that she wasn't on her own anymore. That had her deciding on her next move.

She rearranged her patient schedules, and while she was at it, brought up the topic of taking over her patients for good with the colleagues who had agreed to fill in for her.

Next step—talk to Gran. She dialed, and the receptionist immediately answered.

"The Mom's Place. May I help you?"

"Leah, this is Sophie Calvert." She cleared her throat of its nervous vibration. "I'd like to make an appointment with Gran."

"I'll put you through."

"No." She tried to stop Leah, but too late.

"What's wrong, Sophie?" her grandmother asked. "Are you ill?"

"Not at all, but I need your undivided attention for an hour or so."

"Here? At my office, I mean." Her grandmother's tongue clicked. "Something's wrong or you wouldn't have asked for an appointment. Tell me before I imagine the worst."

"Don't imagine anything. I just need advice." She didn't want to discuss the possibility of working with Gran over the phone. "Don't mention it to Dad, okay?"

"Sure. Ethan won't be mad at me if I hide the fact you're coming home."

Sophie laughed. "I'm depending on you. Will you send me back to Leah, and tell her when you'll have an hour free?"

Two days later she flew to Knoxville, rented a car and drove into the blue-and-green Smoky Mountains beneath a bright sun. Up here spring was slower to take hold. At the baby farm, she climbed out, sniffing the faint sharp scents of young honeysuckle and azalea. Their slightly spicy fragrances sat well with her iffy stomach. That had to be a good omen.

Sophie tucked her hands into the hem of the sweater that had felt too warm in Knoxville but disguised her pregnancy nicely. She mounted the granite steps that led to the resort's entrance. Overhead, tall pines swayed against their maple and oak neighbors, rustling in hushed whispers.

A group of six young women were sprawled in chairs around a sunny table on the terrace, listening to a lecture on quadratic equations. The fees paid by customers who came here looking for extra care, or maybe just time off to pamper themselves during their pregnancies, went to help local teenagers who found themselves in trouble with no real support systems. These girls studying math on the wide cobbled patio would attend college if Greta Calvert had any say about it.

Now that her gran had her mitts on them, these young women were like part of the family.

Inside the glass-fronted lobby, Sophie waved at Leah, who nodded toward Gran's office. Sophie took courage from her own determined footsteps on the polished granite floor. She knocked at the door, nervous for the first time in her life about facing Gran.

She'd have to tell her family about the baby soon. She glanced through the glass at the outdoor math class. She didn't have to worry about being disowned, but no one would be pleased at her stupidity.

Had Ian told his parents? She pushed the question out of her mind. The answer was no longer her business, and she couldn't afford to think of him. She had to get her own life back on track.

"Sophie, is that you?"

Just hearing Gran's voice made her happy. After turning the knob, she leaned around the door and smiled. Her heart swelled and her throat felt too tight to speak. She searched the shadowy room for the vigorous mainstay of her life. "Gran?"

A white-haired woman with a desk as tidy as her pragmatic approach to life put her telephone back into its cradle and hurried through the slashes of sunlight across the thick carpet.

With arms outstretched, Greta Calvert uttered a sound that resembled a sob. Sophie choked back tears of her own as she stepped into her grandmother's hug. Gran would love her no matter how big a mess she'd made.

"Honey, honey..." Greta Calvert sang and cried. Holding on to Gran's deceptively frail body, Sophie let the tears fall for the first time since her wedding.

Everything in the room told her she was home. Her father had built Gran's desk more than twenty years ago. The pictures marching side by side on its glowing honey-colored surface, stacked in lines up and down the walls, slotted unsteadily in corners on the bookshelves, offered a history of Calvert family endeavors. Graduations and baptisms, weddings and rowdy conversation shared across crowded dinner tables. Sophie scanned them all, swimming in memories, hearing echoes of the stories her dad and aunts and uncles told.

Gran kept every gift given to her in love, wildflowers, now dried, her resort guests had collected on their walks up the ridge, and paintings the Calvert grandchildren had done. She even stored pens and pencils in a clay mug Sophie had made in Girl Scouts.

As Sophie composed her emotions, Gran leaned back. Surprisingly tall, she met Sophie eye-to-eye. Her affection eased Sophie's second thoughts.

Everything would be okay. She'd made a couple of dumbfounding mistakes, but Gran had heard stranger stories, and she possessed an unlimited capacity for love. Where Gran forgave, so would the rest of the Calverts.

"Tell me your deep, dark secret, Sophie," Gran said teasingly, as if she didn't believe it could be anything serious.

Just that quickly Sophie got scared. Gran had always known when she'd sneaked an extra cookie or waded in icy streams before winter left the mountains, but a baby put such trivial things as cookies and wet jeans in perspective.

Best get to the point. "Are you still open to having me join you in practice here?"

Happiness flashed in Gran's eyes. Sophie pressed her fingers to her mouth as relief washed over her, but then Gran sobered with a wary question. "Why?"

That wasn't supposed to happen. "I thought you'd be pleased."

Gran urged Sophie onto the sofa and then settled beside her, smoothing a soft, printed skirt over her knees. "What's wrong?" she asked again. "Not more than a few months ago I begged you to come home, but you said this town was too small. You knew too many faces here. You were happy in Washington among strangers.''

Her spin made Sophie smile. ''I doubt I put it like that.''

Clearly not in the mood for a joke, the other woman waited.

''I'm ready.'' Sophie looped her hair behind her ears, trying to look as if she had nothing to hide. She hated disappointing her grandmother. ''I've had enough big city.''

Mysteriously, it was true the moment she said so. As her grandmother searched her face, she realized she might not have been so open to Ian if she hadn't grown lonely. Gran folded her hands in her lap and still said nothing.

An uncomfortable tingle darted up Sophie's spine. ''Where's my rip-roaring welcome?''

Gran traced her skirt's paisley pattern with a delicate, pearl-tipped fingernail. ''You're lying. I never thought I'd see the day.''

Sophie squelched a groan. If only she'd inherited Gran's talent for culling truth from a lie. ''Can't you take my word for it?'' A momentary twinge of sympathy for Ian troubled her as a headache began behind her forehead. She was asking her beloved grandmother to trust her—exactly what she'd refused to do for Ian.

''You're running from something. Or someone.'' Cool, capable brown eyes pinned Sophie to her side of the sofa. "It's that man, isn't it? That Ian." She screwed up her face as if his name tasted bad.

Surprise jolted Sophie. "You don't like Ian?"

"He's not right for you. Not some man who wanders the world without a mat to call his own. I saw you liked him. I should have butted in. I was afraid he'd hurt you, but I trusted your good sense."

Sophie remembered what had kept her out of Tennessee all these years. "Why do you all do that? Ever since the day Mom left Bardill's Ridge, every female in our family, including the 'marry-ins' has tried to save me from myself. None of you believed in my ambition. You were all waiting for me to come to no good because Mom didn't know how to be a mother."

"Nita may have left, but you had Beth and Eliza and me." Beth and Eliza were Gran's other two daughters-in-law. "We should have pretended you had a normal family and you didn't need us?"

Sophie gripped the trim on the sofa cushion so tightly the beads bit into her palms. She'd proved their worst fears about her. Before Ian had come along, she'd been heart-whole and content with her job and her Washington friends. She'd thought she was too smart, too careful to get hurt. But the truth was, she'd never cared enough about any other man.

Even now, three weeks after their sham wedding, she missed Ian, and missing him felt irrational. She'd compromised her pride for him. She'd punched holes in all her best walls of defense, and he'd betrayed her trust.

"Sophie, I can't offer you the job unless you tell me why you want it. I need another doctor—and I want a good one like you—but I'm after someone who'll take over, someone I can depend on."

"Why take over?" The family all assumed Gran would work here until they carried her out feet first. She'd promised she was quitting a million times before. Sophie felt a chill.

"Nothing's wrong. Don't jump to conclusions," Gran said, and kneaded Sophie's hand. The same touch had comforted Sophie all her childhood. "You remember I promised your grandfather I'd retire on our anniversary?"

"Yeah, but no one believed you."

"Grandpa did." Gran laughed, a touch embarrassed. But Sophie knew she had the courage to take the necessary steps. "If I'm not working here, someone as good as I am has to take my place."

"You're sure that's all?"

"Positive." Gran kissed her forehead. "I've done good work and I want it to continue. If you take over, I could help you until you know the place the way I do."

Gran wasn't arrogant. She'd trained at Vanderbilt when most Tennessean young ladies were learning how to sew a fine seam. Despite getting married and soon giving birth to her first son, she'd finished at the top of her undergraduate class and stayed there all the way through med school. Not one of the powerful men in charge of those male-dominated institutions had ever given her a break.

She deserved an honest, long-term commitment from her granddaughter. It wouldn't be fair to take temporary shelter in the mountains. "What if I think it over to make sure?" Sophie asked. "I don't want to waste your time with training and then let you down."

Gran pulled back, satisfied. "Take a few days. Are you staying in town?" She stood, ushering Sophie to the door. She was a busy woman. She made time for family, but she didn't dawdle. Sophie took no offense. She'd learned her work ethic from her grandma.

"I'm on my way to Dad's." She'd decided to tell him about the baby now. Lucky thing Ian was too far away for her father to set an armed posse on him. She'd be lucky if her dad didn't turn the posse on her.

Gran reached for a file from the top of her in-box. "Listen to him for a change. Ethan's a smart man."

"You say that about all your sons."

Gran slid on her glasses and smiled over the half lenses. "Bring him up to dinner tonight. Grandpa will want to see you, too."

Sophie doubted food would be one of her dad's priorities after she dropped her bomb. He'd be too busy trying not to let her see she'd disappointed him. "I'll call if we're coming."

"Fine." Gran nodded at the door. "I'll walk out with you. My next appointment should be waiting."

Gran darted around her as they exited her office. Sophie took her time, studying the spacious waiting room as if she'd never seen it before, the easy chairs squatting, fat and comfortable, in front of the far windows, the hefty ottomans just waiting to prop up a pregnant woman's swollen feet.

She could work here. She already felt her share of family pride in the place.

Several patients glanced up from their magazines. Gran's patrons were usually the only strangers in town and even they couldn't maintain their anonymity forever. They obviously wanted to know who she was.

The pressure mounted. This was for real. These women would be her patients, and she'd be leaving an office full of women in Washington—her first patients in her first practice.

Sophie headed for the door. She'd often thought of how it would feel to work here, but she'd never imagined scurrying home to Bardill's Ridge, pregnant and conveniently married. She flattened both hands on her stomach.

She'd manage fine with the patients, but how would she survive her grandmother's on-the-job mothering? It might be a good idea to end her marriage before Gran discovered it. Greta Calvert believed in family enough to think Sophie should give Ian a second chance.

And the other citizens of Bardill's Ridge? Sophie's mother had left town with a man who wasn't her husband. Sophie could see the heads nodding. *Wild like her mother.*

Nita had never possessed the instincts that guided some moms. Marriage was a piece of paper she could simply burn, and when she had a date, her daughter was usually an inconvenience.

Sophie understood that her mom just didn't "get" motherhood. And while Sophie loved her, she didn't want to be like her.

In D.C., her soon-to-be unmarried state wouldn't provoke a ripple of interest, even among her own patients. Bardill's Ridge would consider such an attitude too progressive to abide within the city limits. Nevertheless, she wasn't about to protect her reputation with a marriage that existed only on paper.

With one hand covering her belly, Sophie pushed open the glass door. She'd be a good mom. Her dad, her cousin Zach, her grandfather and Molly's dad, Uncle Patrick, would be strong father figures in her child's life.

"Sophie?"

Her grandmother's startled voice spun Sophie around on the threshold. Gran's eyes were fastened on the hand covering Sophie's stomach.

Stricken with guilt and regret, Sophie dropped her hand to her side, allowing Gran to study the bulge of her stomach unimpeded.

When Gran looked up, her gaze was a mixture of

happiness and confusion and regret. After a moment she turned away.

"Wait." Sophie could barely speak over her own despair. She'd hurt one of the two people whose love and respect meant more to her than anyone else's.

"Tell your father," Gran said curtly. "And then we'll talk. I just don't want you or a child to be hurt, Sophie."

Sophie stanched the urge to defend herself. She nodded and turned to descend the granite steps.

The weather had changed. The Mom's Place looked less rosy under a now cloudy sky, and a chill breeze mussed her hair. Even the girls had taken their books inside.

Sophie glanced toward her car and froze. Ian had materialized, seemingly out of nowhere. Long and lean, feet crossed at the ankles, he was braced against her car. Her first thought was that he had to be cold in his light camel-colored windbreaker. Then she saw anger in his blue eyes. His mouth was a thin slash of pain.

She walked toward him. "Why are you following me?" she asked. She couldn't control the desire she felt at seeing him, but then stiffened against it. Her body was no longer running her relationship with Ian.

"You're my wife. You're carrying my child. I want to be with you. Take your pick."

"You've prepared a series of stories?" She had to get Ian out of here before Gran saw him and called for family reinforcements. "Let's start with the one where you want to be with me. You're saying that because you think that's what I want to hear. We can drop that whole 'wife' concept, because we're getting divorced. That leaves you thinking you owe something to my baby." She halted, prepared to shove him aside to reach her car door. "You owe the baby nothing. I'm the one who depended on a condom." She was allergic to the Pill, but she'd never explained that to Ian. Who'd have thought she'd need to? "This is my child."

"Mine, too." His dogged gaze devoured her. He might be looking for changes in her body, but his regard turned her heart into a battle drum.

She longed to throw him off her mountain. Her sense of his betrayal was still so strong she wanted to call her cousin Zach, the local sheriff, to chat with Ian about stalking.

"Even if you plan to be the baby's father, you have no business near me until I deliver." She fished her keys from her purse and held them up. "Will you move?"

He straightened, his skin taut across his cheekbones. "I made a mistake." Tired and anxious, his voice softened with a plea that unsettled her. Ian never begged.

"It's too late." She lifted her keys again.

He ignored them. "I'm sorry." She could hear the ache in his tone. "I don't know how to be a husband, but I'll do my best if you give me a chance. How can I convince you?''

"Make me forget you lied about wanting to be one." A horrible truth dawned on her. She actually wished she could forget what he'd said at the church. "I trusted you."

"I didn't lie." He held himself still, his only movement the rubbing of his right thumb against his index finger. One night as they'd lain in a moonlight-painted bed, he'd told her that finger, unnaturally straight from middle knuckle to nail, tingled in cold weather.

She'd never asked how he'd damaged it. Why hadn't she? Why hadn't he told her, anyway? None of that mattered now.

"If I thought I couldn't be with my child any other way," she said, "I'd pretend I wanted you, too."

He opened his mouth, then closed it again without speaking. She suddenly found herself focusing on it. She remembered how it felt beneath hers, moist with passion, seductively destroying that common sense her grandmother had mentioned. She'd glimpsed a future in his kisses. She'd believed in him because she'd thought no one could make love as they had without sharing more than just physical need.

"Sophie." He curved his hand around her forearm. "When you look at me like that…"

He dragged her closer, but it wasn't hard. She forgot to resist. His breath whispered against her lips.

He paused, his seemingly defenseless gaze almost

asking permission. She could break away if only she could remember how to make her feet move. She might have been dangling in midair. She'd made another mistake, putting herself within his reach.

She was about to make a worse one. She closed her eyes and sighed in absolute, physical relief when Ian brushed his lips over hers.

A sane inner voice commanded her to run. She made herself deaf. She hadn't touched him in nearly three weeks, and she'd pined for his hands on her, his kiss, his beating heart pressed against her seeking palm.

This was their strongest bond, and she needed him in ways she didn't begin to understand. He closed the chilly space between them. Sophie slid her hands into the hair at his nape and pulled his head down to hers with strength born of inexplicable longing. Holding Ian was more like coming home than driving up the mountain road had been.

He tightened his arms as if surprised to find her in them. His warm hands bunched her sweater. She breathed in as his fingertips traced her spine, her rib cage, the curve of her breasts.

A moment's shame flitted through her as she welcomed his touch. She'd run from that church because she hadn't wanted to need him. Letting him hold her like this, giving vent to her desire, put the lie to that, but she'd stopped feeling whole without him.

A groan slipped from his mouth to hers, melting her against the car. She arched, claiming him, offering herself. But somehow sanity reminded her where they were.

"My gran," she said against his throat, unable to make herself look over at the resort's open windows.

At once he released her. They were both breathing hard. He caught her left hand. "Where's your ring?" She'd never heard his passion-thickened tone in public.

Bemused, she shook her head.

"Your ring, Sophie." Repeated more harshly, the question finally penetrated her thoughts.

"Nothing's changed." In case he didn't understand, she widened a bland gaze, trying to force him to believe her. "You touch me—I want you. Apparently, I'd make love to you anywhere, anytime, but nothing else has changed, either. I don't trust you, and I can't live with you."

"You can." He rubbed his finger again, his thumb trembling in time with her heartbeat. "We'll learn to trust each other."

"Not in front of our child. I want to do motherhood right."

He reached for her again. Thank goodness he expected her to give in as if she possessed no will of her own, because she caught him off guard, taking his wrists to drag him away from her car door. He didn't seem to be a guy who struggled with women. He was easy to move.

She opened the door and jumped inside, completely unashamed of her healthy fear. Not of him—

of herself and her apparent addiction to him. She wasn't on her own anymore. Time to break bad habits.

She started the engine. Ian planted his hands on his hips, the picture of a gunslinger.

She reversed the car, staring straight into his unforgiving gaze. He'd find her before long. He had a gift for hunting down his quarry. She'd never hidden from anyone before, and how far could she run in Bardill's Ridge?

DUST SETTLED ON THE GRAVEL that had skidded from beneath Sophie's tires. Ian took stock of the faces at the windows of the resort. Somewhere among those reproachful women, Greta Calvert no doubt wished him dead.

He couldn't blame her. He'd screwed up Sophie's life, and he'd certainly want to destroy anyone who ever hurt his child.

He turned away, unable to go inside to reassure Greta, since he had to follow Sophie. Or anticipate where she'd head next. To her father. If she planned to move back to Bardill's Ridge—and that had to be her plan—she'd tell Ethan Calvert about the baby.

Ian already knew the way. If only he'd kept his big mouth shut after the ceremony, they'd be telling her father together. She shouldn't have to face him alone. A sense of guilt made him hurry to his own rental car. Sophie loved her dad, respected him, worried more about his disappointment in her than even

Greta's. Her parents' divorce had driven her to want to please Ethan.

Ian quick-stopped through a couple of four-way intersections on the country roads before he reached town. Three red lights later, he had to slow for traffic at the square. Some of the local farmers had brought early wares from their greenhouses and set up stalls beyond the wrought-iron fence that protected the grass. Their customers upped the small-town traffic.

By the time he reached Ethan Calvert's house, Sophie and her father, a tall man in jeans and logger's plaid, were standing in front of the barn-workshop that rose higher than Ethan's clapboard house. The pair were clearly at odds. Ethan leaned down to say something that made Sophie grimace. Ian didn't think. He just launched himself from the car to protect his wife.

Ethan and Sophie turned at the sound of his slammed car door. Sophie tried to stop him with a hand up, looking like an impatient crossing guard.

"Ian, no. This is about our family."

"I'm part of your family now, Sophie."

She widened her eyes in an urgent, silent appeal that he keep quiet about the wedding. He shook his head. He'd rather saw off his own arm than hurt her again, but she'd made their child the spoils of this fight.

Ethan interrupted their unspoken battle, moving in front of his daughter.

"Dad." She grabbed his flannel-covered arm. "It's as much my fault as Ian's."

"Maybe you don't know how we handle your kind of man down here." A threat of bodily harm quivered in Ethan Calvert's voice.

Ian restrained a ripple of anticipation. Physical danger he could handle all day long, but Sophie had him in an emotional trap, and he had to be smart. He strode to her side. "Tell him everything."

"I have," she lied. A blush drew her father's closer attention. "You've already forced me to break the news about the baby to my dad on the doorstep because I knew you'd hare over here. Now leave us alone."

Ian glanced from father to daughter. Ethan must know how much his divorce had hurt his daughter. He'd surely want Sophie to give wedded parenthood a chance to provide her child with two parents together in the same house. Especially when the baby's father wanted to do the right thing—as detestable as the concept of responsibility might be to Sophie.

Behind them, another car climbed the hill. Ian turned, as did Sophie. It was her cousin Zach Calvert in a Bardill's Ridge patrol car. Her grandmother must have rushed to the telephone.

The sheriff parked beside Ian's car and climbed out. The slow-moving Southern lawman had a talent for kicking the shit out of bad guys. In his frustration, Ian thought a fight sounded good, but it wouldn't guarantee his welcome into the family.

Another cousin, Molly, climbed out of the passenger side. She'd been one of the Calverts Ian had investigated before he'd allowed James Kendall to set foot in Bardill's Ridge. The more the better he thought now.

"Sophie—" Zach settled his cap on his head "—do we have a problem?"

Without waiting for her answer, Molly pushed between her cousin and Ian, her glance setting him on par with a mugger. Molly's parents had abandoned her, and she'd lived on the street until Sophie's Aunt Eliza and Uncle Patrick had adopted her. She knew more about bad people than Sophie.

Molly's abandonment put his own in perspective, and sympathy would have led Ian to be kinder about shutting her down, but Sophie showed no favorites in her habitual resistance to being helped.

She fended Molly off. "I'm fine," she said. "I don't know what you two are doing here."

"Gran." Ignoring Sophie's resistance, Molly looped her arm around her cousin's shoulders.

"Wait a minute." Ethan towered over the two women. "I don't need my mother or my nephew and niece to help me protect my own daughter." Planted at his daughter's side, Ethan looked strong enough to do the job.

"What are you protecting her from?" Ian ignored everyone else.

The sheriff moseyed into the fray. "Our grandmother suggested you manhandled Sophie in the parking lot at the baby farm.''

"Don't call it the baby farm,'' Sophie and Molly said at the same time.

"Gran hates it,'' Sophie added, though it was what she and everyone else called the resort. She didn't want Ian to feel he was part of the family.

"Whatever you call the place,'' Zach said, maneuvering to get in Ian's face, "she said this guy had his hands all over you and I should find out why.''

"Oh, for…'' Sophie twisted out of Molly's grip and swung away from her relatives. "Gran didn't want to believe what she really saw. And, Molly, I'm sorry to tell you she called you because she thinks I've turned into a bad girl, and you might have some pertinent advice.''

Her cousin's pale skin colored, clashing with her dark red hair. "Why does this family believe we should talk about such personal things in front of just anyone?'' She pinned Ian with another pointed glance.

"You just do,'' he answered, "but I envy your honesty.'' He was all set to confess his and Sophie's secret. He'd use every advantage to force a second chance with her and his baby. He waited for her to speak up. The trees around them clicked their branches as if they were counting off the seconds. He knew Sophie was willing him to keep silent. With deep regret and a gut-sucking fear she'd never forgive him now, he did the dirty work. "I need to talk to my wife about our child."

The other Calverts turned as one to gape at Sophie. She seemed to sink, but Ian caught her, willing to lie on the ground for her if she'd get over this and start rebuilding their fledgling life. She found her strength and shrugged him off.

"You knew I was begging you not to tell them." She flexed her fingers as if she'd like to shove him down the mountain.

He glanced at her father. "I'm sorry, sir."

Ethan clenched his hands into fists as shock glazed his eyes. "I don't get it, Sophie. What do you want me to do?"

"I want you to slide him under the biggest saw you own."

Zach took a step. Ian tensed, ready, willing and pretty much aching to fight.

Sophie must have sensed a hint of his desperation. She held up one palm, breathing deeply. "Cut it out." She focused on Ethan, who looked appalled. "I need time to figure out how to handle my life. Dad, I'm sorry."

"Don't apologize, Sophie." Ian knew he was begging, but didn't give a damn. "I didn't tell him to hurt you."

"He's my dad. I'm his daughter. How'd you think he'd feel?"

"I love you." Ethan reached for her, but she backed into Ian. "It's just that your mother—"

"I'm not Mom."

Her voice, ragged with guilt and the fear that she might just be like her mother, forced Ian to act. He pressed her to his side. "Sophie's done nothing wrong. If you want to blame someone, blame me, but we're both trying to make the situation right if you'll stay out of our business."

"You invited them in," Sophie said. "Now they'll give us hell until we agree to try staying married."

"I know," he said.

Rage exploded in her eyes. She tried to break free, but he pulled her hand against his chest and held her. She had to understand his pounding heart wouldn't lie, and he wouldn't expose such weakness to anyone else on earth.

"I'm sorry," he said. "I just want what's mine. I'm fighting for my child as hard as you are, but I'm fighting for you, too. I was raised by headmasters and upperclassmen. I'm going to be this baby's father, and you and I have to do something about our marriage. Can't you just forget what I said to Jock?"

"No." She shook her head, but her sadness was palpable. "I keep asking you, what's changed?"

"I quit my job, and I told my boss not to assign me anywhere else." He still hardly believed he'd done it, and she sucked in a breath. "You understand that kind of commitment, Sophie? Can you match it?"

She shook her head, looking dazed. They were both so tied to their jobs she knew exactly what his leap of faith meant. Commitment. She sighed, shaking her head. "I wouldn't have given up my job," she said as if she didn't even realize the words were coming out of her mouth. "You'd do anything..."

Her father brought his fist up to his chin, rubbing as if he were trying hard not to take a swing at her husband. Ian shifted Sophie out of range and prepared himself to take the punch.

She placed her hand over her father's fist without taking her eyes off her husband. "I guess Ian fits in well enough with the rest of us. He's already an expert at spilling his guts in front of a crowd."

CHAPTER THREE

"ARE YOU—" Ian broke off, aware of their audience. Had Sophie just agreed to start over? In silence broken only by the squeak of the weather vane slowly revolving on her father's tin roof, he stared from Molly to Ethan to Zach. They eyed him and then looked at one another.

Ethan recovered first. "Sophie, I want to send this guy to the hospital right now, but think a minute. Maybe he's talking sense."

With a pained expression, she closed her eyes and Ian stifled an urge to laugh. He'd flown to Bardill's Ridge, convinced he'd lose her for good the second a Calvert laid a loving hand on her. Instead, her family was driving her toward him.

Ethan glared at him in a not-so-veiled warning before he went on. "Sometimes I wonder what would have happened if I'd fought harder to keep my family together. Sophie, your mother was unhappy. I never wanted to hear about that. All that mattered to me was that she'd cheated on me and done it recklessly enough for you to find out." His face reddened. "At least listen to Ian, if he's this serious about trying to make your marriage work. I'm not asking anything more of you.'' Ethan wrapped an arm around his niece. ''Come on, Mol. Zach, why don't we give these two some privacy?'' He herded them toward the patrol car. ''Soph, use the house. I'll be in my shop.'' He paused, his boot heel scraping through the gravel as he eyed Ian with unmistakable threat. ''Where I'll hear if you yell for me, Sophie.''

''I don't need to talk.'' Sophie looked like her father, gazing at Ian with mistrust.

''Your child's dad disagrees.'' Ethan tossed the reminder over his shoulder as he continued to assist Zach and Molly to their car. ''But you shout and I'll be with you in a heartbeat.'' He nodded at Ian. ''Toting my power tools.''

Ian nodded, a sign of respect. In Ethan Calvert's place, he'd also wonder if he was handing Sophie over to the devil.

''How do we know we're not forcing her into a bigger mistake?'' Molly twisted free of her uncle's hold. ''He might not be a decent guy.''

Sophie planted herself beyond anyone's reach. ''Thank you, everyone, but don't worry about me. I've made all the mistakes I plan to.'' Her glance stabbed Ian. ''And I'm perfectly capable of making him see sense one last time.''

Molly studied Ian's face as if she saw all the way into his mind. Finally she turned to her cousin. ''Do what you really want. Don't just think about how good it would feel to throw him out today. Imagine how you'll feel when you look back—and remember how I grew up. My parents pleased themselves, and I got to pick up the pieces.''

Ian had heard the stories about Molly's father and then her mother leaving town without her.

"Let's go, Zach.'' Molly tugged her other cousin's sleeve. Then, with second thoughts in her eyes, she hugged Sophie, who focused a dazed smile on her cousin before Molly stepped back. "And—'' she pitched her voice low "—I'm available for that 'bad girl' talk as soon as you need it.''

Zach took his turn, going toe-to-toe with Ian. "Sophie may technically be my cousin, but she's more like a sister. No one hurts her. *No* one.''

Ian had looked into Zach's mysterious past, too. He hadn't been unable to uncover where the sheriff had learned the martial arts he'd used to disarm a bank robber. He hadn't gotten to the bottom of the silence Zach kept about his military training. But as he met the other man's belligerent eyes, Molly's advice about considering the future echoed in his head.

She was pretty smart. Hurting Sophie's cousin Zach might feel satisfactory in the extremely short run, but a family feud and his own eventual guilt wouldn't further his cause. "I'm glad Sophie can count on you.''

The words nearly stuck in his throat, and Zach's expression called him a liar. It also promised to follow up, but he let Molly drag him back to his car. Still watching, he started the engine and backed out.

Only Ethan remained, reluctant now to leave them alone. He curved an arm around his daughter, ignoring her stiffness. "How do you feel?"

"I'm fine." Exhaustion weakened her tone. She leaned away from him. "I know about pregnancy. It's my job."

"In theory. You've never been pregnant before. You're taking care of yourself?"

"Absolutely." Relenting, she sank against him. "I don't want you to worry."

"I won't."

His obvious lie touched an unexpected chord of loss in Ian. Sophie's family might meddle, but they mattered to each other. He tried to imagine Ethan Calvert telling his daughter he couldn't make her wedding because he had an appointment to pick up some specialty wood for a new project he was building.

Couldn't possibly happen.

"Come on, Ian. Let's get this over with." Sophie led the way across ragged brown grass to the clapboard house that had once been her home.

"Sophie," her father called. Urgency edged his voice.

Ian turned back with her. Ruddy color painted Ethan's face again as the wind whipped his graying hair. He hooked his fingers into the belt loops of his jeans, turning his booted feet inward. "I know you aren't like your mom. I got scared for you."

To Ian's surprise, Sophie's expression hardened.

Aiming a level nod at her father, she opened the door and waited for Ian to enter ahead of her. Feeling a little sorry for Ethan Calvert, he glanced back. With the door in a death grip and her face twisted in fierce concentration, Sophie looked like a woman in pain.

"Damn." She let go of the doorknob with such emphasis the door flew open. "Hold on."

He smiled at her disappearing back, but turned away so she could make up with her dad in privacy. He hunched to avoid slamming his head into the low door frame.

Inside, a wood stove stood unlit at one end of the cold living room. Family photos decorated the opposite wall. Ian resisted an urge to look for pictures of Sophie. Though he was curious, she'd think he was pretending to be an attentive husband.

A fine layer of dust covered every surface. Ian peered through the open door at the brittle grass growing unevenly around patches of dry dirt. Sophie hadn't lived here in a long while. Her town house offered a little clutter, but plenty of welcome. This wasn't her kind of place. Images of her growing up in an atmosphere of neglect made him uneasy.

She sprang up the single step to the threshold, hiding red-rimmed eyes the second she saw him. "Do you want coffee? Something to eat? Dad said Gran dropped off a cake yesterday." She closed the door, and the room grew dim in the sparse light through the darkened window.

"You're hungry?" he asked.

"I'm from the South. Our first instinct in any crisis is to feed the victims. Besides, Gran is the queen of chocolate cake bakers, and making coffee for you and Dad will give me something to do with my hands."

And allow her to keep her back to him while she regained her composure. "What else did your father say?"

She led him down a narrow hall that seemed to shrink around them. "He thinks I waited until too late before I worried about trusting you." They reached a kitchen as bright as the rest of the little house was dim. Wide, clean windows opened to the sun on three sides of the room. "I didn't tell him the whole truth about what happened at the wedding."

He tried to look indifferent. No one had ever protected him before, and he didn't deserve it now. "I appreciate your caution." He couldn't seem to produce a simple thanks.

"Dad has a lot of tools that could harm a man if he got really upset."

Ian couldn't hold back a smile. "I'll try not to make him any angrier." Her wry mood made her seem more familiar. "How about you, Sophie? Are you ready to forgive me and start over?"

She turned, coffee can in hand. "I don't forgive lies—even lies of omission—easily, and I won't forget. Be honest with me from now on, Ian."

From now on? He felt as if she'd punched him, but he crossed the room before he realized he'd moved. "What are you saying?" He took the coffee can because he wanted to touch her, but held back. "We stay married? We go on with our plans from before?"

"We didn't make plans." She loaded a filter into the coffeepot, then took the can back. "Another mistake—and not one I think you and I ever made before we knew each other."

He nodded. "Normally, I like to know where I am, what to expect—how to minimize the risks. You made me forget the rules."

"Same here. I've planned my career since—" She stopped, and he wondered what she didn't want him to know. Her eyes glittered as if tears lay in them. Her scent, flavored by sun and mountain wind, emanated from the top of her head, enticing him. "I always ticked off the steps on my lists before I met you." She busied herself with the coffee. "Let's make rules this time. I stay out of trouble when I understand the boundaries."

"What rules?" What more could he give up?

"I'm moving here." She peeled off the coffee can's plastic lid, still without looking at him. "I see you're serious, but living here is part of the deal. This is a good place to raise children, safer than D.C. or Chicago. And my family is here. I want my child to know family the way I did."

"I thought you grew up in D.C."

"Partly. I stayed with my mom in the summers after she and Dad divorced, and I went to school at

Georgetown and Johns Hopkins.'' She ran water into the glass carafe. ''But my best times were here with my dad and my cousins and my grandparents. I want to come home before I have the baby.''

Sacrificing his job should have been enough. ''I either come with you or take a divorce and visitation?''

She nodded, finally looking at him. ''I'm willing to try, but there's no point in staying married if we aren't going to work at it.''

When she widened her green eyes like that, he tended to believe his whole world lay in them, but he wouldn't pretend he could let her push him around. ''I'll eventually have to take another assignment. How am I going to find work from here?''

''Exactly.'' She poured water into the coffee-maker's well and dropped the lid. ''So you'll travel as often as you do now. My family will help me with the baby.'' She slid the carafe onto the warmer and switched on the machine. ''You could even be killed.''

Her pragmatism almost hurt. Maybe his death would affect her more if it actually happened.

''I'll work at our marriage, Ian. You know I want to be with you, but I let myself forget the important things before. And our baby is important—more than I am, more than you are.'' She shrugged, her skin flushing as if she'd confessed too much. ''Besides, my grandmother is about to retire. I asked her if I could join her at the baby farm, but she needs to know I'm staying.''

"For good?" He looked around. The kitchen was nice, but the rest of the small, stagnant house, with its close-set walls, contained only so much oxygen. "You're asking me to surround myself with people who think I've ruined your life.''

"I'm forcing you to become part of my family.''

She stared at his hands, and he realized he was rubbing his finger, the one that had never set properly after his father had broken it during an argument. Ian had thrown up his hand to defend himself, and instead ended up with a lifelong memory of an idiotic argument and his father's demand for submission.

Just like then, he had no choice now.

"They'll be your family, too.'' Surprising him, she covered his hand, including his broken finger. "Give them a chance and time.''

He pulled away and shoved both hands into his pockets. "What do you really want?''

"You can take me at face value.'' Clearly puzzled, she opened a cabinet and took down a tall glass and a mug. "I told you I want to live here, partly because of your work. I want to come home, anyway, but if we're staying together, it makes sense to be where my family can help with the baby. My job is demanding, too.''

"You obviously made the decision before you thought about staying with me. This is an ultimatum.''

"I am moving home. I—need…" She closed her mouth, making a seam of her lips as if she had to gather strength to utter the word. "Help. And that won't change if you and I are married."

Anger grabbed him by the throat. Only his father had ever dictated to him. He tried to say no—to suggest their child wouldn't be the first to divide time between divorced parents.

But his own confusing childhood stood in his way. How could he consider shuttling his son or daughter between houses without trying to create a family home?

Sophie was right about the Calverts. They'd help her when he had to work. And her grandmother was growing older. A new physician at the baby farm made sense. Sophie at the baby farm made sense. Worst of all, if he refused, he'd be doing it to prove his manhood. To himself.

He'd lost all his options the day Sophie's pregnancy test came up positive. Now he had to live with the consequences—and maybe make something good out of them. Maybe make a real family and a real home for his child.

"When do you want to move?" He stripped his tone to the bare words—no emotion. That was safer.

"As soon as I transfer my practice to another doctor. While I'm arranging that, you can pack up in Chicago—or put things in storage in case we don't make it. Whatever you want to do."

Her expression was innocent even as she suggested their marriage remained a trial relationship. He left the bait where she'd cast it. Time would prove him honest.

"We'll pack you up first," he said. "I don't want you doing all that work on your own."

"I know what I'm capable of physically." She took two sliding steps down the counter, movements she was obviously repeating from the past. She lifted the lid on a round, plastic container and stared, struck dumb, at a rich chocolate cake. "That looks—" her throat worked as she swallowed "—good."

He wanted badly to laugh, and he envied that cake her besotted admiration. She pushed it away with the tips of her fingers. He crossed to the counter and pulled it back. "Take some." When Sophie gave in to temptation, she gave all and then some. She was irresistible.

"I wish I could say no, but I'll eat my fair share." Flashing a pained smile, she took down two plates and served cake on both. But she denied herself even a bite of the moist chocolate while she poured a glass of milk and a cup of coffee.

He watched, seduced. It was all part of the dance. She wanted the cake. It was in reach, but she controlled her appetites. He lifted his mug, determined to remind her of other days and other delicacies. "No more champagne?"

Her blush looked like sunburn. They'd sipped champagne from the hollows of each other's bodies.

"No more," she said, her voice liquid. "Until we learn how to talk to each other with our mouths."

He stared at hers, remembering the silky touch of those full lips, the delicious taste of her. "I like the way you use words already."

She picked up his mug and her glass, leaving a splash of milk that betrayed her trembling hand. He tore a paper towel from a fat roll and wiped up the spill behind her.

"You're the one who said we did everything backward." She set both drinks on the table. "This time we'll learn about each other. We can't go on having sex until we suddenly wake up and can't stand being in the same room."

He frowned, understanding she wasn't just declaring a moratorium on champagne. "Being more conventional won't keep us from making more mistakes, and I didn't say I hated the—"

"Sex? I want more than just sex, Ian." She pulled back a hard wooden chair and sat, staking territory. "If you can't live with waiting until we're both sure we want to be married, we'd better both call lawyers."

Anger rolled over him again, but it was about time he learned to control his emotions around Sophie. "Go softly. I know you think I tricked you into this marriage, but playing house won't help us. I want a wife for myself and a mother for my son."

"Or daughter," she said. "And I have to know we can be more than lovers."

"I tried to hide cold feet because I was afraid I'm the worst thing that could happen to you." Maybe she'd heard all the evidence she needed, but her low opinion of him still hurt. "You meant more to me than the time we spent in bed, but at least it was a connection."

She glared at him. "I don't trust the way we felt."

It was useless to argue. "How long do you see us living as housemates?"

"I'm trying to be your wife." She lifted her chin. "Because you cared enough to quit your job. And… I didn't…" She stopped, her gaze wavering with doubt, but then she seemed to gather strength. "I didn't think about our baby when I left you." She breathed as hard as if she'd run a couple of marathons. "My mom never seemed to realize I was as important as her dates, and I always thought if I had children, I'd put them first."

"You aren't your mother. You aren't anyone but you."

"Don't try to make me feel better. I don't need comfort. I only want to hear the promises you *can* keep."

She sounded as if he'd lied to her all along, instead of making one nearly catastrophic slip. "Why'd you agree to marry me in the first place? Don't you respect me at all?"

"This isn't a matter of respect." She finally speared a bite of cake, but her lust for chocolate had lost its effect on him. "You say you want to be with

me, but you could meet someone you really care for.
I want to know where I stand with you at all times.''

His wife had funny ideas about marriage. ''Why
would I marry you and keep my options open for
another woman?''

She stared until all he could see was the open,
earnest expression that had rendered him stupid in
her grandfather's apple orchard last fall. ''I don't
seem to make sense anymore.'' She opened her
mouth. The fork and the piece of cake slid between
her moist red lips.

Ian gripped the sides of his chair, his muscles
shaking with his effort at control. He wanted to pull
her onto this table and touch her until she turned back
into the woman he'd known.

At last she swallowed her bite. ''I told you what
I need. Why don't you tell me what you want?''

''I'm not crazy about rules, but I'm afraid I'll lose
you if I argue.''

''You're afraid you'll lose the baby.''

A mixture of temper and frustration with her absolute blindness pushed him. ''If that's the way you
want it. Would you have married me if you weren't
pregnant?''

Her game face cracked, and she shook her head
from side to side, pain bruising her eyes. Her blond
hair tangled in messy strands over her shoulders.

''I believed we'd make it work until I heard you
tell Jock you had no choice about marrying me.'' She
flattened her hands on either side of her plate. ''Who

wants to hear on her wedding day that she was an entry in the groom's to-do list?''

Anguish threaded her voice and drew him to his knees at her side. He wrapped his arms around her, elbowing the plate out of his way. ''I never meant what you heard. I was afraid I'd hurt you, but if I could take it back, I would.'' He pressed his lips to her forehead, breathing in her sexy, clean scent, sliding his mouth over her lustrous hair. ''I don't talk like this. I've never let anyone mean so much to me that I can't walk away, but, Sophie, I'm trying to walk toward you, if you'll just let me.''

She dashed tears from her eyes and pried her damp hair away from her cheeks. She looked weary down to the fine bones of her strained face.

He finally understood her fear. She was trying to protect herself and their child, and she believed he'd betrayed her.

''You're worth whatever I have to do,'' he said.

Her mouth was straight and thin, and the loss of joy she'd worn back in that orchard wounded him. ''I've never trusted anyone who lied to me the first time.''

He stroked her shoulder and then passed her the glass of milk. ''I won't hide anything from you again.''

''Good.'' She looked into the glass as if she was reading a murky crystal ball and then set it down. ''I think I'm going to be sick.''

Immediately he rose, his hands clenched. He hated feeling helpless. "What can I do?"

"Wait here and don't bust into the bathroom to help."

He nodded as she stood, growing paler by the second. All the life in this small house seemed to follow her when she left the kitchen.

Mindful of his promise to stay out, he washed their dishes. He was drying the last fork when Ethan Calvert knocked briefly and entered the house.

"Soph?"

"Back there." Ian assumed she didn't want her father's help either. "You should probably wait."

Ethan searched him suspiciously. "What'd you do now?"

He couldn't blame the man. "She's in the bathroom. Morning sickness."

Ethan grabbed the back of the nearest chair. "Let me promise again I will kill you if you hurt my daughter. And if you get yourself killed and leave her stranded with a child, I'm still coming after you."

Ian tried not to laugh. Ethan was serious, and Sophie would be better off if he and her father got along. "I was trying to take care of her when I married her."

"I wouldn't say that too loudly." Ethan glanced over his shoulder. "She's pissed off with you for doing right by her."

"I know."

"Doing the right thing isn't enough." Ethan released the chair. Out of habit, Ian kept an eye on his restless, angry hands. "My daughter deserves better."

"I know." And he'd begged forgiveness in every humiliating way he could think of. Ian wanted to ask Ethan what made Sophie so unwilling to offer a second chance. Just in time, he remembered Sophie was his wife, not a subject who'd hired him to protect her. Grilling her father about her personality wasn't permissible. "I'm serious about our marriage and this baby."

"I remember what her mother's and my divorce did to her, and I don't want her to feel responsible for creating a long-distance relationship between her child and you if she cared enough to marry you in the first place." Ethan came around the table, taking the dish towel from Ian's hand. "But I'll be watching you, and I'm not forgiving like Sophie."

Forgiving? Sophie? Not even her father knew her. "You have nothing to worry about, sir."

"Why are you worried, Dad?"

Ian turned, and Ethan jumped guiltily.

"Dad, were you threatening my husband?"

"Absolutely," Ethan said.

She rolled her eyes. Her smile trembled in a pale face, but she met Ian's gaze with a hint of her old joy. "He's probably serious."

"I assume he is."

She went to the fridge and pulled out a bottle of

water. "I've held enough of a grudge for both of us, Dad."

Ethan moved past Ian to put his arm around her. "Take the time to figure out what you feel for him."

She wrenched the cap off the bottle and stared at Ian as she sipped. He felt like a patient she suspected of malingering. Turning, she rubbed her hand across her belly, provoking a surge of possessiveness that startled him. "Anger is no tool for starting a family."

Ian bit the inside of his cheek. He could have pointed out her mistaken assumptions about his motives. But with both Calverts staring at him as if he'd stolen a family heirloom, it seemed smarter to just shut up.

CHAPTER FOUR

A MONTH LATER Sophie waited while Gran unlocked the small cabin she and Ian were to share on the grounds of The Mom's Place. A less anxious woman might have called the cabin her home, but Sophie felt like running every time she looked at the moving van they'd rented. Their stuff intermingled in there as if they were any normal married couple.

And Gran was no help with her delight in the show. "Your husband's no coward."

With a sense of foreboding, Sophie followed her glance along the gravel driveway, which was overrun by unruly weeds. Ian carried a box bulging with dishes around the van just in time to meet a throng of pregnant women laughing together on their morning stroll up Bardill's Ridge. As they parted to walk around him, their voices floated on the light breeze, and Ian froze. He'd never wavered since that day at her father's house, but the women, with their rounded bellies, surging hormones and burgeoning life, turned him to stone.

"You have to give him points for courage," Gran said.

"Because he's terrified?" A deep flood of relief actually thinned Sophie's voice. Ian's postreconciliation conviction had begun to rub her the wrong way, as if she was slacking because she couldn't stop worrying about their future.

"Because he agreed to take this cabin, anyway. Living up here is scary stuff for an anxious father-to-be."

Sophie could afford to laugh since Ian's look of near panic made her feel less alone. "Gran, he makes his living walking in front of bullets."

"He's never had to raise any of those bullets to be responsible citizens." Gran unlocked the door and ushered her inside. "How did this happen to you, anyway? I assume you know about the birds and the bees?"

As far as Sophie could tell, they'd been rough with a condom in their haste. Gran wouldn't want to hear about that, and it wasn't information she felt comfortable sharing. "A mistake," she said. "Are you sure you won't need this place for a guest?"

"Let me think…reserve a cabin for a possible guest, or give it to my new partner, who's willing to live on site with our patients—or patrons, as the accountant calls them." Gran switched on a light in the cabin's entrance. "I say welcome home."

Behind them, Ian stumbled over the threshold. Sophie caught the sides of the box to steady him.

"Everyone in this place is…" He broke off, looking from her to Gran as if one of them might call on her dad and his power tools.

"Pregnant?" Sophie said. "That's the point. It's a retreat for women whose husbands have gone away or women who need a break."

"Or want to be pampered," Gran said. "Or for the girls who have no other place to go."

"I saw a group of teenage girls collecting leaves down by the bridge. I couldn't believe they were old enough to date, much less have children." Ian hoisted the box higher. "And I'd like a few minutes with the guys who dumped them."

Sophie admired his righteous anger until she remembered he'd married her out of the same sense of duty. She couldn't afford to dwell on doubts that made her feel as if she was doing the wrong thing, so she forced them from her mind. "It's not just the guys," she said. "Those girls have parents, too. Parents who decided not to take care of them. Thank God they have Gran." She hugged her grandmother and then turned her husband toward the back of the cabin. "I think the kitchen is that way, Ian." She pointed down the hall. "Can we take a look at the bedrooms, Gran?"

"I'll bring up the beds next," Ian said. "You could use a nap."

She intended to do no such thing, but her gran's approving nod kept her from arguing. She smiled at both of them as car doors slamming outside made them all turn toward the yard. A line of men trooped up the hill.

"Zach and Dad and Grandpa." Wouldn't you know? Their first day, and already the menfolk had to make sure Ian was treating her right. Sophie almost touched him for comfort, but stopped just before her fingers reached his forearm. He might not understand her family well enough to know he was on probation. All the better for him if she left him in the dark. She curled her hand into a loose fist and tapped the box. "They'll help you unload. Grandpa loves to direct traffic."

"Another pushy Calvert." Ian crooked a smile at Gran. "Sorry. I was trying to tease Sophie."

Gran patted his shoulder with a wicked grin. "You'll say a lot worse by the time my husband moves you in to his satisfaction."

Ian's startled gaze made Sophie laugh again. He turned to her with a glance that reminded her of before—back when they were only having fun. Like a creature of habit, she considered pulling the box of dishes out of his hands so she could throw herself into his arms. Fortunately, the baby nudged her, just at belly button level, and she remembered her new, sober resolutions. She climbed the stairs to safety.

On the landing three doors opened off a narrow hall. She peered into each one. Two bedrooms and a bathroom. Sophie slid her hand beneath her hair and pulled it away from her nape. Two bedrooms.

They needed three. At least they would after the baby came.

She couldn't remember which cabins up here had three bedrooms. She glanced down the stairs. How could she complain? The house came rent free from her grandmother and the resort's board. They'd cleaned it for her and Ian. The gold hardwood floors smelled of polish. The walls reeked of fresh paint.

Her heart beat faster as she crossed the master bedroom and opened the closet door. A walk-in might be large enough to turn into a nursery. But not this one, built in the late fifties. It was dark and small and, thank heavens, smelled of paint, rather than the musty scent of long disuse.

She backed out, hearing Gran climb the stairs. By the time the baby came in another thirteen weeks, she and Ian might be sharing a room, anyway, so the shortage of bedrooms wouldn't matter.

The mere suggestion of trusting him that much nearly choked her. It might be wiser to make sure they had another room if they needed it. She hurried back to the hall to meet her new boss. "Where's the third bedroom?"

Confusion clouded Gran's eyes. "There are only two."

"We need three."

"Three?" Gran cocked her head and hurtled to the right conclusion. "One for you, one for Ian and one for the baby."

"Yes." She flicked a panicked glance toward the

empty stairs, feeling guilty for exposing the true state of their marriage.

"Now I'm really curious." Gran also lowered her voice, closing the distance between them. "You don't sleep with your husband?"

"Sophie, can't you advertise our sleeping arrangements in the local paper?"

She jumped. Bodyguards should clatter around the house like normal people. Instead, Ian startled her again, stepping partway out of the shadows the sun cast through the round window above him on the landing.

"I'm sorry." His body was striped in dark and light. He probably knew she couldn't see his face. "I'm a little desperate." She rubbed her stomach in a reflex action. "Besides, Gran can keep a secret."

Her grandmother stared at Sophie's belly. "Who'd believe me, anyway?" She looked up, a thoughtful, sad expression in her eyes. "You two have bigger problems than I thought."

Ian grunted in disgust. "Sophie, if you don't mind, I'd prefer we work on our marriage privately. And I hope you won't be insulted, Greta, but I'm including you as a person who has no say about what happens in this house."

Sophie had to catch her breath before she could utter a shocked sound. "Don't talk to my grandmother like that. I'm the one who—"

"No, he's right." Gran gripped Sophie's shoulder.

"I'm your grandmother, not your conscience, but think about the marriage you really want."

Sophie had never really wanted marriage after she'd helped end her parents'. And she'd never trusted passion because her mother's passion for her lovers had made her such a careless parent. How was she supposed to trust a paper marriage and a passion that had already robbed her of all semblance of rational behavior?

When she didn't say anything, Ian turned his head to look at her. Tension added a terrifying vulnerability to his face. Sophie mentally nailed her own feet to the floor. She longed to touch him, to smooth away the anxious lines. She loved her family dearly, but she owed him loyalty, too.

"I'm sorry," she said again.

He nodded. "If you want to talk about it, talk to me. We'll work it out—whatever you need."

She felt her grandmother behind her. "Okay."

"Sophie, come show us where to put this couch!" Zach yelled from downstairs.

Gran tore herself from the thick atmosphere in the small hall. "Something must be wrong with Seth," she said, "if he's not telling them where to put your things."

Silence held after she left. Sophie stared at Ian, unwilling to give in. "We have to be careful this time."

He shook his head. "This separate-room plan won't work. All it'll do is put distance between us."

"Sane distance. We should have tried that from the start. You've said so yourself."

"I don't want it now. You're the one who demanded commitment, but you're making impossible terms."

"I will commit, but I can't sort lies from the truth when we're—" She stopped. *Making love.* The words stuck in the back of her throat as images of Ian's nude, needful body made her weak. "I'm doing the best I can."

He hesitated, his mouth open.

"I am," she said. "I have to be sure before I sleep with you again."

"I don't see you ever being sure." But the irritation banked in his eyes. "I'd better go downstairs before your family decides I'm a slacker, as well as a ravisher of innocent Calverts."

Grateful for the reprieve, Sophie fell into step behind him. "I've always liked your sense of humor."

He stopped and turned, and she bumped into him. Despite her best intentions, she didn't move away from the pressure of his arm against her breast.

"Where are you going?" he asked. "Stay up here. I'll bring up the bed and the bedding, and you lie down. You drove twelve hours yesterday, and I don't care that you're capable of lifting the light stuff. I couldn't stand to watch you doing it."

Sophie arched her eyebrows. "You've got to be kidding."

"Give me a break. Just once, do as I ask without forcing the sensible alternative down my throat."

"How about a sensible compromise?"

"Damn it." But a smile warmed his eyes.

She laughed. The sexual energy between them had to go somewhere. "How about if I put the kitchen together? You all bring in the boxes, and I'll unpack and wash everything and put it away."

He stuck his hands into his back pockets. "Why can't you let me take care of you?" He touched her cheek, the tips of his fingers burning her.

"I have no answer." All she could think of was how good his hand felt on her skin.

With a shrug of regret, he let go to start down the stairs. Suddenly he looked back again. "No one else needs to know about the separate rooms."

"Deal." She traced the hard muscle of his shoulder. Touching him even so briefly was an astounding relief. "I wish I hadn't told Gran."

"It doesn't matter. I trust her."

He continued down the stairs, disappearing through the open front door before Sophie could make her feet move. *I trust her.* That was a hell of a thing to say so effortlessly.

SETH CALVERT WASN'T HIMSELF. He resented his wife's approach to retirement, but Greta maintained a blissful ignorance of his problem with her attitude. Alone in the cabin's living room with the moving boxes and Sophie and Ian's mismatched furniture, he listened to the din of his family making jokes over pizza. As Greta laid out yet another new scheme for Sophie and the baby farm, he dwelled with bitterness on the hard facts.

His wife of more than forty years assumed he was the last person who needed her.

They'd finished unloading Sophie's things two hours ago and then they'd shared their makeshift dinner. Zach's wife, Olivia, and Molly had brought spoils from Big Tom's Pizza.

Ethan, barely stopping to eat, had already whacked together a couple of new shelves that looked as if they'd always hung on the kitchen walls. Greta had pronounced herself satisfied with yellow-checked kitchen curtains she'd whipped up on Sophie's sewing machine.

"Just so the ladies don't feel tempted to peep in on you," she'd said.

It was time to go home. But Greta lingered. Seth rubbed his chest, where loneliness had begun to ache like actual physical pain.

Last fall, as a gift to him on their fifty-fifth wedding anniversary, Greta had promised to find someone to take her place up here. Then she'd found something wrong with each applicant until Sophie had shown up.

From Greta's conversation all day, her plans for settling Sophie into her new office, the changes they could make to the patient schedule, the new programs they would enact, it was obvious Greta would keep her hand in until Sophie found the courage to evict her grandmother from the premises.

He couldn't count on any such luck. Greta had been Sophie's surrogate mom since the day Nita had packed her bags and left Bardill's Ridge. Far too aware of how easily a girl could lose her mother, Sophie would do nothing that might hurt Greta.

Which left him where he'd been for fifty-five years—last on Greta Calvert's list of priorities. It hadn't been so bad while he'd sat on the circuit court bench. Even in Bardill's Ridge, the criminal element had kept him busy, but he'd retired over a decade ago. Since then he'd discussed retirement with Greta almost every day.

He'd persuaded her to agree their time had finally come, but now she didn't seem to want it. Ambition had pushed her into a world women had rarely inhabited in her youth, and her drive still rode her like a demon.

He pushed off Ian's plaid couch. "I'm going home," he announced.

"Grandpa?" Sophie poked her head out of the kitchen. "What are you doing alone in here?"

"Not much room left in there." He sounded petulant, but he was too tired, too sick of wanting the wife who took his waiting for granted, to care. "Tell your grandmother I've gone home, would you?"

Sophie must have heard the peevishness he couldn't seem to hide. She wove between boxes to catch his arm. "What's wrong?"

What kind of man ruined his granddaughter's first day home? He wasn't that childish in his tarnished golden years, was he? "Nothing. I have a little research to do. I'm writing an article for the *Tennessee Law Journal.*"

"You and Gran work too hard." She hugged him without realizing she'd hit that particular nail soundly on the head. "But I'll let Gran know you've gone." Compassion filled her eyes. "You know, she'll get over being so excited, but for now I'm flattered."

He hugged her back. "Flattered? What are you talking about? I've never heard you admit to a moment's self-doubt before. You're like Greta that way."

"The Mom's Place is just as much her child as Dad or Uncle Patrick or Zach's father." She patted his arm absently, as if she was looking inward. "I don't doubt myself, but I'd hate to let Gran down. Last-minute jitters, I hope."

His resentment of Greta's distraction faded before his concern for their granddaughter. "She held out for you because she believed you were the one to take over. You're going to improve the services here."

"Improve?" Sophie opened the door but clung to it with an uncharacteristically shy smile. "I doubt Gran believes anyone could care for the baby farm better than she has, but I'll always be able to ask her for advice."

No doubt about that. Rubbing his chest, he turned toward the grassy driveway. "Say good-night to the others for me."

"Why don't you wait? Olivia says her dad's down here visiting, and he's watching Lily and Evan tonight." Evan was Zach and Olivia's son. Lily was Zach's daughter from a previous marriage. "He made some sort of date with Aunt Beth, so she and Zach and Olivia are about to leave. You could drive down with them."

"I'm fine on my own." He tried to picture her suggesting something similar to her grandmother.

"I just thought you might lead them down. Night, Grandpa."

He ignored his granddaughter's faintly anxious tone. Reassuring her took more energy than he could spare.

AFTER EVERYONE ELSE LEFT, Greta stayed to help store dishes and glassware. Stationed between the women, Ian took the newly washed and dried china from Sophie and passed it to Greta.

Sophie seemed distracted, but finally she spoke up. "Gran, what's wrong with Grandpa?"

"What do you mean?"

"I thought something was bothering him. He's not sick or anything?"

"Funny you ask. He's been moody, but I have a theory. I wonder if maybe he retired too early. He seems bored, but I can't persuade him to take up a hobby. He writes a little now and then, a few articles for the law journals, but other than that, I think he spends most of his time waiting at home for me.''

"Waiting for you?" Sophie leaned around Ian with a sharp glance.

He frowned, seeing new reasons to dread living among the Calverts. Flaws in the family structure would drive Sophie crazy, and any extra worry for his wife aroused his strongest urge to protect her.

"Did you talk to Seth?" Ian asked. "I saw you walk him to the door.''

She seemed startled that he'd noticed. "He claimed he had some work to do on an article, but I honestly thought he seemed annoyed.''

Greta sighed with almost too much emphasis, as if she'd suffered long and needlessly. "He wants me to retire right this very minute. You know. You were at our anniversary last fall.''

"He set a deadline?" Sophie asked.

Ian shook his head. Sophie must be blind if she thought Greta would accept a time limit, even from Seth.

"I've explained I have to show you how things work up here.''

Sophie put down her dish towel and turned her grandmother away from the cupboards. "You should go home, Gran. Now.''

Greta's face stilled, as if Sophie's audacity stunned her. Just then the phone rang. Ian ducked between his wife and her grandmother.

"The phone's on," he said. He and each of the Calverts had checked for a dial tone about twenty times apiece today, all with Sophie's pregnancy in mind.

He didn't have the knowledge or confidence of an OB/GYN. In Sophie's eyes, he might not have advanced any farther along the evolutionary scale than Cro-Magnon Man, but he didn't want to be stuck on a mountain, miles of winding roads away from the nearest hospital without a telephone. "I'll answer it in the bedroom."

"Don't you want me here?" Greta asked Sophie as he left them in the kitchen.

He ran up the stairs to Sophie's room and picked up the receiver from the table beside her bed. "Hello?"

"Son?"

His mother's tentative voice shocked him. He'd given her and his father the number, but he hadn't actually thought they'd use it.

"Mom, how are you? Something wrong with Dad?"

"Not at all. He's mixing martinis, and we thought we'd wish you luck in your new home."

Why? He couldn't help wondering after they'd ducked his wedding, though that had turned out to be a blessing in disguise. He had yet to tell them about the baby. They'd screwed around with his life plenty, and he planned to keep them away from his child as long and as much as possible. The most effective diplomatic strategy seemed like a bland truce that kept them on the other side of the Atlantic.

"Thanks, Mom. How's the golf these days?"

"Fine. Your dad has a tee time at Saint Andrews next week, so we're heading over to Scotland for a few days. I'll see some old friends from the diplomatic service while your father plays."

"Sounds good."

"Do you like your new house? You didn't tell me much about it."

He glanced at the boxes stacked along the uneven plaster walls. "It's fine. We'll probably find something of our own after we settle in, but this works for now." No need to explain that Sophie had insisted on taking the house on the property as if she expected him to disappear and leave her in sole charge of a mortgage.

"Good. Good. Your father wants to say hello."

"Put him on. Take care of yourself, Mom. Have fun with your friends."

"Ian," she said, "be happy. I hope you'll be very happy."

Her unnaturally formal tone implied his father wasn't mixing his first batch of martinis for the evening. Either that, or tears were strangling her. Ian felt better putting his money on the booze.

"I am happy, Mom. I hope you'll meet Sophie soon." In a year or so, when he and she were both capable enough parents to protect their infant from his snobbish, pseudo-aristocratic mom and dad.

"Son?" His father's usual bark made Ian jerk the phone away from his ear. "I hear you're settling into the honeymoon cottage."

"Yeah, that's right. Golfing a lot, Dad?"

"Never enough, son, never enough. Got a tee time over at Saint Andrews next week. Your mother has some plans. Shopping, a reception at the embassy, that sort of thing."

His father's bonhomie rarely failed to raise Ian's hackles. Tonight was no exception. "Sounds great." He rubbed his fist in the sweat that beaded on his forehead. "Listen, I've got to stock up on some groceries, so I'll talk to you later. Thanks for calling."

"Glad to. See you soon, son."

"Good."

"Hello to that bride."

His father rarely spoke in complete sentences. Ian had long since learned to translate. "I'll tell her." He dropped the phone into its cradle but considered pulling it out of the wall. Bad plan, his dad would have said.

Ian patted his pockets, searching for car keys. Tomorrow would have been soon enough to buy supplies, but purchasing bread and milk and a late newspaper would take him away from the "honeymoon cottage" and from Sophie. He could pretend life was normal with his parents or with her, but both at the same time? No mortal man was that strong.

He hit the stairs at a run and barely stopped in the kitchen doorway. "I'm heading into town for provisions. I'll be back in a while." He broke off. "Well, you know how long I'll be better than I do. Good to see you, Greta. Thanks for all the help."

"Wait." With one word, Sophie demolished his escape plan. "Gran's leaving. I'll come with you."

"Aren't you tired?" He tried not to look as if he hoped so. A fast drive without his wife or her family might make him fit company for the rest of their first night at home.

"I'm fine." He must be one hell of an actor. She didn't seem to notice he wanted to go alone. "Ready, Gran?" she asked, all sweetness.

"I guess." The older woman rooted in the piles of discarded brown packing paper for her bag, then turned it up with a faintly aggrieved expression. "We still have several items to discuss, Sophie. I'll meet you in my office at nine tomorrow morning?"

"Nine?" Sophie grabbed her own purse and all but shoved her grandmother out of the kitchen. "What time will you be there?"

"Seven, but I plan to clear my desk before you arrive."

"I'd better observe. The sooner I learn all my duties, the sooner you'll be a free woman."

"You sound like your grandfather."

"I was thinking you might not be hearing exactly what he says to you."

Greta puffed up like a cat who'd padded into a nosy interloper. "I understand my own husband."

"Okay." Sophie assisted her grandmother through

the front door, casting Ian an exasperated glance that included him on her side of the skirmish.

He stumbled. Since she'd told him about the baby, he hadn't felt natural with her. Since their wedding he'd felt as if he was in a play, performing badly.

But with one glance she'd turned him into her ally.

"Ian?" Already halfway to the car, Sophie looked back for him.

He was still standing in the doorway. Greta continued to her vehicle, still badgering Sophie in a tone that hovered on the sweet mountain breezes.

"You coming?" Sophie asked.

He felt as if she'd shouted for help. Damn. He could use a charger and some armor. Something to mark the occasion with more importance than merely locking the door and pocketing their house keys.

CHAPTER FIVE

THE DARKNESS BEHIND THEM fell away like a blanket pulled off a bed. Ian parked at the edge of the well-lit square. Beyond the wrought-iron fences, the farmers' market stalls stood under undulating tarps, set up for morning business. The Bardill's Ridge courthouse and the small shops around the square lent more light to the clean-swept sidewalks.

Sophie pushed the car door open, trying not to notice how the couples passing, some with children, some on their own, turned their heads to stare at her and Ian in his unfamiliar car.

"How do they always know when you're new?" Ian asked.

"When you live here, even part-time the way I did, it's hard to pretend you don't notice new people." She smiled. "I used to feel suffocated, but tonight Bardill's Ridge is home."

Ian nodded, but being under the community microscope made him seem different, on edge, as they got out of the car.

"Sophie," said a woman in front of the hood. About Sophie's age, she'd paused with one little girl on her hip and another child, mostly hidden in a mound of lacy blankets in a big stroller. She had her hands full, maneuvering her family while her husband studied Ian.

"Lisa?" Sophie said the name almost before she remembered the energetic young cheerleader who'd been a peripheral kind of friend. Sophie'd talked her through high-school chemistry. Lisa had taught Sophie how to apply eye shadow without looking as if she wanted to audition for clown school. "Lisa," Sophie said again.

"I heard you were back." Lisa pressed her cheek to her older daughter's silky black hair while the man at her side took the stroller. "Dee's in Molly's kindergarten class."

"I'm so glad to see you." Sophie remembered Ian and went around the back of the car to his side. "This is my…" The word stuck in her throat, but she forced it out on the second try. "My husband, Ian Ridley. Ian, this is Lisa Conroy."

"Detner," Lisa corrected. "And this is my husband, Dave. Sophie and I were in school together. She saved me in chemistry."

"You made me socially acceptable," Sophie said with a laugh.

Both men chuckled vaguely and nodded at each other, obviously sharing the notion that women's talk could be enigmatic. But they shook hands, and Sophie warmed to Dave's friendly smile. He was the first man in Bardill's Ridge to treat Ian as a possible friend rather than a womanizer.

"Nice to meet you both," he said.

"Were you in Sophie's class, too?" Ian asked.

The other man shook his head. "I'm a civil engineer. I came to work on a public dam project that fell through, but I met Lisa and never left. I work with the road commission in town."

"Is it true you're staying?" Lisa asked Sophie. "I thought you'd never come back here for longer than a visit."

Sophie hesitated. A public pledge squeezed her into the commitment she'd made. She swallowed, forcing a smile. "You know how marriage changes the way you look at your life. I'm ready to settle down, and Gran's ready to let one of us help at The Mom's Place. The time's right." She turned to her friend's baby in the stroller, avoiding Ian's gaze. She didn't really want to know what he thought of her little speech. "Boy or girl?" She looked up at Dee in Lisa's arms. "A brother or sister?"

"That's Tommy," the little girl said, and then buried her face in Lisa's neck.

Laughing, Lisa twitched the blanket back to show off her son. Sophie and Ian voiced appropriate approval over a boy whose head looked enormous to a pregnant woman. Fortunately his wide, gummy smile made up for it.

Her own baby was going to make all the changes

she'd made to her life worth it, but she hated having to force them down Ian's throat, too.

After a phone-number swap, Lisa and Dave moved on with their children, and Sophie turned Ian toward Ritz's Food and Sundry with a touch on his forearm.

"Can you see us crowing over ours?" she asked. It was hard to imagine, hard to believe unequivocally that they'd be together that long.

"I noticed you didn't mention him."

"Her," Sophie said. "The mother always knows."

"Not if she doesn't let the ultrasound technician tell her."

"I always know." She was actually about fifty-fifty, but Ian was so smug with his unapologetic yen for a boy.

"You know I don't care which we have," he said, as if reading her mind.

"Seriously?" For some reason it mattered. A man couldn't help what he wanted, but her only interest was in having a healthy child. She just thought of the baby as a girl.

"Seriously." He surprised her, flattening his hand against her stomach as he followed her onto the sidewalk. "You're not ashamed of your pregnancy?"

"Never," she said staunchly. "But isn't our marriage enough news for now?"

"The marriage is big news," Ian said, "but I wonder if you're hedging your bets. Maybe you can get rid of me, and people will just remember a blank spot for my child's father, some guy they saw on the street…what was his name?''

Sophie stopped, shocked that he didn't at least know her better than that. "I'm scared." Why not admit it? "But I'm not a total fake. I thought twice about coming here as a single mom only because I don't want to be Nita's daughter, who shamed Ethan with a pregnancy of longer duration than her marriage.''

He searched her gaze. "You worry about the damnedest things. Why do we care what anyone else thinks of us? Even the fine citizens of Bardill's Ridge.''

She lifted both brows. "When you put it like that…but, Ian, there's something else. I don't want you to dislike my mother, and you're going to if I don't shut up about her.''

"Your mother didn't go completely wrong. You were with her part of the time.''

She nodded. "She doesn't have inherently maternal instincts. But she has loyal friends, and you have to be a good person to manage that, and I love her. I'm trying to tell you she's not a bad person.''

"I understand." He took her hand "We're blocking traffic.''

"Wait.''

He looked down, a question in his eyes.

"You'll always be my baby's father.''

He stared at her, his jaw tight. Finally he kissed her forehead. She caught his sides. The waistband of his jeans scraped against her palms, and she sighed, longing to pull him closer, but he was already moving toward the store.

He pushed open the squeaky screen. The wooden door inside stood wide, letting early-summer night into the store.

"Evening, Sophie," Mr. Ritz called from his position behind the deli slicer.

"Hey. Good to see you. Mr. Ritz, this is my husband, Ian."

"Hello," Ian said. The wind had whipped his curls into a frenzy. It had been a while since he'd had his usual short haircut.

"Nice to meet you. Of course I've heard the rumors about you two moving in up at the baby farm."

"Well, Gran's finally retiring," Sophie said.

"Hard to believe."

"Isn't it?" She cruised to the vegetable bins while Ian disappeared down one of the aisles of metal racks. She tucked greens and tomatoes and a selection of fruit into clear plastic bags before she found Ian studying the canned green beans.

"We're not eating that." She tapped the can that appeared to have hypnotized him. "We can get fresh."

"You're a lot like your gran, aren't you?"

She tried to read his expression. "Are you laughing at me or insulting me? Don't you like Gran?"

"She's great, but she's pushy. You both think you know best, and you don't like input." He pushed the can back onto the shelf. His arm brushed hers and she tried not to shiver. Even with such minor contact, she felt his strength, and she wanted her share of it. "You even have to approve the green beans," he said.

She smiled, still uncertain. "I am right about them. Let's come back to the farmers' market tomorrow."

He took the fruit and vegetables she'd selected and began to head for the cash register with her. "You don't want to buy all this tomorrow?"

"I only got enough for a salad for lunch." She wavered a second and then gave in to the urge to stroke the bright red flesh of the tomatoes through the bag. "Or maybe for tonight."

"After all that pizza?"

"I can taste these tomatoes."

"It's the dressing you're after."

She almost stepped back. "You watch what I eat?" She made dressing from a recipe Gran had made since her own childhood.

He took her hand again. "How can I help but notice? You all slop it on as if it's liquid gold."

She threaded her fingers through his, overwhelmed by a sense of shyness and desire that mingled like lightning and thunder. She was working on instincts she never trusted when she was with Ian.

"I'm glad you pay attention." She smiled. "It feels like a good sign."

"I want to know you." His heat and scent invaded her space, replacing her craving for tomatoes with an implacable need for him. "I never meant to hurt you."

"You didn't. You make your living as a watcher, and I'm a little fascinated with your methods. I have to observe, too, to know what's going on with a patient's body, to make sure her pregnancy progresses normally."

"I meant at the church. You've never let me apologize."

She unlinked their hands and smoothed his hair away from his forehead. He wouldn't like knowing she could see his emotions. "It did hurt, but you've apologized since."

"I'm still not sure you understand." Turning her hand, he pressed his lips to the mound of flesh beneath her thumb. "I'm a bad risk for the kind of marriage you need, but I should have told you, instead of Jock."

"Now who thinks he knows best?" Each beat of her heart seemed to pulse in the back of her throat. "Let's both hope you're wrong."

"DAMN IT. Stupid, flipping flowers." These blooms were determined to cling to their stems. Ian glanced at the cabin up the hill, inadvertently pointing his penlight at the window where Sophie was washing dishes again.

It did hurt, she'd said, and he'd felt guilty, so here he was in the dark, collecting posies.

He straightened from the poisonous-smelling

daisies and found honeysuckle wrapping itself around the wide, chunky trunk of an oak tree. With his small light, he could hardly see the topography. He took a hesitant step onto sloping ground and slid down a deeper ravine than he expected. The wet grass clung to his clothes and his arms. Swearing again at the honeysuckle, he took out his knife and sawed off a few strands.

Lifting his fist full of wildflowers, he inspected them with his light. Not too impressive, but Sophie might appreciate the effort. He closed his knife before he tried to climb the slippery hill. Better to avoid a homemade appendectomy.

At the house, he wiped the mud and grass off his feet on the edge of a porch step. Seeing his bedraggled bouquet in real light, he considered tossing it back to nature.

But he couldn't kill the wildflowers for nothing. He went inside and found Sophie waiting in the kitchen doorway.

"What were you doing out there?" In the dim hall light, she switched her gaze between him and the ratty flowers, and then she blinked with unfeigned amazement. When she was off balance like this, he believed she might come to need him some day.

"Oh," she said.

"I know." They were pretty bad, and his man-handling had loosed a sharp smell that battled with the sweet honeysuckle fragrance. "I should have bought some in town."

"No." She straightened her shoulders, regaining her bearing. "I like the natural look." With quick footsteps, she moved to him. "I saw your light and thought you were securing the premises or something." A soft smile belied her defensive posture of the past several months, and she took his offering. "Maybe a bodyguard needs practice."

She hugged the bunch of flowers to her chest as if she actually wanted them. Her happiness made him strangely self-conscious.

"I tracked in some mud." He kicked off his shoes. "But I'll clean it up. Do you have everything you'll need in your room tonight? Do you need me to carry anything else upstairs?"

"I'm not an invalid. My family must be rubbing off on you." She headed back to the kitchen.

He grinned. "No, but your dad's threats scared me." He wouldn't have made the joke before she'd taken his flowers. Were they making progress again?

The kitchen floor was cold beneath his sock-shod feet. She bent to hoist a vase from one of the packing boxes, and he discovered he liked the curves her pregnancy had added. Feeling like a voyeur, he crossed to the sink.

"Found it." She brandished the glass container like a trophy. "Thanks again, Ian. This place needs fresh flowers."

"Let me just add one more thing about that night in the church." Her acceptance, when he'd half expected laughter, must have greased his tongue. "I never meant for you to find out I had any doubts because I knew I'd get over them.''

She started to look annoyed, and he wished he'd kept his yap shut.

''I can work with the truth, but I felt like an idiot because I believed in you. And when a guy makes me feel idiotic, I don't want to be around him.''

''It was never my intention,'' he said, stiff again.

''I see that now.''

''Marriage is going to be work.''

Her eyes asked if he'd just figured that out, and now he felt like the idiot. Unlike her, however, he didn't have an urge to run.

''I like hard work,'' he said.

''Me, too.'' Sophie glanced at the clock ticking on the wall behind his head. ''Speaking of which, I'd better get to bed so I'll wake up in time to meet Gran at the office.''

''Good night.'' Letting her climb the stairs alone was going to be difficult. He belonged up there in his wife's bed, lying next to her, learning the changes their growing child was making to her body.

''Night.'' Faint color blotched Sophie's cheeks. It didn't feel normal to her, either. ''I'm sorry I have to start this way, but I want to be sure we're making actual decisions for the right reasons.''

She wanted honesty? Looking at her, wanting her, he had some to offer. ''Learning to be apart now that we're married is ridiculous, but I'm willing to do what you need.''

She tiptoed to kiss his cheek. "This isn't what I want." Her voice dropped into a husky tone he knew too well. It was persuading him he didn't want to do what he knew was best for her.

Taking her shoulders, he eased away. "I'll see you in the morning."

"Okay." Her voice sounded smaller.

He wanted to explain, but how many times could he beg one woman to slice him with the cold edge of rejection? He concentrated on wetting a stretch of paper towel to clean the mud he'd tracked into the front hall. Sophie climbed the stairs. Once he heard her walking overhead, he breathed a sigh of relief.

IT HAD BEEN AFTER DARK when Greta decided to go to the office for a few minutes, instead of heading straight home from Sophie's cabin. She wanted to put together a few files, some notes for Sophie's first day.

Leah, her receptionist, had already left when Greta had unlocked her office. She'd called home but had to leave a message when Seth didn't answer. Sometimes he went over to the Train Depot Café for dinner if she was late.

Knowing his meal was provided, she buckled down to work. Her procedures for prenatal care brought to mind some guidelines she'd put together for nutrition. The nutrition handouts reminded her she'd set up two files, one for the women, one for her adolescent patients. And so it went. Each item she wanted to discuss with Sophie in the morning made her think of another subject she needed to cover.

Setting a stack of files on the corner of her desk, she nudged the clock her grandson Zach had sent her from Monte Carlo when his Navy ship had taken port in the Mediterranean. She grabbed at the timepiece and couldn't help noticing the spread of its old-fashioned hands. "Oh, no." She twisted her watch. It also read 11:17 p.m.

She grabbed the phone. Guilt seemed to thicken her fingers, making them too clumsy to dial. After three rings Seth picked up the receiver on his end.

"Were you asleep?" she asked. "I'm so sorry. I've been planning for tomorrow and forgot the time."

"I'm not asleep. Why would I be asleep before my wife comes home? You do plan to come home tonight?"

His resentment was obvious. Greta's first instinct was self-defense. "I have to provide Sophie with the information she'll need to take over. You know that. I'll only be this busy for a few more weeks at most."

"I don't believe you anymore, Greta. I can't even imagine you believe yourself. Your heart and soul are buried in the brick and mortar up there." She smiled as he paused to take a breath. He sounded a little annoyed, but he did understand. "You bring home the leavings you think are good enough for me. Distracted conversation. An occasional meal a man couldn't buy in the best restaurant in the biggest city. But I don't give a damn about the leavings.''

He didn't understand. ''Seth, you're upset.'' She couldn't believe it. The heck with defending herself. She'd somehow hurt her husband. ''I'm trying to do what you've asked me to. The sooner I turn over this information, the sooner we'll have time to ourselves.''

''Greta, I'm going to bed now. Good night.''

''Seth, wait.''

''I've waited long enough. Good night.''

''No—I'll be there in a few minutes.'' She grabbed her purse, skewing another stack of files. Tucking the phone beneath her chin, she rummaged for her keys. The receiver clicked in her ear.

He'd hung up on her. What did he mean by that? She hit redial. He picked up right away, but she didn't let him speak. ''I don't know what's wrong with you. You're insulting me.''

''Good night, Greta.''

''No.'' For some reason she needed him to agree she was only doing what he'd asked her to do. ''What's your problem with me preparing for a turnover? Should I just dump the files on Sophie and let her sink or swim?''

''She's a smart woman.''

He stopped, and she had the feeling he was trying to imply Sophie was the only intelligent woman in this conversation. ''How dare you, Seth Calvert? I'm your wife, not your maid. I'm sure you've eaten.

You're in a warm, tidy house. You have a soft bed that I made up this morning. I'm working. I don't have your free time, and I don't expect you to crack the whip over my head as if you're scheduling my hours.''

"Work yourself up, woman. You aren't about to convince me, but as long as you believe you're doing the right thing, what does it matter? I'm the fool for thinking you can change after fifty-five years of marriage. Now I'm going to bed, and I'd rather you didn't disturb me again."

"Are you telling me to sleep in the guest room?"

"I'm asking you to be quiet when you decide to come to our room."

"I'll be extremely quiet."

"Thank you." And he hung up again. As if he had a right to. The man spent too much time on his own. She'd known he was too young to retire at sixty-four. Good Lord, was it fourteen years ago? She'd tried to suggest as much to him, but he wouldn't listen. He never listened to her good sense.

She wiped at the moisture in her eyes. She'd been staring at her files so long her eyes were watering.

IAN WOKE ON HIS FEET, blinking to clear sleep-filled eyes, reaching for a gun in the holster he wasn't wearing. Someone was trying to batter down the front door. He veered, his feet sticking to the bare wooden floor. He'd dreamed he was on an assignment gone bad, but reality came back with wakefulness.

He pulled on jeans and a sweater he'd left on the back of a chair and threw open his bedroom door. Across the hall, Sophie's door stood open. He could see her bed already made.

"Sophie?" Sleep made his voice sound odd even to himself. Where was she? The clock beside his bed read barely after six. The narrow road that wound between here and the resort took some time to maneuver, but not three hours.

Had she and her grandmother entered into a competition for who could reach her office first? Sophie liked to prove herself, but did she honestly feel she had to show Greta she was woman enough to take over the job?

Fists bounced off the door downstairs again. He glanced at the phone. He'd like to call his wife, but what if his impatient visitor had something to do with Sophie? What if she'd gotten hurt driving in the near dark?

He bounded down the stairs, his heart beating in panic. He opened the door violently, and Ethan Calvert stepped back.

"Sophie," Ian said.

"What about her?" Ethan rebalanced a long piece of polished wood on his shoulder. "You sleeping in today, boy?"

Ian relaxed against the door frame. Sophie wasn't hurt. Her father would have known. "I guess I'm getting soft.'' He reached for the board. ''Let me help you.''

''I'm fine.''

''So that's where Sophie learned it.''

Ethan paused, but the board kept moving, just a few inches, and he grabbed it back. ''Learned what?''

''She won't ask for help, either. Why is that?''

Ethan ignored the question. ''I made her a couple of bookshelves. She said to set one up in the dining room and one in the living room. She didn't tell you?''

This family apparently thrived on competition. Ethan liked being more in the know than his daughter's husband.

''She must have forgotten. Can I help carry in the pieces?''

''There are two stacks in the back of my van. Take your pick.''

He chose the stack still completely covered by a canvas tarp. The cold ground and sharp rocks bit into his bare feet, but he didn't stop to put on shoes. Ethan had started to put up his shelf in the dining room.

Ian set his share of the parts in the living room. Ethan had decorated the shelf fronts with figures, primitive cuts of bears and trees and running water that suited this cabin and the ridge around them. Love for Sophie gleamed in the care her father had given the furniture.

Ian couldn't help stroking the smooth wood. How did a man build something like this? And Ethan had worked fast. After Ian finished carrying in all the pieces he'd found beneath the tarp, he joined his new father-in-law.

"I'll put the other one together."

"If you're awake now. Need some tools?" Ethan asked.

"I have some of my own."

Ian was slower—less familiar with the project, possibly more reverent with the wood. Ethan strode in before he'd half finished.

"Do you really always get up this early?"

Ethan laughed. "No. I just wanted you to know I think you're a soft city boy. Need some help?"

Ian heard an offer of friendship in the other man's honesty. And he didn't have to be a Calvert do-it-yourself-or-die kind of guy. "Thanks."

"We should install a new doorbell. The one you have hardly makes more than a click."

Ian glanced up, meeting Calvert green eyes that measured him. "Sounds like a good idea."

Nodding, Ethan knelt beside him in jeans almost faded to white and leather work boots, shiny with time and use. "You don't have to treat this like glass. I built it so you two could take it with you when you find your own place." Ethan got busy with his cordless drill, but stopped between screws. "And I expect the kid'll be chewing on it in a year or so."

That image was enough to make sweat pop out all

over Ian's body. He didn't always manage to connect the growing bulge in Sophie's belly with a flesh-and-blood child who'd depend on him. He set down his drill and gripped his knees to hide trembling hands.

"You're going to do that, right?" Ethan ignored Ian's hands so emphatically Ian knew he was caught. "Find a place of your own?"

"You're asking about my intentions?" He let go of his knees and picked up his drill again.

"I have to believe good intentions made you marry my daughter and then chase her down here after you lost her in D.C. If I doubted you wanted to do the right thing, you'd probably be wearing this by now." He waved the drill that was more like an extension of his own hands. "I'm asking about your plans."

"We haven't planned further than the baby's birth." Ian looked his father-in-law square in the eye. "And I'm really not comfortable discussing plans with you before Sophie and I talk."

"See, now that's where this whole situation goes haywire for me. Put down that tool, son." Ethan sat back and waited for Ian to do the same. "My daughter makes lists for laundry day. Getting pregnant, marrying you—that wasn't part of any list my Sophie ever made."

Ian considered putting the drill through his own head. He wasn't about to discuss unforeseen, uncontrollable physical need with Sophie's father. "I can't explain. I never made so many mistakes with one person, either.'' Her dad looked as if Ian had insulted his daughter. ''I'm talking about myself, not Sophie. She's not the mistake. I regret we didn't approach our marriage and the baby the conventional way, sir, because I didn't want to hurt Sophie or your family or mine, but I wouldn't change anything now.''

Self-disgust dried Ian's mouth. He sounded more like an accountant than a man who loved his wife, but what did Ethan Calvert hope to gain from this conversation?

''I'm starting to see why my daughter dumped your ass at the altar.'' The other man picked up his drill again. ''Let's try it this way. Is this a halfway house for you, or are you two planning to buy something here? How do you intend to support my child and yours?''

''I don't have an assignment right now, but I've saved enough money for time off so Sophie and I could settle in.''

''Did Zach's father-in-law fire you?''

He couldn't blame the guy for assuming he was irresponsible. ''I quit because I want to be with my wife, but I will work again.'' Ethan Calvert must not know his own daughter if he thought she'd give up her job and live off what Ian could provide. ''I'll take care of Sophie and *our* baby.'' He couldn't help emphasizing the ''our.''

Ian had no idea if he'd passed the quiz, but he resented having to take it. He fastened the last shelf into place, taking cover in the drill's racket. Ethan held his spot on the floor until Ian sat back on his haunches and tested the bookshelf for sturdiness.

"How about coffee?" Ethan asked in a less aggressive tone. "You got any of that yet?"

"Yeah."

"Not instant."

An offer to share coffee didn't rate high as an apology, but face it—Sophie's father wasn't doing anything Ian wouldn't have done for his own daughter. Might have to do someday, if he and Sophie had a girl and some guy like him staggered into her life.

He felt a taste of Sophie's morning sickness. "I could use a cup of the real stuff myself."

CHAPTER SIX

THAT NIGHT Sophie parked behind Ian's car, but she couldn't force her fingers to move from the steering wheel to the door handle. She was so tired she couldn't tell if her whirling stomach came from morning sickness that was supposed to have ended weeks ago—but hadn't—or exhaustion.

She pressed the back of her head against the seat rest, trying to stretch her neck muscles. Closing her eyes, she hoped her grandmother, who'd dragged almost as much as Sophie, had gone home, instead of preparing work for tomorrow. She was tempted to call her grandpa, but when she opened her eyes to reach for the phone, she noticed Ian fiddling with something on the front porch.

Sophie couldn't manage to turn on her phone, so she glanced at its digital face. The battery was dead as a doornail. And she might match it for energy.

Scooping up her jacket, briefcase, purse and the dead phone, she climbed out of the car. "What are you doing?"

"Installing a doorbell." He turned. "But don't

touch it yet. It might shock you into the next county... What happened to you?''

''Not looking my ravishing self, huh?'' She lumbered up the stairs, and when Ian set down his drill and reached for her armload, she gratefully handed it over. ''I don't mean to challenge your skills, but are you good at wiring?''

''You're scaring me. What's wrong?'' He nudged her toward the door. ''Come inside and put your feet up. I'll get you some tea. I picked up some of that herbal stuff you like when I went in to town today.''

''But did you talk to an electrician?'' She let him tug her through the door and ease her into the puffy chintz love seat that had been her first comfort-furniture buy after med school. She grabbed his sleeve as he turned away. ''Hey, stop ignoring me. Are we talking fire hazard?''

He looked down. ''Sorry. I was wondering what I'm going to do if something happens to you out here in the middle of nowhere and you need medical care.''

''The office is only fifteen minutes away, and town isn't more than twenty-five.''

''Which is fine when you're healthy. If something happens, we're in trouble.'' With tenderness that made her heart leap, he eased his sleeve out of her grip. ''I can wire a house, so set your mind at ease. I can also set a broken ankle or stitch up a knife wound or dig out a bullet. But I've never delivered a baby.''

Sophie tried to avoid his eyes. She tended to forget how to think when she noticed how intensely he looked at her—as if she was the only woman he'd ever truly wanted. "If the worst happens, you can hike through the woods for Gran. That'll cut the trip by nearly ten minutes."

"During work hours, you'd be with her anyway." He took her teasing as she meant it, with a smile. "But I'll keep my compass handy."

"Wait. Why do you keep running away?" She reached for him again, but he was farther than the tips of her fingers. She pulled her hand back and smoothed her skirt over her aching thighs. "You eased my mind about the fire hazard. I'll tell you I'm extremely good at my job. I could talk you through it if we had to. I'm not worried at all."

Something changed in his eyes, a shifting of color or emotion she couldn't decipher. "I'm not re- lieved."

His voice shook a little on the "relieved." Sophie bit her lip, trying not to laugh. "Good thing noth- ing's going to happen, huh? About that tea?"

With a brief nod that emphasized his strong, blunt chin, he turned toward the kitchen, muttering some- thing about house fires and counting contractions. Just inside the kitchen, he leaned back into the room. "Don't touch that doorbell till I tell you."

She sank deeper into her beloved chair, smiling as she held in a huge bubble of laughter. "I'm probably a bad person, but I love watching you wrestle with doubts.''

''Not a bad person, but a touch vindictive.'' His smile softened the blow. ''Have me set up security for a meeting between two heads of state. Ask me to protect your grandmother from an enemy she doesn't even know about. I'll be fine. Don't ask me to deliver a baby.''

''And the wiring?''

He laughed, and she liked the husky, rumbling sound of that even better than his worried tone. ''I just haven't checked that yet. It'll work perfectly.''

''I suspect it will.'' Sophie closed her eyes. ''I could use a nap more than a cup of tea.''

The phone at her side interrupted.

''Leave it,'' Ian said. ''I'll tell whoever it is you're still out.''

''It might be Gran. She couldn't seem to fit in everything she wanted me to know today.'' She picked up the portable and tapped its on button, but then she covered the receiver. ''She didn't let me see one patient.''

''Didn't let you?'' He sounded as if he hadn't heard correctly. ''How did she stop you?''

''They're her patients. She's having a problem letting go.'' She moved her hand off the speaker and said hello.

''Sophie?''

Nita always said her daughter's name as if not entirely certain she remembered it. Sophie braced herself. It wasn't that she didn't love her mother, but she'd always hoped her mom would come to love her more like a daughter than a confidante. After Sophie'd walked in on her and "the other man," Nita had never seemed to realize there were grown-up secrets she should keep from her child.

Sophie had spent most of her childhood either wishing her mom would come home alone or hoping she wouldn't detail the "exciting" adventures of a single, twentieth-century woman.

"Mom."

"I heard about the wedding."

"Did you?" Nita's low-pitched, slightly accusing voice warned Sophie to apologize and prepare for a small spate of wounded maternal love, but for the first time in her life, she was too tired to make the proper move in the mother-daughter Olympics. "Who told you?"

"Aren't you sorry you didn't?" Nita sounded as if she'd suffered a deep wound. "That's what I wonder."

"Ian and I wanted to keep it private." She hoped that was apology enough.

"Surprisingly, Beth Calvert let me know."

"Aunt Beth?" Zach's mother.

"Apparently she and Eliza were sampling the local 'shine and got to thinking I had a right to know."

"What?" A drinking party that extreme didn't sound like Molly's mom, either.

"Well, maybe they're putting together a reception for you and they invited me."

"Mom." The picture became crystal clear. "Did either of them mention the word *surprise* in connection with this reception?"

"Oh." Nita sounded faintly amused and only a tinge repentant. "Maybe Beth did." She charged back in. "But you kept a big secret from me. I might as well blow one for you."

Sophie's exhaustion swept back, full force. She curled into a ball, facing the back of the chair. "That's not the way it's supposed to work."

"I love you, dear."

Sophie felt as if she were trying to choke down the Rock of Gibraltar. At least her mom had prepared her for talking to a child who declared his love the second he got caught with his hand in the cookie jar.

"I love you, too, Mom, but you should stop and think before you…" Never mind. Replaying the broken record about thinking before she acted never helped. "You remember Ian, don't you?"

"Yes, but you said nothing about marriage. Do you love the man?"

Sophie sensed him, too close in the other room. For all she knew, he'd bugged every phone in the house to exercise his wiring skills, and he'd listened in on the whole conversation. She wrapped her palm around the receiver's rounded edges. "I married him," she said. "What does that tell you?"

"That you're probably pregnant."

"Mom!" How could she be the only person who'd guessed? But then, everyone else had always believed she was conscientious.

"So you are. Don't sound so shocked. Remember, I've heard all your antimarriage speeches. You'll never need another human being to make you whole. You don't believe two people can be totally necessary to each other. Well, something had to make you change your mind. And I've been pregnant. Pregnancy changes a woman's priorities."

Sophie was shocked. Her mother did understand her fears. Gripping the phone more tightly in sweaty palms, she tried to be friendly for the sake of her husband and child. "I am going to have a baby. Are you coming to the reception?"

"Of course. I called to ask what you need in the way of a gift. I mean the two of you have lived alone so long you probably have everything you need, or you know exactly what you want."

A hollow metallic crash in the kitchen supplied the answer to her mother's question with a touch of drama Nita would have loved. The old silver teakettle they'd found at the back of a kitchen cupboard flew past the door, followed by a dish towel and a blue stream of curses in Ian's sexy voice.

"A teakettle," Sophie said, "with an insulated handle." She looked away from Ian, still swearing as he aimed a hiking boot at the kettle and scooped up the towel. "I like the ones that whistle," Sophie added.

"That was easy. I have one other thing in mind for you, too."

Her extra thought refocused Sophie on their conversation. "You don't have to and, Mom, don't mention to Aunt Beth or Aunt Eliza that you've told me about the party."

"I'm not completely insensitive. I wouldn't dream of telling them. But trust me on this other gift. You'll love it."

A cold chill quivered down Sophie's spine at light speed. Terrifying images of lingerie for pregnant women lodged in her head, but she didn't dare mention she'd hate opening such a thing at a reception in front of every Calvert on the mountain. Her mother wouldn't be able to resist the idea.

"Thanks, Mom."

"Gotta go, sweetie, but look for me at the party."

The line clicked in Sophie's ear. She hung up and twisted around to set the phone on the table. Ian was leaning against the kitchen doorway, comfortingly large, sympathy shining a warm light from his eyes.

"I'll add a small plate of kippered herrings to a tray with your tea," he said.

Wonder robbed her of speech. The tomatoes were one thing, but there'd been moments lately when she'd known if she couldn't find a supply of those nasty little fish, she'd have to start smoking her own. "You noticed that, too."

"The cans stink."

"Oh, sorry. I try to remember to wrap them in a plastic bag before I throw them away."

"I can live with it."

"Thanks," she said, and as he turned away, "Ian, remember to act surprised when my dad's family shows up with a party."

"Your mom's a piece of work."

"Yes." She couldn't argue, and she was too tired to explain her mother's me-me-me tunnel vision.

"Sophie?"

"Hmm?"

"I shouldn't have said that. Sorry."

"It's okay. She's just different."

"At least she never took up golf."

His tone teased, but Sophie shuddered. Would they be lousy parents, too? They'd both been single-mindedly tied to their careers until they'd collided with each other.

FROM THE LANDING above the glass-paneled front door, Seth watched Greta turn the doorknob several times before she dug in her purse for the key. Silver glinted between her fingers as she tried, unsuccessfully at first, to insert the key. God forgive him, his wife's nervousness pleased him.

After the accusations she'd shouted at him last night when she'd finally come home—that he was trying to control her, that he'd ruined his life with retirement and he just wanted her to ease his boredom—he was the last thing she wanted.

Just as his anger reached a slow boil that had grown as familiar as sleeplessness or hunger, she tried to look through the mottled top of the beveled door glass. Optical illusion showed him her face in a series of puzzle pieces. Worry pinched her nose.

He never locked the door when he was home. She'd rattled the handle for endless seconds before she'd begun to search for her own key. She assumed he wasn't home.

She opened the door to the whisper of air-conditioning escaping. She sniffed, but she'd find no aroma of dinner cooking—a greeting she'd taken for granted in the past few years.

"Seth?"

He was too angry to answer. After she'd flounced to the guest room last night, she still expected to come home to the pliant husband who'd twiddled his thumbs waiting for her—for years. This morning he'd actually considered packing his things and moving down to the bed-and-breakfast their son Patrick ran with his wife, Eliza.

Greta looked up the stairs, but Seth was still determined not to say anything else he couldn't take back. He eased into the shadowed corner of the landing. She searched the stairs as if anticipating a trail of socks and the jeans he'd worn since the day he'd last sat on the judicial bench. Jeans Greta had announced last night that she hated.

What else had she grown to hate about him?

"My Lord," she suddenly said. She pushed away

from the door, her face twisted with alarm, and started up the stairs.

In that moment he forgot she'd walked out of his bedroom for the first time in their marriage. Fifty-five years of loving her, waiting for her, depending on her even when she'd let him down, softened his anger. She needed him. Without thinking he ran to meet her. "What's wrong?" He slipped on the top step, barely caught himself before rocketing head-long into her.

Immediately her expression relaxed. "Seth." Relief nearly rendered her voice unrecognizable.

His fate was sealed. He had to stay and fight it out. He loved her. She loved him. He couldn't afford to move out and take a break at this late date in their marriage.

"I'd never leave you, Greta." He grimaced, considering how badly he'd wanted to when he'd awakened alone in their bed this morning. "At least, I wouldn't take the coward's way out and disappear."

Tears slid from her eyes. "No. You'd leave me a note and phone numbers where my attorneys could reach yours."

"How can you assume that about me?" He shook his head. "I pay attention to detail, but you mean more to me than phone numbers for a lawyer."

She climbed the last two stairs and leaned into him. Her soft white hair tickled his chin. Her hands, strong enough to bring life into the world, held him with the tentativeness of an uncertain welcome.

"You mean everything to me," she said, his Greta, who'd always known how to run her world with no help from anyone, speaking through tears.

"We'll work this out." He curved his hand around her shoulder. "It's a rut in the road, like others we've faced. After fifty-five years, a rut—" even one that looked like the Grand Canyon "—can't pull us apart."

"All my life I've needed to work. I have to learn to take down-time without feeling guilty."

Her work came first. Trying not to let it would be the challenge. Seth tried hard to swallow a sense of betrayal. She didn't realize how deeply her words cut. What kind of man had to beg his wife to come home?

IAN DELIVERED TEA and smelly fish and then started the only meal he knew how to cook. Chili that had even drawn Zach's father-in-law, a media mogul accustomed to cordon bleu cookery, to the kitchen on the cook's day off.

In the middle of chopping onions, he noticed how quiet the house seemed. He set his knife on the blue plastic chopping board. He'd made Sophie promise to rest, but he wouldn't put homework assignments past Greta Calvert. Sophie might be nose deep in one of the files that overloaded her briefcase.

She wasn't.

Still sitting straight in the chair, she'd fallen asleep, her mug of tea cradled in both hands in her lap. Far from glowing with hormones, she looked half-dead with exhaustion. Even that night in the church rest room she hadn't been this pale.

Ian hesitated. Touching her felt like taking liberties, but that was his baby rounding her belly, and he had a right and a need to care for them both.

He eased the cup onto the coffee table and took the foul-smelling fish back to the kitchen. After he'd sealed them firmly in plastic and tossed them into the garbage, he went upstairs to his room to sort through his unpacked boxes. He came up with lanterns and books and dried food packs for camping before he found a fleece blanket that he pressed to his nose. It smelled faintly of his apartment in Chicago and of an open fire, but it should be warm enough to make Sophie comfortable.

The thick walls of their cabin kept the house cool during the day, but up here on Bardill's Ridge in early summer, night could be chilly. He descended the stairs more slowly than he'd climbed them. At the bottom he had a clear view of the living room, cluttered by a few boxes and furniture that hadn't found a final resting place. Still sitting up, a testament to her iron control, Sophie slept on, her head to one side.

A surge of tenderness startled Ian. He'd watched her before, sleeping in his bed or tucked against him as he'd barely clung to the edge of the full-size bed she'd kept since childhood. His need to be with her then had astounded him, but tonight felt different.

Sophie was his wife. If he was capable of love, he had to learn to love her. Not just for a few stolen moments, not only with the passion that seemed to grow more possessive each day she carried their child. He had to love her and their baby enough to establish a real family.

Ian spread the fleece and gently wrapped it around Sophie. Taking her rounded shoulders in his hands, he eased her against the cushions on the roomy chair. Her hands curled into the blanket. Not opening her eyes, she sank as far as she could manage into the padding and muttered a sound that resembled "thanks." Ian stepped away, trying not to fully wake her. He stared at his palms, warm from holding her. If theirs had been a real marriage, he'd wake her and wrap his arms around her and remind her of the need that had brought them together in the first place.

She wasn't ready, and he had to make himself wait. He rubbed the back of his hand across his mouth and tried to think of her as a client. If she'd hired him to protect her, he'd be handing her his speech on setting a healthy schedule. Tonight she'd be more comfortable if he finished the chili and woke her in time for dinner and an early bath and bed.

A sick client made his job more difficult, and Sophie was damn close to being ill. She might have a heaping helping of the Calvert-family energy on a normal day, but moving, marrying and changing her entire life had obviously taken more out of her than she knew. Yet, if he suggested she do less, she'd try to prove she could do more.

He had to find a way to care for her without letting her in on the secret. Cooking was a constructive first step. And since she'd fallen asleep, it was her own fault if he let her nap to replenish a store of energy.

After the chili began to bubble, he quietly emptied the rest of the packing boxes and put their contents away. The task taught him how little time he and Sophie had spent in their own kitchens. Together, they didn't own enough pots, pans or dishes to fill up the few cabinets in their new home.

When he ran out of goods to unpack downstairs, he gave the chili a stir and returned to his room to unpack. His stash of towels looked lonesome in the narrow hall linen closet. His books overloaded the top of his dresser and the flimsy shelf beside his bed. He wouldn't be able to leave them there, anyway. Soon the baby's things would need the space.

Working the riddle of what to leave in boxes, he heard the phone ring. He ran to Sophie's room to catch the call before it woke her.

As he picked up the receiver, he heard her saying hello. His boss, Adam Quentin, asked for Ian.

"I'm on," he said.

Sophie hung up in mid-yawn.

"Ian, I know you told me you weren't working for a while, but I have an assignment. A client who asked specifically for you."

"I can't." Sophie wouldn't take his disappearing for a job as a sign of devotion.

"You didn't resign from the agency when you left the Kendall assignment."

"Don't start, Adam. I warned you I needed time off."

"You've already had almost a month. I'm asking for a few days. Big bucks for us, and I'll pass on a commission to you."

"It's not the money." He had enough. What the hell had he had to spend it on all these years?

"I know. You're newly married. You have better things to occupy you, but this is a good job. It won't take more than a week."

"Don't try to sell me."

"I need you to escort a courier who's taking a CD to Washington, D.C. It's proprietary software, but the company that's hiring us wants it hand-carried. They've had so many intrusions they don't trust their own fire wall. You know D.C., so you won't have any prep work."

He was tempted. Other than the initial setup for a protection assignment, he liked the short, sweet jobs best, and no matter what he said about money, a guy who hadn't worked in a while could use a salary. "Don't couriers generally know how to take care of themselves?"

"Yeah, but for this one, they want backup."

"For software?"

"That's what I said." Adam laughed. "But they

insisted they want us. Seems as if industrial espionage in that sector can be serious.''

"I'll have to talk to Sophie."

"You'll let me know once you get the wife's permission?"

Adam's jab felt good, like a sharp crack in the ribs should. "Right—when Sophie says I can come play."

"Great. I'll be at the usual numbers. No rush, but I need to know by Friday, so I can set up someone else if Sophie says no."

Adam never knew when to rest a joke. "Friday's tomorrow."

"Yeah, so let me know tomorrow."

Adam hung up and Ian made his way slowly down the stairs. He was in deep trouble. Sophie would accuse him of running.

With his blanket neatly folded in her hands, she joined him at the bottom of the stairs. "Adam Quentin? He's your boss, right?"

Ian nodded. "He offered me a short job. A quick trip to D.C. and back." Her bland look exposed nothing of her feelings. "You can come with me and see your friends."

"Gran would have a heart attack if she thought I was homesick already." She stopped, apparently focusing inward. Suddenly she grabbed his hand and placed it on her belly. "Feel that."

He waited, holding his breath. He knew she'd felt the baby's movements for several weeks, but his child seemed to play hide-and-seek with his old man. "Nothing," he said.

"Wait a minute."

He waited, to no avail. Except that Sophie's gaze softened.

"I'm not trying to be difficult, but how do you protect someone on a quick trip?"

"I'm actually ensuring delivery on a package."

"You're working as a courier." She stared at his hand and then met his eyes with a challenge in hers. "Is that safe?"

What had she seen in his hand? Six-guns? Silencers? The last thing he wanted was to worry about Sophie worrying about him. He lied. "No problem at all." No job came with a promise of safety, but this one sounded innocuous, and he didn't intend to make her more anxious.

"You want to go?" She sounded as if she didn't care.

He tried to reassure her with nonchalance. "It's a day up and a day back, and Adam's been understanding about the time I'm taking away from the agency." She still appeared to feel nothing. "Are you angry?"

"It's your job." She looked down at the blanket she'd folded nearly small enough to fit in a pocket.

He tweaked it from her hands. "I'm not running out on you. I have to work, same as you. We came here for your job. I have to leave for mine."

She lifted her head and her eyes raked him, searching for the truth as if he always lied. "As long as you're not grateful to escape from duty." Almost before the last syllable left her mouth, she bit her lip with regret.

This was starting to feel like the same-old-same-old. "I'm not lying." He tried to sound sincere, but she also made him feel guilty. "Duty is the farthest thing from my mind with you."

"I want to believe you." She gripped his sleeve, not quite touching his skin, but establishing contact. "I don't want pity."

He turned his hand, catching both her wrists, and easing her against his chest. "Don't you know how ridiculous it is to talk about pity? I'm here. I came here practically on my knees. I want us to be together."

She went limp, contouring her body to his. He held her tighter, incoherent with need as he ran his hands down her back. She sighed, to his surprise, pressing a kiss to the ridge of his collarbone.

He longed to reassure her. He opened his mouth to promise nothing could happen, but thought better. Promises kept screwing them up.

"I'll try not to doubt you," Sophie said. "And I guess calling you a liar isn't part of our deal." She lifted her head, smiling with funny self-awareness.

He hugged her again, wanting her mouth beneath his, afraid to push her that far. He contented himself with a fervent kiss on the top of her head. He drank in the scent of her hair, its softness and vibrant texture. As his fingertips reached the curve of her breast, he had to let her go or beg for more.

"I'd better stir the chili. How do you feel about cheese toast?"

"Cheese toast?" She looked interested. "I like anything with cheese on it."

He eyed her incredulously. Back in Washington, she'd owned the most extensive takeout menu collection he'd ever seen. "Haven't you ever cooked? Even bread with cheddar cheese, under the broiler?"

"Sounds delicious. I'll make it."

"No." He started her up the first stair step. "Change out of your work clothes. You'll do dinner one night when I'm tired." Or too delirious to care what his expectant wife ate, now that he understood her lack of culinary knowledge.

"Thanks. And thanks for the nap. I was exhausted. I don't know how Gran does it."

"Give yourself a break." She looked back, questioning but not on the defensive. "You act as if you're supposed to deliver babies, including ours, rebuild the cabin, run your gran's baby farm and maybe establish a clinic in downtown Bardill's Ridge."

A smile lit her weary eyes. "Great diagnosis from the man who's out to save the world one possibly fatal situation at a time." She undid her top shirt button. "I kind of like that clinic idea."

Grinning, he headed for the chili pot. "Megalomaniac."

CHAPTER SEVEN

ON THE LAST DAY of her first week at the baby farm, Sophie trailed her moody grandmother through the crowd of lounging patrons sprawled in the armchairs outside her office.

Greta tried to shut the door behind her, but Sophie caught it. Gran glanced over her shoulder, distracted. "We're through for the day, dear. You can go home."

"No, I can't. Gran, you have to start letting me see patients. For one thing, you've grown so impatient with the staff, I'm concerned you're edgy with the moms, too."

"Never." Gran dropped into her chair. The glow from her green banker's light painted shadows beneath her eyes. "The patients—patrons deserve our best care and our first attention."

"What's wrong with you, Gran?" Sophie took the chair on the other side of her desk. "Or should I ask what's wrong with me? Are you disappointed in my skill?"

"Not at all. I knew you'd be good the first time I saw you at your office in D.C., and besides, I've known you all your life. I followed you through your schooling. You're perfect for The Mom's Place.''

"Then why are you so reluctant to let me start?''

"I'm not. I've been preoccupied. I can't turn over my patients when I'm so—''

"Patrons, and I think you're trying to distract yourself. What's troubling you?''

Greta opened her mouth. Fear ran through her gaze and she gave up. "I can't talk about it, but you might be right. Maybe I am using this place to avoid thinking about my own predicament.''

"Are you sick?'' Sophie felt a little like Gran, jumping to conclusions, but something serious had to be wrong. "Is Grandpa?''

"Nothing like that.'' Greta came around the desk and hauled Sophie to her feet. "I won't burden you. It's a matter I need to work out for myself. I like to fix what I've broken on my own.''

"You don't have to. You have a large family and too many friends to count. If I can't help you, talk to someone who can.'' Having finished high school at sixteen, undergrad work at nineteen and her residency at twenty-four, Sophie had worked with women who'd considered her too young to understand their dilemmas. "Try Aunt Eliza or Aunt Beth.''

Alarm tightened Gran's face. "No, and don't you talk to them, either. I don't need anyone's advice, so don't you go and sic the family on me.''

Sophie surrendered, putting both hands in the air.

"I won't, but you need to talk to someone. You aren't yourself."

"I'll work my way through it. How do you think I managed before you came home, miss?"

A smile took Sophie by surprise. "You haven't called me that in years. And you were clearly on your best behavior when I came home before now."

Greta returned a grudging smile. "I lured you back here. I admit it."

"But now that you've won, you don't want me to work?"

"All right, *you* win, you win." Greta rubbed her forehead. "We'll discuss the patients tomorrow."

"No." Sophie took a stack of files from her grandmother's desk. "You'll go through these and you'll assign me half the patients—patrons. We'll never get used to that." She settled the stack in front of Gran and then went to the cold fireplace. "I'm going to light this. We'll be here another hour, and whoever's on duty at the front desk can make sure the place doesn't burn down after we leave."

"Thank you, sweet. I appreciate it."

"Do you have matches or a lighter?"

"In the break room."

She found matches and a mug of the fragrant, fresh coffee that a satisfied p-a-t-r-o-n had donated to the refreshment room. Sophie added a moist pumpkin-walnut muffin and thought about tucking in with her grandmother, but she didn't need the comfort food or the calories.

She sniffed Gran's impromptu snack, enjoying it vicariously as they discussed the cases she'd be handling. Their talk evolved. They laughed over the new doorbell Ian had installed and the fact that the cabin was quickly becoming home.

"You've both begun to settle in," Gran said.

"I haven't had time to think, you've kept me so busy."

"Not too busy? Are you feeling well? When do you have your first appointment with Dr. Sims?"

"Next week, but don't mention it to Ian if you see him. He's going to be out of town, and I don't want to reschedule."

"I'm glad he wants to go with you."

"I'm carrying his baby, too." After the words spilled out of her mouth, Sophie stared at her grandmother.

"You've just now figured out he has an equal stake?" Gran laughed out loud. "Maybe you're not such a great physician, after all. We have to read our...patrons' minds. Why are you reluctant to reschedule if Ian wants to accompany you?"

"He's supposed to be gone for a couple of days, but sometimes that stretches into more time away. I just want to make sure everything's all right."

"You're feeling healthy?" Gran adjusted her silver-rimmed glasses for closer inspection. "You know what we tell our patients. Science is fine, but we care how the mother feels, too."

"I'm fine, but I'm due for a checkup. Ian can come to the next one."

"Why's he taking this job now? He should be with you and the baby."

"It's what he does, Gran." She held back a sigh. She was going to miss him. She'd grown used to sharing the little house.

Her dread as the day drew nearer meant he was becoming part of her life. Funny, she hadn't considered the painful aspects of a working relationship—longing for an absent husband.

"You're going to miss him? Excellent."

"You're smug." Sophie patted her grandmother's long fingers. Greta nodded in agreement, so self-satisfied she made Sophie laugh.

"I'd think you'd be glad you don't want your husband to leave. You weren't so sure of him at first."

Sophie tensed. She wasn't Greta Calvert's granddaughter for nothing. Despite recent events, she kept her personal life mostly off-limits. "I'm working at the marriage, but I've also just realized he'll always be leaving me and the baby as long as he keeps this job. And later, when our daughter is older, I'll have to explain why Daddy works so far away so often." She rubbed her stomach absently. "Not to mention the fact he makes his living throwing himself in front of people who are in danger of being hurt or killed."

Greta stacked her files neatly. "I thought the point was to keep anyone from being hurt, including himself. Has he been injured in the past?"

"I don't think so." Why hadn't she asked? "I might not want to know."

"You're afraid and that's natural, but Ian can put your mind at ease if you talk to him. He faces danger every time he goes to work. He'll know how to explain his job to you so that you don't have to be afraid." Greta tapped tomorrow's files on her glass-topped desk again. "You just have to know when to ask for help, dear."

Sophie waited for her to realize she'd analyzed a problem that must be a family trait.

"What?" Greta asked, apparently mystified.

Sophie leaned across the desk and wrapped her arms around her slender grandmother. "We're both intelligent women, but we share a blind spot."

Greta removed herself from Sophie's embrace as if she were offended. "Explain. That makes no sense."

"It wouldn't to someone who's attained your years and success without ever asking another living soul for assistance."

Greta cracked a wicked Calvert grin that had softened almost every face Sophie loved most.

"I've asked," Gran said. "But I've never been cheerful about it."

IN THE MIDDLE of knotting his tie for dinner at Seth and Greta Calvert's house, Ian stopped to admire the blue streak of swearing that came through Sophie's door. Trying not to laugh, he crossed the hall and knocked.

"Sorry," she said. "I can't zip this skirt."

"I like it when you talk dirty," he said without thinking. Well, flirting had to come up between them eventually. He reached for the door handle. "Mind if I come in? I'll help you."

"Thanks, but I'm changing."

"Maybe you should buy new clothes."

"Where? I could pick up some overalls at Kleman's Bargain Basket, but Bardill's Ridge hardly features shopping."

"You could come with me to Knoxville when I fly out tomorrow."

Silence met his suggestion. He didn't push.

"That's a good idea. I could drive you over if Gran doesn't mind." She opened the door, swathed in a black dress that crossed in a low vee over her breasts and then floated toward her calves. "What if we're wrong about the reception?" She plucked at the material and then let it flutter out of her fingers.

"Your grandmother told you to dress." Her newly voluptuous body distracted him. He wanted to touch her, to feel his baby's movement beneath her bare skin, but he never reached her in time to feel a hint of movement at all. In a normal marriage, he'd have the right to sleep beside her and expect the occasional kick in the kidneys from his unborn child. He forced himself to meet her eyes. "If you showed up in a pair of those Klemen store-bought overalls, she'd lecture you.''

Sophie padded across the wooden floor and a pale Oriental rug to rummage in her closet. ''Are you making fun of Gran?''

''I don't think so. I like her even when she's bossing us around. What are you looking for?''

''The wrap that goes with this. I'm not showing off my bulgy belly all night.''

Ian's good humor faded. ''Why?''

She locked one slender hand around the door frame and turned, hearing the hurt in his voice. ''I wasn't thinking. I'm just out of sorts, and I feel fat. Sorry.''

During the past week, she'd lost the drained look that had worried him the week before. Her face seemed thinner, more vulnerable, but maybe that was the heartfelt apology in her green eyes.

''You look more beautiful than ever to me.''

A smile slowly lifted her mouth, stretching the skin across her high cheekbones. ''I'm going to assume you don't have to say that, and you're not under the influence of my cleavage, even though you're staring,'' Ignoring his embarrassed grimace, she dove back into the closet and then grabbed something with a shout. Turning, she spun the diaphanous wrap around her shoulders. ''And thanks. I needed to hear it.''

''Since I'm in your good graces, can I hold your hand?''

She took his. "I'd be grateful. I haven't worn high heels in about five months, and my center of gravity's gone south."

"You don't look that pregnant for almost twenty-nine weeks."

"I feel it—especially in these shoes."

The heels were high and pointy with thin straps that clasped each ankle in a completely insufficient black-velvet hug. He cleared the lust from his throat. "I'll go in front of you, just in case."

"I plan to fall on you if I topple down the stairs."

"It's good to have a plan." He released her hand, fearing his palm might be sweating like a schoolkid's. She rested her fingers against his shoulder. He'd like to think she wanted to touch him, not that she really needed his help. Whatever her motives, she let him take her hand again as he led her through the front door and then locked it behind them.

"You've got your surprised face ready?" she asked as he opened her side of the car for her.

"I'm not going to practice it for you."

"That's okay. We need to look sincere, not practiced."

"You could be wrong. This may just be dinner with Seth and Greta."

"I hope not. Every time anyone in my family asks us over, I expect them to jump out and yell 'surprise' at us." She pulled the seat belt over her shoulder.

"I've never seen you like this," he said, bemused

and somewhat charmed by her concern that he put on the right show.

"I'm not like the others. My family, I mean."

"Yeah?" He'd like to see anyone come between her and "the others." He shut her door and crossed around the hood to get in on the driver's side. "How are you different?"

"I didn't live here full-time." She wrapped her shawl more tightly around her shoulders.

"Living with your mother made you different?"

"I'm the outsider, the visitor." She looked away as if admitting her doubts was almost too difficult.

Ian switched on the car. "It's all in your head. No one treats you like a visitor. Visitors are pampered. Your father threw you at me, and your grandmother disapproved of both of us. They didn't care if their opinions sent you all the way back to D.C. that first day."

She turned her head so fast her hair swung over her shoulder. "You don't get it, but I'm glad you clumped the two of us together."

"How else would I think of us? You're hard to convince."

"I'm honest." She waggled her hands impatiently. "And I can't explain the way I feel. Everyone who's lived here all his life is part of the main group. I'm a single and my mom is another single, and we all get together, and I can feel the difference in the way they treat me. They're a little gladder to see me, a little doubtful I'll stay, a little more careful with my feelings.''

She made him nervous when her true emotions broke the surface. ''Let's get back to you and me,'' he said. ''When are you going to stop being surprised I see us together?''

She faced the dark in front of them. His headlights picked out branches and grass, the occasional bloom. He couldn't see her face clearly. ''I don't know,'' she said.

''This is our home. I'm your husband. You're my wife.'' He hit the switch to set the lights on bright. ''You should practice repeating all that in front of a mirror. I'd like to know you believe it, too.''

''Do you practice?'' She sounded as if she wanted the answer to be no, which it was.

''I don't have to. I already believe.''

He'd never meant anything more. He glanced at her. A small smile touched her mouth before she gave her attention to the windows.

''You know, I think I'll ask my dad about having some gravel hauled up here.''

''Gravel?''

''It keeps the road from washing away on such a steep hill.''

''I'll talk to him tonight.''

''If he's there,'' she said. ''He won't be if it's just dinner with Gran and Grandpa. I say tonight's the reception because she knows you're leaving. She'll want it out of the way.''

"She thinks like you, then. Business first?"

Sophie's mouth gleamed, moist in the moonlight. "I guess she does."

He broached a subject that had bothered him more as his departure neared. "I wonder if you should ask Greta or Molly to stay with you up here."

"Huh?"

"While I'm gone." The car finally rocked to a halt on level ground. "With this lousy road and the lack of neighbors, I don't like leaving you alone." He glanced at her. "I'd say that whether you were pregnant or not."

A battle ensued in her eyes. With a shrug she offered a smile. "The big forest scare you, city boy?"

Nodding, he turned the car onto the ridge road. "Maybe a little. I'm not expecting a horror movie, but you might lose power or the phone, or you could need something you can't reach."

"I appreciate your concern, but I'm fine. My dad would laugh at me if I asked someone to baby-sit. Gran would think I've gone soft. And I really don't need a keeper."

"I'm trying to take care of you." Why wouldn't she let him?

"I'll be fine till you come home."

Home. Her soft voice reached across the car and wrapped him in an acceptance he hadn't known from her since their wedding. It distracted him from her refusal to accept his advice, but it felt good.

"Something's changed your mind about me," he said.

"Working with Gran every day, I see how reluctant she is to let go of the reins, and I think she and Grandpa have argued about it. They disagreed about the time she spent up here when I was a kid, but she always said she had to put in extra hours to make the place succeed. There were the employees and the young girls who'd have no place to go if she failed." Sophie paused as if reluctant to reveal the next part. "I've started to wonder if I'm a little more like her than I knew, and I figured you and I don't need to rehash the same argument for nearly sixty years. Every couple has an argument. The one they come back to, but I'd like to break that habit early. I want to accept you."

Relief slapped him with head-rocking force. Their child stood a better chance at a well-adjusted life if he and Sophie could dismantle their defenses and make their quiet truce a marriage.

"Aren't you going to say anything?" Sophie asked.

"I'm glad," was the truth and the best he could manage. His throat felt too tight, and he didn't want to make wild promises she might later think he'd broken, such as *I'll stop trying to overprotect you because you're carrying my child,* or, *We'll make this marriage real. We'll learn to love each other.*

"I guess that works." Sophie twisted to face the window, a hint of testiness in her tone. "Sounds like something any guy in these mountains might say after a woman's bared her soul.''

Ian laughed. He couldn't stop it in time to worry that laughing might offend her. As if he'd touched her, she turned back to him, and the dim light painted her bewildered smile. Maybe he looked as dazed as he felt, because she laughed, too. And he'd never heard sweeter music.

THEIRS WAS THE ONLY CAR in Gran and Grandpa's driveway as Ian parked.

"I guess I was wrong," she said. "No one else is here. Apart from the fact I'm afraid I'll let them see we already know, I'm starting to worry the surprise will shock me into labor when it comes."

"Can that happen?"

"No. I'm grousing."

He appeared to sag in relief. But he quickly righted himself. "The food will be good."

"And we don't have to cook it. Always a benefit." She opened the door and climbed out, making sure her shawl was clear of the door.

Her grandparents' two-storey brick house rambled along the side of the ridge, the somewhat misshapen product of more than a hundred years of Calvert building whimsy. As they reached the stairs that led to a wraparound porch, lights flashed on all over the hill.

"Motion sensors," Ian said as Sophie jumped. "I like that."

"Tell Grandpa you approve. He was probably hoping to keep us from tripping and breaking our necks, rather than shining a light on a burglar, but he'll be proud you think he's safety conscious."

"Keeping you from breaking your neck is a safety measure."

"I won't always be pregnant." It was hard to think beyond when the baby came. She couldn't blame him for suspecting she'd be perennially pregnant, too.

"Give me your hand. These treads are narrow."

He'd hauled her up and down stairs all night, but honestly, she liked the rough texture of his palm against hers. In fact, she gripped his fingers more tightly than she needed to. Not that she'd admit it if questioned.

"Do we ring the bell?" Ian asked at the top.

"I used to storm in when I was a kid, but it doesn't feel right now." She pushed the lighted button beside the door.

Immediately the floorboards inside squeaked. Beveled glass distorted her grandmother's white hair and smiling face, but the woman turned into Gran as she swept the door open.

"Evening, you two. I hope you brought your appetites." Gran hugged Sophie until she struggled for breath.

"You just saw me a couple of hours ago." But she hugged back, in response to Gran's need for affection. Had her grandparents argued again? The terse conversations she'd overheard this week were starting to worry her.

"You both look so lovely," Gran said.

"Ian's handsome." Sophie spoke in a loud whisper, teasing both her husband and her gran.

"Yes, he is. You're a lucky woman."

Ian's chuckle broke midstream as Gran wrapped him in a loving clinch, too. "Are you all right, Mrs. Calvert?"

"Greta." Gran let him go. "I'm fine. Just happy to see the two of you looking relaxed together. Follow me. Seth did something mysterious with brie and cranberries and some sort of a bread shell this afternoon. I've been scenting it since I got home, and I can't wait any longer." She peeked over her shoulder. "You don't mind eating in the kitchen, do you, Ian?"

"I'll eat Calvert cooking anywhere."

"Except mine." Sophie earned a wry grin from her husband.

She reached for his hand again, hoping he'd be comfortable with his first real dose of the Calvert matriarch and patriarch, up close and personal. A stray wish that her grandparents would enjoy him tonight crossed her mind. She felt silly the moment she acknowledged the thought, but she couldn't shake it. She wanted him to feel part of the family, not one of the singles.

Gran led the way to the kitchen, holding the swing doors open behind her. The moment Sophie set foot into the light, movement and sound erupted around the large room. Family burst from behind the long, butcher-block island and the even longer rustic pine table her father had built in his youth.

"Surprise," they all shouted, entirely out of unison.

Sophie backed into Ian's solid chest. His arms closed around her, and his chuckle vibrated down her spine.

"Where are your cars?" she asked.

Aunt Eliza, in a voluminous Worship The Cook apron, flushed from her labors, pounded for silence on the butcher block. "Where are our cars? Not thank you for this party and for all the lovely gifts we've stashed in the living room? Not I'm glad to see all of you together for the first time since I've come home?" She turned to the rest of the family. "Let's scoop up those gifts. If we do a gift grab, we'll all take something home."

"Can we, Dad?" Zach and Olivia's son, Evan, seemed eager.

"You can't play with the knives," his sister, Lily, answered for her father. "You're not a circus guy, you know."

Confused, Sophie looked to Olivia for an explanation.

"The circus was in Knoxville, and they had a knife thrower."

"You'd think they'd be careful about suggesting such things to children," Zach's mom, Beth, said.

Sophie looped an arm around each of her opinionated aunts and then sampled a lively round of affection from all the other Calverts. She lost track of Ian until they both ended up at the cranberry brie end of the tastily laden table.

"They must have hidden their cars," he said in a low voice so close to her ear he drew goose bumps all over her flesh.

With powerful discipline, she just managed to avoid begging him to follow up on the tingles. "You may feel you have to get to the bottom of this, but you'd better put a lid on discovering their hiding place until we see if we don't want the gifts."

Molly brought them plates and napkin-wrapped utensils. "We're eating buffet-style tonight. Help yourself."

"Sit down, Sophie." Ian tried to take her plate and silverware. "I'll bring you something."

She evaded his hands. "You underestimate my current appetite." Besides, she belonged at his side, making sure her family treated him right. Woe betide the cousin who acted as if Ian were an outsider who'd "compromised" her.

All progressed well. They met Zach over Aunt Beth's world-famous coleslaw. "You're not hogging your mom's slaw, are you?" Sophie asked.

He passed her the spoon. "She brought me an extra dish I've stashed in the fridge downstairs."

"You have to try it, Ian. You'll never eat anything else as long as you live."

"There's nothing to it." Aunt Beth always protested as if her coleslaw fame bewildered her. Nevertheless, any Bardill's Ridge function brought clamoring cries for her specialty. "You just chop it up and… I'll give you the recipe, Sophie."

Ian had unwrapped his silverware and he tasted a bite from the helping Sophie dished onto his plate. "Mmm. I have to side with my wife. You take that recipe, Sophie."

Everyone at their end of the room laughed, and Sophie gave in to a sense of relief. Zach joined Ian in a low-voiced, abbreviated discussion of his latest assignment. Sophie finished piling her own plate high and went in search of her grandmother.

She finally spotted Gran, atypically alone on a tufted chintz ottoman across the living room from Grandpa. She was picking at a sparse meal.

"Not hungry?" Sophie sat, sending her grandfather a worried glance.

"I helped Seth finish when I got home from work. For some reason cooking always depletes my appetite."

Sophie tucked into a yeasty roll. "What I'd give for a problem like that about now."

"And I'm afraid I sampled while I performed the ritual ooh and aah at your grandfather's skill for carving the turkey and ham. That man thinks he deserves a medal for wielding an electric knife." Shaking her head in wifely exasperation, Greta studied the contents of Sophie's dinner. "You are watching what you eat?"

Sophie wafted the mother lode in front of her. "Mostly veggies."

"And two bread servings, I see."

Aunt Eliza's yeast rolls were as irresistible as Aunt Beth's slaw. Brazenly Sophie tore a bite off one, glancing at her grandfather again, and changed the subject. "Why are you two maintaining positions on opposite sides of the room? Are you on the outs?"

"Not at all. He's having a word with your uncle Patrick about the bed-and-breakfast. He's hiring their dining room for some dinner the circuit court retirees are planning."

Sophie suspected more behind weariness in her grandmother's smile, but she knew the family rules. Gran meddled. Everyone else stayed out of her business.

"You know," Sophie said, "Ian and I were talking the other night, and he mentioned an idea I'm interested in pursuing."

"Good." Gran's smile became even more strained. "You two should work together now you're married. A good marriage comes from team effort." Her glance washed over her own husband before she managed to focus on Sophie.

"You're starting to scare me, Gran." She didn't dare say more because Grandpa kept sending them touchy looks Sophie wanted to question. At a more judicious time. "I don't think Ian and I could do much together. He might set up security for a new building, but a dead bolt ought to do the trick in Bardill's Ridge. He mentioned opening a clinic. He was half joking, but I think it's a good idea. Most of the patrons at the baby farm have their own OBs, and they go home to deliver. That's the only qualm I'm feeling about moving here, and I think we could offer a real service to the town. Most of the women who live here have to leave to have their babies.''

Gran knotted both brows. ''You couldn't work at The Mom's Place and downtown at the same time.''

''I'd need help.'' Sophie tasted Aunt Beth's cole-slaw and restrained a moan of sheer delight as sweet and sour mingled in her mouth. ''But think what we could add. Dr. Fedderson's a good G.P. and I'd talk to him about the impact on his practice, but our neighbors could use access to an OB/GYN.''

''I don't know.'' Greta whisked off her glasses and rubbed her thumbs down the sides of her nose. ''I think you overestimate Bardill's Ridge. I'm not all sure we could support a clinic, and to be honest, I'm not sure people would like us taking business from Tom Fedderson. He's delivered half our family.''

''I don't want to poach. I'd like to expand on what he can offer. He's in his sixties. He might want to lighten his load.''

''You think a person of a certain age is no longer capable? Listen, Sophie, I'm glad you've brought this up. You're doing a great job. The patients—I know, damn it, they're patrons—accept you, but I don't think you should try to overhaul medical practice in Bardill's Ridge the second you set your pregnant foot in town. Don't you have enough to keep you busy as it is?''

To Sophie's astonishment, tears surged, burning into her eyes. Her gran's response stung like the slap it was.

As if appearing out of her need, Ian materialized at her side. ''Ladies—'' he slid to the floor at Sophie's feet ''—you're awful deep in conversation.''

Sophie curved a grateful hand over his shoulder, realizing for the first time that he was an ally all her own. He dropped his arm across her knees. ''Give me one of those rolls, Sophie. You don't need them both.''

She handed over the unbitten one, managing a watery, grateful smile.

''Excuse me.'' Greta rose, a tornado taking shape. Without a word, she buzzed out of the living room.

''Whatever she said, she didn't mean it.'' Ian palmed the roll absently. ''I've watched the way she's avoiding Seth. You might be right about them.'' He curved the backs of his fingers against Sophie's cheek. ''You're the light in her eye.''

''She discarded the clinic idea and somehow that spilled over into rejecting me, too.'' Gran had never been so harsh. Her accusations had pitched Sophie back into those strange childhood days when her mother had seemed to dislike her simply because Nita didn't want to have a child.

CHAPTER EIGHT

"YOU'RE SERIOUS about the clinic?" Ian took Gran's place on the couch beside her. "You have time to start a clinic with all your other work?"

"At least you only doubt my ability, not my motives."

"I don't doubt you." He bit into the extra roll. "I've never been a pregnant woman's husband before, and I probably have stereotypical ideas about how I'm supposed to look after you. But starting a new business seems extreme when you're about to become someone's mother."

Impatience sent a sharp response halfway from her brain to her tongue, but her grandmother's unthinking comment a few moments earlier made her stem an emotional response. "I wouldn't do anything to endanger our child, but the clinic's a good idea. I just don't want Gran to resent me for it."

"Why would she?" He stared at her grandmother, who was whipping back and forth between the counter and the kitchen table within their narrow view through the door. "I don't see her resenting a medical facility that might help her community."

Sophie looked for the woman who'd always been her mentor. "Something's wrong. She's already cleaning the table, and half the family hasn't stopped talking to eat yet." Sophie frowned. "And even you noticed something's bugging Grandpa."

"Do they usually stick together at a family party?"

"Not necessarily, but she tries to push him around, and he does what she wants before she can think to ask. It's a dance they've always done. I'm wondering why no one told me Gran and Grandpa weren't getting along before I came home."

"No one else seems to see a problem." Ian looked around the room, studying expressions, body language. Sophie enjoyed watching him work. His attention to people interested her. "Either nothing's up with Greta and Seth," he said, "or they've changed so gradually this feels normal to everyone except you."

"What should I do?"

He gaped, evidently as shocked as if she'd asked him to peel off half his skull. "You're asking for advice? From me?"

"Are you teasing, or am I that difficult?" She rubbed at the moisture that had seeped as far as the corners of her eyes.

"A little of both." He stroked her forearm, trailing a series of disturbing shocks over her skin. "But give me a second to assess your options."

"You know how to handle people. What would you do?"

"If I were trying to keep her alive, I'd ask someone to replace those flimsy lace kitchen curtains with thicker, dark material. If I thought something was bothering her, I'd ask."

"That's a brick wall. I did ask."

"And she brushed you off?"

She nodded, setting her plate on the coffee table. "I'm not hungry anymore."

Affection added warmth to Ian's laughter. "I don't believe you, but I'll take up your slack." He picked up her fork and started on the infamous coleslaw. "You're right about this stuff," he said around a bite.

"I'm right about Gran, too." She leaned back, enjoying his proximity. She only had to stretch her hand out to touch him. "I don't want to hurt her, but this is a good idea."

"Before you commit, Sophie, think about the time it would take."

His serious expression made her wonder if he was right. "I don't have to do it by myself, but I'm not sure what to do if Gran's against it."

"Maybe you should leave Greta alone. You may talk to Dr. Fedderson and find you're encroaching on his territory, anyway. As for Seth and Greta, until she wants to talk to you, you might be making things worse."

"Did you train in psychology?"

A reflective grin widened his mouth. "No, but you're like her. How did you feel when the family came after you at your dad's?"

She hated admitting anyone had a better plan, but she nodded. "You're right. I wanted them to go away and let me sort out my own life. She says nothing's wrong, but she's obviously stretching the truth."

"I have a different perspective than you. If people lie to me, I usually ignore what they tell me and then I force them to follow my rules." He shrugged. "There comes a point when they know I'm right and they can do as I say or they can die."

She shuddered. It wasn't the part of his job she most liked to think about. She faced the possibility by pretending not to care. "But ultimately, you can't make them talk?"

"I don't care as long as they don't walk the edge of the safe house roof or print our phone numbers on a public rest-room stall."

"That works for paying clients, but we're talking about my grandparents." She took comfort from the solemn eyes that had mesmerized her the second she'd met him. "Gran and Grandpa are the soul of this family."

He set down his fork and dusted his hands on his legs, unintentionally drawing Sophie's gaze to the pull of his trousers across his thighs. Seeming not to notice, he took her hands in his, imparting strength she gratefully borrowed just this once.

"Are you worried about them or about yourself?"

The blunt question in Ian's most quiet tone forced her to face herself. "I seem selfish because I made so many demands after our wedding, but I was trying to protect our baby and myself in case you weren't serious about us." She glanced from Gran, whose smile looked as if it might shatter at the slightest provocation, to Grandpa, dexterously avoiding his wife. "Sure I'm concerned about my family, but I don't want my grandparents to be unhappy. Something made Gran angry with me, and it wasn't just the idea of the clinic."

He looked from Seth to Greta. "You still can't do anything about this. You wouldn't want even Greta to come to our house with the idea she could fix everything."

"Maybe, if I knew she could fix it once and for all."

He draped his arm around her shoulder. "You're fooling yourself. You could lop off a leg and you wouldn't ask your grandmother for help. You don't even want her to know you could need assistance. And deep down you know that only they can fix their problems, just as you and I are working on ours."

Maybe she was a selfish woman, because his warm, hard body put everyone else in the house into the distance. She liked Ian touching her as if he had a right. She'd been harsh and defensive and foolish to insist on separate bedrooms, and she was lucky he'd cared enough to stay.

"I wish I'd been more understanding with you."

He looked down, his eyes shadowed, his mouth temptingly firm. "What are you—"

Beyond him, down the front hall, the doorbell rang. Sophie looked up at the sound, discomfited to find Molly's gaze intent on her. With a knowing smile, Molly stepped away from her mother to speed down the hall.

"Sophie," Ian said.

"Hmm?" She was still watching Molly, the cousin who'd offered to explain the consequences of being a bad girl. The second Molly opened the door, she retreated as if an armed intruder had greeted her from the threshold. Sophie couldn't hear all she said, but she caught the name. "Nita."

Sophie rocketed to her feet. "My mom."

"Where?" Ian rose beside her.

"At the door." She braced herself for her mother's opinion of Ian. "Where's my dad? I haven't seen him yet."

"He drove to Maryville to pick up a restoration project, a sideboard."

She eyed him in surprise.

"I spoke to him this afternoon."

"How often do you talk to him?" Ian's friendship with her father diverted her from her mother, chic in a suit of silver silk.

"I asked if I could help with the sideboard when I get back." Ian looked faintly self-conscious. "I don't have a lot to do up here while you're working.

He was impressed I didn't kill you or myself or burn down the house with the doorbell I installed.''

''So was I.'' Sophie tugged at his sleeve, sliding her hand into his. ''But I'm even more impressed you're making friends with my father.''

His eyes widened with interest. She felt closer to him than she had since their wedding.

''Don't get too excited,'' Ian said with a strange intensity. ''He'd agree to anything to keep an eye on me.''

She leaned into him but watched her mother's shimmery progress down the long hall. ''I just want you and Dad to be comfortable with each other, but, Ian, are you bored up here? Is that why you took Adam's assignment?''

''No.'' He pointed toward her mom, who'd stopped at the edge of the living room. ''No one's welcoming her. Maybe we should.'' He slid his arm around Sophie's waist and headed them both toward the doorway.

She kept up on legs that wobbled. Who knew what her mom would say—in front of the whole family? Ian's arm around her made her feel better prepared to face whatever came next. The knowledge troubled her. She looked up at his determined profile and let herself relax. Sometimes having a protective husband was a fine thing.

''Mrs. Calvert.'' Ian shook her mom's outstretched French-tipped hand, and Sophie realized she'd never explained her mother's marital history.

"Franklin," Nita said. Brad Franklin had been her second husband. "You must be Ian."

"Nice to meet you."

According to long-established tradition, Sophie waited for her mother to make the first move. Nita had perfected an embrace that brought her close but kept her perfectly coiffured blond shoulder-length curls out of danger.

Sophie accepted the affection her mother could afford. "Hi, Mom. I'm glad you came."

Nita studied the less than exuberantly welcoming Calverts scattered around the room, peering in from the kitchen or over the banister from upstairs. "You're the only one who shows any sign of being happy."

"Did they expect you?"

"Probably not. I was invited, but I imagine they thought I'd just send a gift." She pulled Sophie close again. "Which I brought. It's in the car."

"You're not staying in Knoxville this time?" Sophie asked as talk stuttered to a start around them.

"No. At a bed-and-breakfast down the street from Eliza and Patrick's. Do you think anyone here could offer me a drink?"

"What would you like?" Ian asked.

"Whiskey, straight up."

"Mom." Sophie understood her mother's thirst in the face of her former in-laws' disapproval. "Don't make it worse."

"All right. Wave the soda bottle in the general

direction of my glass.'' She reached for the nearest sofa, as if her grasping hand led her feet toward it. Sophie followed but hovered at her side, a dutiful audience. ''Where's Ethan?'' her mother asked.

''On his way. He had a job in Maryville.''

Nita arched a flirty smile. ''I should have coordinated my plans with him. We could have met on the road and carpooled.''

And initiated a whole new ice age. ''Good idea, Mom. How long are you staying?''

Nita's smile collapsed. Disappointment filled her eyes. ''Are you hinting I should leave already?''

''Not at all.'' Sophie leaned into the chair's arm and restrained an urge to press her fists into the pressure at her temples. ''I'm making conversation.''

''I know it can be an effort.''

''Mom, I'm glad you came. Let's drop the subject there.''

''Sorry, but everyone in this house would be happy to hold me down and pin a scarlet letter to my breast.''

Sophie froze. As the person who'd accidentally exposed her mother's affair, she couldn't joke about that subject.

''I'm sorry, honey. Did I bring back a bad memory for you?'' Nita chuckled, sounding nervous. ''It's okay. I'm over it.''

''That's a relief.'' Sophie spoke more sharply than she'd meant to. She sprang to her feet. ''Are you hungry?''

"Starving."

Sophie snatched her own plate off the coffee table and her mother followed her back through the buffet line. Food was a much safer subject.

Greta was the first to approach them. "Nita, I'm happy you joined us this evening."

Seth appeared at her side, providing a husband's rescue just when it was most necessary. "Nita." He took her hand in his but then quickly let it go. "Did you drive straight from Knoxville?"

"Yes, and I'm staying in town. Good to see you, Seth. Greta." Patrick, her former brother-in-law, and his wife, Eliza, joined them. "How are you?"

Molly inserted herself between the growing cluster and Nita. "Aunt Nita," she said. "Nice suit."

"I always dress in armor when I come up here."

Laughter rustled, ending with Ian who was the only one who sounded as if he meant it. "I'll carry your drink, Mrs. Franklin," he said.

"Thanks, but I suspect you should have made it an IV."

Ian measured her with a look and then glanced, concerned, at Sophie, who shook her head. Drinking was not one of her mother's problems.

"Maybe we should sit so you can eat, Mom."

"I'd like to be out of the way. I forgot how everyone stares at me here."

Sophie had always assumed her mother enjoyed the attention. Hence her sweeping, prodigal-returns attitude.

"Soph—" Ian set the whiskey on the table in front of her mother "—I see Ethan. I'm going to talk to him about the sideboard."

He departed on a wave of now-familiar Ian scent that made Sophie follow him with her head and at least half her heart.

"More like he's gone to warn your father."

"If Dad's not expecting you, Mom…"

"You've always taken his side."

What did she expect? He hadn't cheated. "I'm on your side, too. Tell me about your trip. How'd you get time off work with such short notice?"

"I've trained an excellent staff." Nita dressed windows for Becks, a major D.C.-area department store. "They'll be fine without me for a couple of weeks."

Sophie tried hard not to suck in air as if her mother had socked her in the gut. "A couple of weeks?" To talk about babies and marriage and the good old days? "You've saved up your vacation."

"You're dismayed that I'll be here so long." Nita set her plate on the table beside Sophie's. "But I have even more time left for after the baby comes."

"You're overly sensitive because we're in Gran and Grandpa's house."

Her mother tapped the side of her nose. "Maybe. I do hate being in this house again." She turned with a smile full of brilliant white teeth and moist red lips. "But you're worth any punishment." She leaned in. "And I'm pleased with Ian."

Sophie braced herself.

"He's a looker, Sophie, and so expressive—in his body."

"Mom." Her worst nightmares, full-blown in reality. Her mother had always felt free to discuss her own boyfriends' attributes. All of them.

"I know." Nita smirked as if Sophie's "prudishness" continued to amuse her. "You don't like to discuss intimate matters. But I *am* your mother."

Moments like this tempted Sophie to push her mom headfirst through the nearest door and insist she never return. "You know how we've talked about maintaining a relationship?"

Nita sat back. "I remember discussions that continue to astound me. How you can talk to your own mom like that…"

"You are my mother, not my girlfriend."

Ian's firm hand on Sophie's shoulder provided a warning. She looked up and saw that her voice had risen high enough to attract spectators. Meeting her husband's concerned gaze, she barely restrained herself from yanking him over the sofa to join her.

He turned his head slightly, redirecting her attention, and she took in her father's anxious expression.

"Hi, Dad," she said. "Look who's here." Nice, hysterical note. She coughed. "Mom."

"Nita." He used the Calvert tone of challenge he reserved for his ex-wife.

"I came for Sophie and Ian's reception."

"So I see." He strolled around the couch, taking

Sophie's free hand even as he focused on Nita. ''Don't even think Ian's business trip means you're staying with Sophie.''

Sophie groaned silently. Only her mother could trick her dad into making a mistake like that. Nita flashed a quick look of interest, and Ian stiffened.

But she shot Ethan a false smile. ''I'd never force myself on our daughter.'' Her next pointed glance suggested a mother should expect a welcome in her daughter's home.

''We don't really have room, Mom.'' Sophie imagined her mother's overblown reaction to Ian's separate bed. ''We're getting a nursery ready.''

''You can breathe again, Ethan.'' Nita picked up her drink and inhaled a slug. ''Even I don't go where I'm not welcome.''

''The room is a mess,'' Ian said. ''Our house is small, and we both had extra furniture. It's all stacked in there.''

Nita gazed at her husband, annoyed. ''See? That's all anyone had to say—if you wanted to warn me without being rude.''

''I can see you didn't know about Ian's leaving, so I should have kept my mouth shut.'' He apologized to Sophie and Ian with a regretful smile before he took on Nita again. ''Since you've taken a room in town, I don't know why we're even talking about it.''

Sophie recognized impending disaster, but music

from the kitchen saved them all. She slid around on the sofa. "What's going on?"

The strains of "When I Fall in Love" filled the rooms. Eliza and Patrick followed the song to the kitchen door, arm in arm. Beth stood with Zach and Olivia on the other side of the threshold. A cousin from Greta's side excused her way through the bodies, taking her daughter toward the bathroom. In the space she left, Sophie saw her grandparents dancing, too close for light to sneak between them.

Their tension completely dissipated, they leaned into each other, moving as one. Greta's expression, soft with love, squeezed Sophie's heart. Seth, his arms tight around Greta, was a tender reminder of how a man loved, protected and longed for his wife.

Sophie stood, breaking free of her parents. She moved toward the kitchen, filling the gap between her aunts and their families.

Marriage could work. Her grandparents had problems, but the man and woman floating around their kitchen clearly didn't want to be anywhere else.

Someone came to stand at Sophie's shoulder. When Ian slid his arms around her waist, she pulled him closer.

"Feel better?" he asked in her ear.

She shivered, her legs going weak. She might have fallen if he weren't behind her. Somehow she stayed where she was, resting against his hard, lean body, instead of begging him to take her home to one of their two bedrooms.

She cleared her throat. "My mom's arrival causes a side effect. She makes any married person in my family appreciate a normal spouse."

"She's her own person."

But Nita had never been happy, never satisfied like Sophie's gran and grandfather were with each other. Not with Ethan or with Brad. Sophie wondered which blood ran more strongly in her veins—the Calvert brand that featured love of family, or her mother's, where a hunger for something new always called.

She hoped to be like her grandparents. The rest of the family had disappeared for them. Fifty years fell away. They'd loved like this from the moment they'd met, through raising their own family, establishing themselves in their hometown and finally, coming to retirement with mixed emotions. One feeling ran steady. Their love made the whole family possible.

"Ian." Sophie backed him away from the others, twisting so that he had to lower his head. "That's what I want," she said. "I want to be like that for our grandchildren one day."

He seemed taken aback, but Sophie didn't mind. Her grandparents' kind of commitment took consideration. She wouldn't want him to jump in and claim they were on their way.

Just then, he took her hand and led her to the two French doors that opened onto Gran and Grandpa's deck. The moment they were outside, she felt as if they were also dancing. In the night, he took her in his arms, and she knew he felt what she did. They couldn't wait another second to hold each other.

"I want it, too." His voice thick and thready, swathed her as tightly as his arms. "Maybe tonight we really start over. I won't push you, but I want a real marriage." He pushed one hand between them, stroking her stomach with a possessive touch that lit needful fires within her body. "I want to feel our baby in your belly. I want to know you're my wife."

Sinking against him, she forgot everyone inside. His arousal was hard to ignore. She wanted him, too. Desire made the complications they'd faced since their wedding seem simpler.

Ian pressed his lips to her cheek, moving them as if speaking words she couldn't understand. She stretched, loving the heat of him, the breath he took against her, the longing only he made her feel.

She was content. She could bear to think of asking him to return to her bed. She'd begun to trust him again.

AT HOME THAT NIGHT, Ian tried to persuade his wife to let him carry in the gifts from their reception. As usual, Sophie accepted no quarter because of her pregnancy, and he couldn't find words diplomatic enough to tell her to take it easy because she looked tired. After all, women who looked tired rarely wanted to hear about it.

As he eased a box of her grandmother's china out of the car and she scooped out the quilt Eliza and

Beth and Olivia and Molly had made, Nita drove up. Ian straightened first.

"You don't think she's inviting herself to stay?"

"I wouldn't put it past her." Sophie hugged the quilt. "But she never did get her gift out of her car. Maybe she's dropping it off."

He doubted it. Nita wasn't as bad as her reputation, but there was a definite method to her madness. She knew how to get her own way.

"Keep her out here," he said.

"What?" Sophie looked alarmed. With an armload of quilt, she managed to grab his sleeve.

"I'm going to strip my bed and shove some extra boxes in the room."

"I didn't think." Sophie sounded desperate. "I know I don't deserve your help, but please don't let her know about the separate—"

"That's what I'm going to fix. Stall her."

"Thank you."

He leaned down and caught her mouth in a swift kiss, lingering, drawn by the sheer pleasure he found in her soft lips. His heart raced, his breath went short, and he damn near dropped the china to take his wife in hungry arms. Nita's unsteady footsteps reminded him she'd arrived, and for once, Sophie wanted him to protect her.

He ran without caring if his escape gave them away.

CHAPTER NINE

SOPHIE HURRIED to her mother. Bewildered, Nita stumbled a little as she returned her attention to her car.

"Will you help me, honey? Although I really think the box is too heavy for either one of us." Reaching in, she pulled her keys from the ignition.

Nita headed toward the trunk, her narrow skirt and high-heeled pointy shoes hampering her stride through the gravel. She fluffed her hair. "I know I said I wouldn't horn in on you and Ian, but I got to thinking."

Not that big a surprise. Her mother waited for the explosion, but Sophie nodded and then realized Nita could hardly see her in the moonlight. She was so intent on keeping her mom out of the house she couldn't afford to be upset over the change in her plans. "What about your reservation?"

"Ah, you know me better than I know myself. You already guessed I'd feel I should come up here, but you shouldn't be alone with Ian gone. You need me."

She'd needed Nita when she was fourteen, when

her company hadn't compared with an attractive man's. At twenty-nine, staying alone in her own home no longer scared her. "I'm fine, Mom." She glanced at the house. Ian's window was on the other side. She couldn't even see shadows through her bedroom window on the second floor. "Maybe we'd like to be alone our last night before he leaves."

"He'll only be gone a few days." As if that settled the matter, Nita poked at the trunk with her key. Still enduring her mother's jabs after all these years, Sophie felt a little sorry for the car. Finally, with a metallic slide, the key went in, and the trunk popped open. Her mom wrestled with a large, long box.

"See? I knew it was too big."

"Leave it, Mom."

"No. I'll bring it in. Ian can come back for my things."

Sophie didn't know what to say. Years of trying to maintain a relationship with her mother weighed in one hand. Pity, because the rest of the Calverts couldn't come to terms with Nita, made her turn toward the cabin.

She opened the door and planted herself in front of the stairs to keep her mom from going up. "Want some coffee?"

"Do you have a beer?"

"Probably." Her dad's favorite brand had turned up in the fridge in much the same way he seemed to turn up at odd hours.

"I could use a beer after all that hilarity."

Sophie eyed her sharply.

"I know, I know." Nita set down the box. "You love them. They're fun for you, but I can't enjoy myself when I feel all that hatred directed at me."

"No one hates you. They love Dad and me, and they just don't like the choices you made when you left."

"It was all so long ago. I say get over it." Nita tapped the top of her unwrapped box. "What do you think?"

Sophie finally looked. "A child's car seat. That's great, Mom. We don't have one yet."

"Well, what did you think? I'd wait till the kid's born to give you something?" Nita did a rendition of "Wipeout" on the box. "I'm determined to do the right thing by your child."

"Good." She hoped being a grandmother was a more instinctive response for her mom than motherhood had been.

"Good? That's all you have for me?" Nita twisted her mouth in a little-girl pout. "I thought you'd be glad I wanted to make up for my shortcomings."

At a thump overhead, Sophie concentrated on not glancing at the ceiling. "I don't dwell on shortcomings." Not entirely the truth, but she did try not to worry about the kind of maternal instincts she'd inherited. "I'm grateful for the car seat. You chose the safest brand." She covered her belly with both hands. Her marriage so far had been based on the baby. Tonight, her mind was on her husband. "But

I'm thinking of Ian right now. He's leaving tomorrow. He didn't expect my family to spend the night." And neither had she. She'd anticipated a different kind of farewell.

"If you don't want me..." Nita let the rest of her sentence tail off into silence while she shrugged out of her jacket. Finally she said briskly, "I'll get a knife from the kitchen so we can open this box."

And that settled that. Sophie opened a beer for her, and they both admired the new seat. Sophie ignored both the thudding upstairs and her mother's repeated questioning glances.

At last Ian came down, his expression calm but his jacket missing, his dark tie loose in the open collar of an equally dark shirt. He stopped to gaze at the car seat box, his hands on his lean hips.

Sophie didn't care what had taken him so long. She simply wanted to complete the undressing process he'd started in his rush to move things.

"Where've you been?" Nita asked. "We almost forgot you. Would you mind bringing the rest of my things in from the car?"

Sophie laughed nervously. "Mom," she said, "I think you should stay at the B and B tonight. You can come back tomorrow morning."

"It's all right," Ian said.

Sophie gaped at him. Nita here tonight was anything but all right. His dark-blue eyes sent her a message. Frustrated, she assumed he'd managed to stuff enough of their belongings into the guest room to

make their marriage more convincing, but she still
didn't want her mother under her roof tonight.

"It's all right," he said again. "A little messy,
Nita, but you're welcome to use the guest room. I
put some sheets and pillowcases on the bed in there.
You'll have to navigate the packing boxes."

"Still haven't unpacked, Sophie?" Nita stepped
around her own contribution to the box population
in their cabin. "Well, you'll find time eventually. My
daughter will gladly get you a beer, Ian, after all your
hard work. You didn't have to tidy up for me."

"I know where the beer is." He paused at Sophie's side to rub her shoulders. "You're tense. Go
on up. Nita," he said, "the remotes for the television
are on that table at your elbow. I still have to pack
for my trip tomorrow. Sophie's exhausted, and I'm
driving to Knoxville at about five in the morning."
His rueful glance at Sophie acknowledged that she
wouldn't be coming along now. "I'll bring in your
bags, but then I think we're calling it a day."

"I'm sure I can entertain myself." Her voice was
pitched a little high as she fumbled with the remotes.
"Two? Could you show me how these work?"

"Sure. We both want you to feel at home. Soph?
You going up?"

Sophie stood as if in a trance. She spun slowly on
her heel, rocking a bit unsteadily. The full weight
of what her mother's staying in the guest room
meant hit her. Ian would have to sleep in her room.
With her.

She climbed the stairs and opened the door to find Ian's bedding and clothing strewn across her floor, his scent hanging in the room. She carried his shampoo and deodorant, and all the other personal items he'd dropped in a towel on the floor, to the bathroom.

Then she picked up his clothing and began to fold, grateful to perform even so small a task in return for his keeping their secret from her mom.

WITH HIS MIND on his wife, Ian settled his mother-in-law on the living room couch with instructions for all the electronic equipment she might use. She dialed up a retro movie on the satellite he and Ethan had installed, and he thanked her again for the car seat.

Nita patted the remote, looking perfectly comfortable in her tight silver skirt and blouse, her hand wrapped around the beer bottle. "I'm fine for the night. I'll find my way to bed later. Don't you bother with me."

Her smile actually flirted, but Ian assumed it was a reflex action. Nodding, he headed where he wanted to be, upstairs with his wife. On the landing, he paused to knock at the door. No doubt Nita found a man knocking at his own bedroom door suspicious, but Sophie's feelings mattered more, and she might appreciate warning.

She snatched the door open and grabbed his arm to drag him inside. "Don't knock. She'll hear you."

"I was just thinking of you." He stopped dead.

She'd tidied all the stuff he'd tossed into the room and taken a shower. She was now wearing a Seattle Mariners T-shirt he'd thought he'd lost around Christmastime. "You stole my shirt."

Sophie colored from the neck up, making him curious about what went on below the collar of his faded shirt. The last time he'd seen her in it, it had fit her differently. Did she need those striped flannel pant-things?

"I forgot." She crossed her arms defensively beneath her breasts. "You know how we were back then." She tried to sweep her hair off her face, but whenever she showered, it seemed to swell with curls and humidity, and it simply tumbled against her soft skin. "Every time I saw you might have been the last time. I was afraid..." She tugged at the shirt's hem. "I took it because I wanted something of yours to remind me, just in case."

He laughed, pulling her close. She came with resistance, but he sensed embarrassment rather than rejection. "I wasn't complaining. I like knowing I mattered to you." He kissed the top of her head, his heart hammering. Being close to his wife reduced him to a mass of physical responses he couldn't control. "You didn't have to put away my things."

"What if my mom had barged in? She might have insisted on a tour."

"I would have said no." He rubbed his cheek against her hair. "You have that option, too."

"No means so much to my mother." She put her

arms around him. "You've lost weight, and I'm gaining."

"You look gorgeous, and you feel even better." He ran his hands down her back, knowing she must be aware how she aroused him. "I can't get enough of holding you."

His chest muffled her chuckle. She tilted back her head. "I missed you, too."

After all that had passed between them he was tentative, brushing his lips against hers. That swift kiss outside, partly to claim her for Nita's benefit, hadn't satisfied a single desire. He needed time to taste Sophie, to remember the million different ways her body responded to his. To feel what it might be like to have everything he'd ever dreamed of—family, real love—forever—if he could make his marriage work.

Sophie opened her mouth and he groaned, need surging almost uncontrollably. Kissing her now, in the privacy of their room, simply because he wanted to make love to his wife, changed everything they'd ever been to each other.

He pushed his hands beneath her shirt, seeking warm skin. She muttered his name and arched against him, making him aware of the new curves that cradled their baby. Her waist, though thicker, begged for the caress of his hands. He claimed her, possessive as he held her and their child between them.

"Do you think I'll ever feel him kick?"

"Her," Sophie said with her usual assurance, smiling as she flattened his palms against her stomach. "I don't know why she's shy with you." Sophie brushed her lips along his jawline, her touch featherlight yet so seductive he shook with longing and wrenched his hands out of her grasp to hold her again. "You'll catch her anytime now," Sophie said.

He couldn't talk anymore. With his mouth, he sought the column of her throat, the curve of her earlobe, the pulse beneath her ear.

As she trembled, he laughed against her skin. "You taste good." He cupped her heavy breasts. "Can we get rid of the shirt?"

She stepped back, but finished undoing his tie, instead. It hissed as it slid through his collar, then she tossed it over his shoulder and started on his shirt buttons.

"Not mine," he said. "Yours."

"They're both yours."

"The one you're wearing."

She pushed his shirt off his shoulders. "You're wearing more."

He reached to unbuckle his belt, but she leaned over his hands to follow the thin line of hair down his breastbone with her tongue. His breath hissed in this time, and he tangled his fingers in her hair, cupping her face.

"Finish with the pants," she said, her skin hot against his.

He could follow orders when they suited him. His

pants and belt thudded to the floor. He followed them, wrapping his arms around her. On his knees, he tugged the flannel pajamas down her hips and helped her step out of them.

Her hips were still narrow. Her thighs trembled as he kissed the waistline of her silk panties.

"Wait, wait," she said. "I'm ahead of you again."

"Will you shut up and let me make love to you?"

Instead, she laughed, throwing back her head with the pure joy he'd sorely missed. He climbed to his feet and urged her onto the bed, following her to the mattress. With his knee between hers, he leaned on one elbow and shucked his shirt. Hers went next, joining his on the floor.

Her sweet gaze, trusting, intense and hungry, captured his. With one hand on the back of his head, she pulled him into a kiss that made him forget to be gentle. He pushed her underwear down her legs and helped her remove his boxers.

But then he stopped, his body arrowed above hers.

"What?" Her voice, thick and urgent, nearly pushed him over the edge.

"We're going too fast. Shouldn't I be more gentle with you?" He ran his hand down her side, eagerly learning the new shape of her body.

She shivered, pressing his fingers against herself. "No."

He kissed the deep-blue vein that ran from her collarbone to the peak of her breast. Even her skin looked different, more translucent. Her nipples were rounder. He sucked gently, shuddering when she groaned. She offered her other breast, and he curved his hand around hers, tasting her until she whispered his name in a savage demand.

She reached for his hips and pulled him over her. He moved slowly, intent on the pleasure in her voice. It was different this time. He needed her as badly as ever. He wanted her more, but he also wanted more for her. They weren't playing around. They were husband and wife, one in this room away from the rest of the world and her loving octopus-family.

Inside these four walls, in each other's arms, they were the only family that mattered. She was all to him as she cried out his name, clenching her hands on his hips. Still, he held back.

What if this feeling, this joining, was all in his mind? What if she didn't feel it? He lowered his head to her breast again, pushing one hand above her head so that he nearly controlled her movements. She arched, working against his control. With her free hand, she clasped his head, gasping his name.

Suddenly she broke free of his hold and wrapped her arms around his neck, her legs around his hips. He pushed her, holding his own need at bay. He wanted this wedding night to be more real to her than any moment they'd ever spent together.

"Ian, please," she said against his ear. "Please."

The plea undid him. He barely remembered in time to hold his weight off her. Sophie. Sophie. Her name repeated in his head, in his mouth. He kissed her over and over, gentling as his heartbeat slowed little by little.

"I'm here," she said against his mouth.

He couldn't help smiling at a concern that wasn't like her at all. Before they'd made love with very little thought or concern. She'd always assumed he'd be fine. He hadn't considered what she'd remember.

"What's funny right this minute?" She sounded slightly disgruntled, though her flushed face and brilliant eyes said otherwise.

"You were worried about me." He took her mouth with a husband's conviction.

She stilled, but only for a second. "I think you worried first," she said, and kissed him back until he was willing to admit whatever she required.

WAY TOO EARLY IN THE MORNING, Sophie waved her husband goodbye and wished she was going with him on that shopping trip. Ian put his arm out the window and waved just as the mist swallowed him and his car. She'd decided she couldn't shop as if her mother hadn't come to visit.

Behind her, the door opened. She steeled herself for commentary, hoping they hadn't been too noisy. "Morning, Mom." Nita was perfectly turned out in today's theme—gold. A gold band holding her hair off her face, gold threads in her cashmere sweater, gold pumps peeking beneath bone gabardine slacks.

"Good morning." Nita held up a delicate china

cup. Part of the gift from Gran that Ian had carried in the night before. "I made coffee."

Sophie smoothed her T-shirt over her stomach. "I'm off the stuff for now. Thanks, anyway."

"Off? Oh, yes, that caffeine stricture during your pregnancy." She sipped from the cup. "I'll drink an extra cup for you. What's your plan for today?"

"I want to meet Grandpa for lunch." Sophie consulted her watch. She had hours before Grandpa would show up at his usual lunch spot, the Train Depot Café in town. "I need some business advice, and I think he'll be there. Do you mind if I call him?"

"Not at all. I have a date myself." Nita looked pleased. "With your father."

Sophie grabbed the rail that bordered the porch steps. "You could knock me over with a feather."

"You're just a little off balance, that's all."

Sophie smiled. "Cute, Mom. Tell me it's not odd that you and Dad, who can barely stand breathing the same air, twenty-one years after you left, are sharing lunch today."

"I insisted on meeting in public," her mom said. "I've persuaded your aunt Eliza to make us lunch. Meeting in front of family will drive your father crazy, and the B and B's dining room is much safer than his house. We won't be tempted to bean each other with our plates."

How could she argue? "Good plan." Sophie hauled herself up the steps. "Come inside. I'll make toast and juice. I need something to get me through a shock like this.''

''And you're probably tired, too.''

Nita sounded knowing. Sophie blushed, but then she looked back over last night and went all mushy inside. She wasn't usually the type to go mushy.

Last night had been different. As passionate as ever, maybe even more so. But those hours in Ian's arms had been spiced with a new generosity of spirit. They were no longer just taking from each other. They were both learning to give.

SETH CALVERT HID a grin as his granddaughter eased into a green-vinyl-clad booth, which was a tighter squeeze than it used to be. He squeezed her hand. ''I should have taken a table, but since you asked me not to tell your gran about our lunch, I'm keeping a low profile.''

''This is good.'' She adjusted her jacket around her swollen tummy and glanced at the steady stream of customers. ''I like the privacy.''

The Train Depot Café was what its name suggested, a café built in the no-longer-used depot that had housed the old Bardill's Ridge train station. A long Formica counter served farmers perched on fat green stools. A chalkboard above the open cooking area displayed today's specials. Seth passed Sophie one of the laminated menus that stood in a chrome rack on their table.

''What'll you have?''

Her lips curled a little, in the way women had of showing their morning sickness.

"I'm not sure. I'm not feeling that well."

"Your gran always said crackers did the trick."

"I'm crackered out, Grandpa."

Their server, a boy who looked too young to have a steady job, came to the table. "What for you, Judge Calvert?"

"Coffee and something…let's see, how about tuna on toast, Sophie?"

"Dry tuna, if it's white with no oil." She shut her menu. "Sorry to be so fussy."

"That's okay," the teenager said. "You want that, too, Judge?" he asked, clearly unwilling to believe a man could choke down such a meal.

"Yes, and a glass of milk for my granddaughter."

The kid nodded at Sophie and left them. Seth waited for her to start. She didn't.

"What did you want to discuss?" he asked as she readjusted her silverware for the fourth time. "I know you said business, but your gran handles everything up at the baby farm."

Sophie looked at him, surprised, but smiling. "She wouldn't like to hear you calling it that."

"She wouldn't be that stunned. She's never believed I respected her calling to work up there."

Sophie narrowed her gaze, the same green eyes almost every Calvert was born with. "Are you being sarcastic when you say she has a calling, Grandpa?"

"A little." He took a glass of milk and a glass of

water from their server and passed them to her. She drank deeply of the water. "Are you all right, Sophie?"

"Fine." She slipped her napkin from beneath her cutlery and spread it on her lap.

"I don't interfere up at the resort."

"I really wanted to ask your advice." She lifted the water glass again and almost drained it.

"But you're nervous?" He worked her problem out loud. "You don't really want to talk to me, but you have to. This has something to do with Greta."

She nodded. "That covers the harder parts. Ian and I were talking one night and he mentioned a clinic. Just as a joke, really." She leaned closer and lowered her voice. "He may think I work too hard."

"Let me welcome him to my club."

Sophie sat back with a frown. "What?"

"Your gran works too hard, too. It's time she let go up there, and I know she trusts you." He and Greta had never aired their differences in front of their children or grandchildren, and Sophie was in no shape to be the first to hear of his discontent. "What about this clinic?"

"I thought about opening one down here in town. Ian was kidding, but I think it's a good idea. Most women in Bardill's Ridge use an out-of-town OB when they're pregnant, and the others use Dr. Fedderson. He's good, but why wouldn't he welcome a clinic with a dedicated OB/GYN to lighten the load?"

"He might not." Seth sat back. "He might think you're cutting into his practice."

"I'd talk to him about it first. And who's to say his current patients would consult us? But Bardill's Ridge is a growing area. A lot of young families are moving up here. I'd like to provide them with a choice."

"Could you survive strictly on new patients?"

She blinked. "I haven't thought everything through. Maybe I'd ask Dr. Fedderson if he'd like to share space. But he's not my problem yet."

"Greta is?" She had to be kidding. Greta had talked occasionally about opening a practice in town.

"She said I was moving too fast, that the town isn't ready for a change like that. I got the feeling she resented my bringing up the idea."

Seth set his teeth. Of course. Because Greta knew he wouldn't stand for her dabbling in a brand-new enterprise, and she couldn't bear the idea of not being part of a new clinic in Bardill's Ridge.

"What do you think, Grandpa? You know Gran, and you know the town. My first question is about her. Is she okay?"

"She's fine. Perfectly healthy, just a little anxious about retiring. You know she was already pregnant with Ned when she was in college." He flinched as even the mention of his late son brought back the pain of trying to comfort Beth and Zach after Ned's death. "She's always worked with a full plate, and she's envisioning days sinking into years with absolutely nothing to do.''

Sophie caught his hand. "Are you all right?" She squeezed pretty hard. "I'm starting to think I've come between you and Gran."

"Not a chance. Don't take so much credit for yourself. She'll find plenty to do."

"O-kay." She injected the syllables with doubt. "What about the clinic? Do you think it would be a good idea? Would people here resist it?"

"I think it's a great idea if you include Fedderson in the planning."

"But what about Gran?" The bell above the door tinkled a warning. Sophie peered over his shoulder, guilt spreading a mask over her face.

He turned, already expecting to see his wife in a snit. He wasn't disappointed. She marched to their booth, completely ignoring the café's other customers, who spun in their seats to watch the free floor show.

"You lied to me, Seth Calvert. You told me you were eating lunch with Patrick."

He glanced around. Their son Patrick usually came here for lunch, but wouldn't you know? Today he was nowhere to be seen. "I'm sorry, Greta. I knew you wouldn't like me talking to Sophie on my own."

"It's my fault, Gran. I asked Grandpa not to mention—"

Her eyes glinted with real pain. "And you, Sophie. Why would you go behind my back to your grandfather as if I were a child who couldn't understand this clinic business? I know you're talking about the clinic.''

''But I also wanted to talk about you. I'm worried.'' Sophie tugged Greta into the seat beside her. ''You haven't been yourself since we started working together, and then you got angry over the clinic idea, as if you thought I was stealing your business. That just isn't you, Gran. I thought Grandpa might be able to tell me what was wrong.''

Maybe he couldn't get through to Greta, but their granddaughter could. Greta paused a moment. Sophie's concern bothered her.

''Well, your grandpa can't explain, because nothing's wrong, except I'm starting to suspect the people I trust don't trust me.'' She stared across the table with an animosity Seth had never seen before. ''Starting with you, Seth Calvert. If you weren't so busy acting crazy to get your own way, no one else would dare.''

''That's enough.'' He stood, digging his wallet out of his back pocket. ''Greta, you're coming with me. You want the truth, Sophie? Your grandmother and I don't agree on where our lives are headed right now, and all of a sudden, we're discussing our private affairs with you. Greta doesn't want you to start planning the clinic because she can't stand not being part of it.''

He was already ashamed of himself when his wife shot to her feet. ''You're darned right I'm coming with you. I'm going to straighten you out once and for all. I am not the lunatic you imagine. A lot of women don't want to give up rewarding work to pander to their husband's every whim. You pander to mine for a change.''

''I have, Greta, for fifty-five years.'' He took money from his wallet and tossed it on the table. ''It's my turn now to have my own way.''

He glanced at Sophie, and the tears in her eyes damped the fire on his temper a little. ''Sophie, honey, I'm sorry.''

''I'm the one you should apologize to,'' Greta said, ''talking about me behind my back.''

His wife's outraged sputtering turned the flames back up. He stalked from the restaurant. So what if she didn't follow him home? They'd never walked away from each other in mid-argument, but it might already be too late to hash this out.

CHAPTER TEN

HER GRANDPA'S DEPARTURE seemed to suck all the available oxygen from the unnaturally silent café. Sophie stared at her grandmother, who returned her gaze but clearly wasn't seeing her. She said nothing before she followed in her husband's wake.

Sophie felt the eyes of the town upon her. She didn't care what they thought. She waved down the kid who'd taken their order and settled with him, and then she hurried out to her car. The second she shut her door, she started dialing her grandparents' house on her cell phone. The answering machine picked up. Of course they couldn't have made it home yet.

Would either of them ever go home again? What had she caused? Did she have to bring bad luck to every married couple she knew?

She dialed again and got the machine. "It's me. This is my fault. Don't blame Grandpa. I shouldn't have asked him to meet me without telling you, Gran. And I probably overreacted to our talk about the clinic." She felt like an eight-year-old, begging her mommy not to leave. "Please call me and tell me you're okay. I'm worried about you."

She drove to their house. Cupping her hands around her face, she tried to see through the dark garage windows. It was empty. Only the sunlight and the birds and the buds on the trees waited with her outside the tall, brick dwelling that housed everyone she loved most. What the hell had she been thinking? Only of herself. Only of what she wanted.

She had to make changes before the baby came. She had to learn to put the people she loved first, even when what she wanted—the clinic—seemed like the right thing to do.

She turned toward home. With any luck, her mother might still be out at lunch with her dad. But this was a no-luck day. Her mom met her at the cabin door again.

"How was your meal with Seth? Your father and I have declared a truce. Since we both want to be grandparents, we thought setting terms would be wisest. And look." She pirouetted. "No knives anywhere. I think your father's finally grown up."

"Mom, I can't listen to you say things like that about Dad today. He wasn't in the wrong."

"A woman has many reasons to look outside her marriage for sustenance."

"And some women choose an excuse that gives them permission. I'm not saying both people don't play a part in breaking a marriage, but you could have left him before you started an affair with another man."

"You're too hard." Nita swept back inside the cabin.

Sophie hung back on the threshold while the summer breeze wrapped her in the familiar sounds of rustling branches and long grass, whose blades whispered against each other.

"You're right, Mom." She twisted out of her jacket and entered the cabin. "I am too hard, because it's none of my business, and I'm sorry. The past is between you and Dad. I don't know what happened, but I love you both, and I should have just asked you not to talk about him to me."

"What?" Nita jackknifed off the sofa where she'd already flung herself.

Sophie jumped.

"You love me?"

Sophie's heart broke. Even so, she found it harder to say the second time. "I've always loved you, Mom."

Her mother wrapped her in a real hug for the first time in probably twenty years.

"Your clothes, Mom."

"What are dry cleaners for?"

As if she secreted oil or something. She'd meant she didn't want to wrinkle her mother's clothing, but some things never changed. "I can't breathe."

"Oh, sorry." Nita backed off. "You have gained a pound or two. How far along are you?"

As if offended for her, the baby kicked so hard Sophie grabbed her sides.

"Sophie?"

"I think she cracked a rib."

"It's fun now to feel all that life going on inside you, but from here on the work starts. And then she'll be on your mind the rest of your life."

The baby seemed to be drumming with her heels. Sophie wished Ian were here. No one could have missed this display. "Am I on your mind, Mom?"

"Well, yeah." She said it as if Sophie must be nuts for not knowing.

IAN MET HIS CLIENT, Andrew Hawthorne, at a little sandwich shop in Great Falls the night before they were to drop off the software. Ian and the courier discussed their plans at dinner.

"I don't even know why they hired you," Andrew said. "I know it's financials, but I can hand-carry a CD as well as the next guy, and I'm assigned to security. They picked me because I can bench-press more than my boss in the company fitness center."

"I don't need to know what's on the software," Ian said, "and you shouldn't be so willing to discuss it." The other guy looked sulky, but Ian found he didn't care so much for short jobs when they meant leaving his pregnant wife behind. He wanted to take care of business and go home.

After they ate, Ian sent Hawthorne out ahead of him so he could check to see if the other man was being followed. The coast seemed clear enough. He headed back to his hotel. In his room, he sprawled on the bed and dialed Sophie on his cell. Her voice flashed images of last night in his mind. An uncomfortable hunger took hold of him.

"What'd you do today?" he asked, trying not to sound as desperate as he felt for her.

"I had lunch with Grandpa, and then our little soccer player broke most of my ribs."

"What?" He loved the joy in her voice, but he felt left out. "I'm never going to feel him move."

"You'll have plenty of time when you get back home."

"Well, I like the sound of home." And that she assumed it was his now, too.

"Good. How's your stuff going?"

"Fine, but I already wish I hadn't taken the job. I've managed to switch my flight, so I'll be in Knoxville by nine tomorrow night. I should make it to the cabin by ten-thirty."

"I'm glad."

Her relief sounded too intense. Something was wrong. "Did you have a good lunch with Seth?"

"Fine."

He waited for more. She volunteered nothing. "You don't sound as if it was fine."

"We'll talk when you get back. My mom's calling me. She wants to start the movie we rented."

"Okay." She was pulling away from him as if he had no right to pry, but he didn't want to argue over the phone. "See you tomorrow night."

"All right."

He hung up, dissatisfied.

The next morning he picked up Hawthorne at the Metro station at Rosslyn. An odd thing happened. Sophie kept showing up in his head, getting between him and his client.

In the subway car, sitting across from Hawthorne, he had time to stare at the dark walls they sped past, wondering why his wife still held back. He seemed to be acclimating to sharing their life more easily than she.

Ian tried to clear his family from his mind. He turned to Andrew. "We're on time as long as your counterpart shows up."

"He'll be there. We're just two guys passing a baton at Union Station."

Ian glanced from face to bored face among their fellow passengers. The courier ought to shut up. At Union Station they left the Metro car and headed upstairs toward the coffee bar.

He kept his client a few steps ahead of him. All this for software. A man stepped away from the bar, and Ian's guy held out his hand, the CD case extended. But the man he was handing off to didn't match the photo Adam had faxed to Ian.

Ian stepped between the two men and reached for the CD. A second too late.

The new guy turned and bolted for the nearest exit. He had the CD. Ian shot after him. Hawthorne tried to trip Ian, but Ian ducked the move.

Damn. Over software.

He shoved through the double glass doors that had barely shut behind the other guy. He was still reaching as the man jumped into the front seat of a cab. The CD was close enough to touch. Without thinking, Ian threw himself at it. He grabbed it and slid along the open door, onto the hood. A random taxi shouldn't have been moving so fast—unless the driver was in on the scheme, too.

Ian slammed into the windshield, breaking the antenna that slapped him in the face. Still calculating how to get out of his first job gone really bad, he learned that fear tasted like metal in your mouth. He had too much to lose now.

Images of Sophie passed through his mind as safety glass broke around him. He pulled up his legs, slid off the car and hit the road, rolling.

Sophie. She'd wanted him to turn down this job. He thought of the baby who'd never moved in his hands.

Oil from the road filled his nostrils. Sophie would never trust him again. Sky, swirls of blue and white and gray filled his eyes. Pain swiped everything except Sophie aside. Sophie and their unborn child.

His ankle broke with a crack like a piece of brittle wood. His shoulder seemed to catch fire. The road scraped his shirt off.

Need, like a well, opened within him. He had to see Sophie again. He was falling in love with her.

Dark liquid welled up on the pavement in front of his eyes, and he smelled his own bleeding body. He couldn't move. "Sophie." He couldn't tell if he was saying her name, or if it just screamed inside his head. Blackness took her away from him.

"YOU'RE FINE, JANEY." Sophie pointed to the machine that counted all 145 beats per minute of Janey's baby's heartbeat. "I know it's scary to fall." Janey was only fifteen, and terror pooled in her eyes as the fetus in her belly struggled hard enough to cause waves in her teenage mom's skin. "But you've clearly annoyed the baby. She's too strong to be hurt."

"How can you be sure, Dr. Ridley? Something bad could happen any second." The young girl valiantly controlled tears. She grabbed at her stomach. "I didn't want her at first. Now I'm getting paid back."

"Nothing's wrong. You're thirty-seven weeks along. We can hear that the baby survived your tumble down the front porch, and the worst thing we have to fear is that you'll go into labor." She'd checked Janey on Thursday, and the girl hadn't been effaced. No sign of dilation. Her daughter hadn't even dropped yet. "I'm not going to check you right now, because your body's been through enough, but we're going to sit here together and listen to the baby, and if you have any pain, we'll go from there."

Sophie reached for a wipe from a box on the pale blue counter. "Let me clean your knee. You tore your jeans."

"Is my mom outside yet?"

"You want me to check?"

Despite having only a learner's permit, the girl, one of Greta's outpatients, had driven herself because her mom had said she couldn't leave her job.

"No, stay here. I told her to just yell my name if she came."

Sophie crossed the room and opened the honey-colored door. "We'll make it easy for her."

"She says Sunday after church is her best time for tips."

How could that be? Most people had children to get ready for school the next day. "How about your dad?"

"I don't want him." Janey looked sullen. Sophie recognized the look. She'd felt that way about her mom once.

"How about the baby's father?"

"He went in the Army. He's supposed to come back for us after his training." Janey's tears rolled down her face, toward the collar of her straining, green knit shirt.

Sophie smiled her best I'm-perfectly-capable smile. "I guess you're stuck with me."

"Thank you for coming. When I couldn't get hold of Dr. Calvert, I thought I was going to have to drive to Knoxville."

"What about Dr. Fedderson?"

"He didn't answer his phone either, and besides,

I've been seeing Dr. Calvert because my mom didn't want Dr. Fedderson to know.''

About the baby. Small-town fears of being shunned for a child's mistake. Ridiculous. "I don't think he'd care, Janey.''

"You don't care, do you?''

Sophie planted her hands in the small of her own overworked back. "That you're pregnant at fifteen?'' She shook her head. "I'm worried about your future.'' She adjusted the monitor across Janey's stomach. "About the baby's future, but I guess you know what you're facing.''

"I'm getting a clue.'' The tears poured out again, and Sophie handed her a box of tissues.

Footsteps started down the hall to the office area. "We're back here,'' Sophie said, but it wasn't Janey's mom who showed up. "Grandpa.'' Sophie knew instantly that something was wrong. "Gran?''

"No, but she's coming.'' He glanced at the girl on the paper-covered table. "Janey, how are you?''

She scrambled to yank her shirt over her belly, and Sophie stepped between them. "You shouldn't be back here, Grandpa.''

"I know. Janey, do you mind if I stay a minute?''

"No.'' The girl stared at the monitor as her baby's heart sounds grew fainter. "Dr. Ridley?''

"It's just the monitor.'' Sophie adjusted it while her grandfather looked away. Sophie pulled a robe out of a cabinet to cover Janey better. "Gran's okay?'' she said as if her heart wasn't pounding faster than the baby's.

"Yes."

Nita. "My mother?"

"Just give me a few minutes, Sophie."

Janey grabbed Sophie's arm. "What are you talking about? You didn't call him because something awful's wrong with me? You don't need a lawyer or something?"

Sophie pushed her own fear to the edge of her mind. "Grandpa was a judge, Janey. He doesn't even remember being a lawyer." It must be bad. He didn't argue with her. But she didn't want to scare this young woman anymore. "You're fine. Have you thought of a name for the baby yet?"

"After today, I'd call her Sophie if it didn't sound so old-fashioned."

"Thanks." Sophie's mouth ached as she tried to smile. She didn't dare look at her grandfather. Only two more names came to mind, and she couldn't stand anything happening to Ian or her dad.

She heard more footsteps.

"How about you?" Janey pointed at Sophie's stomach. "Do you have a name?"

"My husband insists it's a boy, but I say we're having a girl. We haven't talked about names yet."

"You don't know which it is?"

"No. I looked away during the sonogram, and he asked not to be told."

"Janey, I hear you had a little problem."

Gran. Thank God. Sophie whirled but didn't quite meet her grandmother's eyes. The truth would be there.

"She's fine. The baby's heart is beating at her normal rate." Sophie concentrated on the monitor readout. "Plenty of movement. I checked Janey on Thursday and she wasn't effaced or dilated. I haven't done an exam tonight because of the fall, but I promised we'd hang around and listen a while."

"Good idea. Mind if I listen, Janey?"

"I'm glad to see you, Dr. Calvert."

Sophie slipped out the door, past her gran and grandfather, her own tears already escaping. She hurried to her office and dragged her grandpa over the threshold before she shut the door. "Tell me." She choked on the last word, crying too hard to stop because he looked so serious. His pale face terrified her.

"Ian's going to be fine."

"No." Her legs buckling, she started for the floor, but Grandpa grabbed her and eased her onto the couch. "Is he—"

"I don't know exactly what happened. But he told me to tell you he's going to be fine. I'm supposed to repeat it until you believe me."

Her head swam. Fear made her sick, cramping low in her belly. She dropped against her grandpa's chest. "What happened? Is he lying? How bad is he? Did someone shoot him?"

Seth rubbed the back of her head, and the steady

movement helped a little. Sort of like repeating that Ian would be fine. "His ankle is broken. He dislocated his shoulder, and he has some other cuts and bruises, but he's fine. He made them call me when he couldn't find Ethan."

"Grandpa, I'm going to him. Tell Gran I won't be in tomorrow." She pulled out of his arms, already on her way to the door.

"He's coming home. He discharged himself from the hospital."

She rubbed both hands over her face. "Why would he do that?"

Her grandfather pulled her back to the couch. "He wants you to see he's okay. I have his flight number in the car. Just sit here until I'm sure you're all right, and then we'll figure out what time we can expect him tomorrow."

"I'm meeting his plane."

As Seth held her, she noticed his hands were shaking. "He doesn't want you to be upset. That's why I'm here. Just wait for him at home. He's coming as fast as he's able."

"Are you all right, Grandpa?" She didn't care for his wan color. "Let me take your blood pressure."

"Are you out of your mind?" He sprang back from her. "I was terrified you'd lose this baby or go into labor or something. I'm seventy-eight years old, and I've never delivered a child. I didn't want to start with you."

"I'm healthy as a horse. I just don't want my husband to be dead."

"Greta said that would be your reaction. But don't start trying to doctor me."

"Let me at least get you some water."

"Water, I'll take."

"Maybe you could help Gran while I get it. We're just trying to occupy Janey's mind."

Grumbling, he did as she asked. Janey seemed a lot happier, chatting about school like any other fifteen-year-old. Sophie positioned her grandfather in a chair across the table from Gran.

"I'm going for water. Anybody else want some?"

"I'd like a bottle," Janey said, and Gran nodded, too. Sophie tried to draw her grandmother's attention to her grandpa, but Gran didn't seem to notice.

"Grandpa, the flight information?"

"On the front seat of my car. I'll get it."

"I could use the walk." Again she tried to alert her grandmother, but Gran was totally focused on Janey.

Sophie tried to look normal as she passed by the patrons on her way to her grandfather's car. They said hellos and good-evenings, but no one seemed to notice anything was wrong.

She climbed into the car's front seat, scooping a piece of paper off the upholstery first. Ian's plane was due to land at eight-thirty in the morning. Where was he sleeping tonight? She'd left her cell phone in the treatment room, but she found her grandfather's in the glove box.

She dialed Ian's number and got the "this customer isn't answering" message. What kind of a man broke half the bones in his body and then turned off his cell phone?

Sophie folded her arms on the dashboard and leaned her forehead on them. A good cry would make everything more bearable except she'd have to explain a sobfest, and Janey couldn't take much more tonight.

Ian was probably asleep already, doped up on painkillers and too dumb to stay in a hospital where he clearly needed to be. But she could hardly wait to touch him again—to make sure he was alive.

She sat up. One thing she could do right away. She dialed her aunt Eliza's number. Molly answered.

"What are you doing there?" Sophie asked.

"Mom and Dad are having a 'date.' I'm looking after the place. What can I do for you?"

"A massive favor. Can you take in my mom for at least one night?"

"I'd be glad to, but my mother might toss her clothes into the street the second she shows up. She holds a long-term grudge when anyone wrongs the family."

"I know she doesn't like having my mom under her roof, but she'd really be helping me if she'd reconsider this once. Ian's had an accident. I'm going to pick him up at the airport tomorrow, and I'd like my home and my husband to myself for twenty-four hours."

SEEING SOPHIE made even the wheelchair bearable. Ian couldn't reach her on his own two feet, but what mattered was holding her in his arms again. Feeling the warmth of her body and their growing child. He couldn't wait, but every time he checked his watch, time seemed to move more slowly.

The plane took forever to taxi to the gate, but at least they helped him off before anyone else. Sophie was waiting on the other side of the security barrier, surprisingly graceful for such a pregnant woman, heart-wrenchingly beautiful, but he suspected she'd be beautiful to him no matter what she looked like.

Something within Sophie had bewitched him from the moment he'd met her. Something that had to do with passion and spirit and longing that no one else had ever answered for him. Maybe it was as basic as their mutual need for a strong and loving family. He simply accepted that his future now lay with Sophie.

With all that in his face, he allowed a man to push his wheelchair to her feet. Rather, she stopped the wheelchair by dropping to her haunches in front of it.

"Ian." She leaned into him, resting her hands on the arms of the chair. She kissed him as if she hadn't seen him in years, and he couldn't care less about the crowd parting around them. With his hand to the back of her head, he claimed her with the certain knowledge she would belong to him for the rest of their lives.

Laughing, she leaned back, and the crazy woman had tears on her eyelashes.

He rubbed them off, careful not to smear her makeup. She wouldn't like sporting a raccoonish look.

"I'm okay," he said. He caught her chin and kissed her again. "I'm okay now."

"Excuse me, folks." The guy at the wheelchair handles interrupted them. "We're causing a traffic jam. What say we talk about this in some out-of-the-way spot?"

Sophie hoisted herself to her feet. "I'll take over from here. Thanks for your help. Where do I turn it in?"

"Someone will help you get him into your car."

Behind him, they switched at the controls, and he was moving again. "Should you be pushing this thing, Sophie?"

"It's this or check beneath your cast to make sure they did a good job up there. Which hospital did you go to?"

"George Washington, but I don't remember the doctor's name." He knew she'd ask. "It's in my paperwork."

She grunted.

"I owe your grandfather for breaking the news to you. What can we do that he'd like?"

"Force my grandmother to take a long vacation with him."

"I still have the condo in Chicago. Do you think they'd like a big-city vacation?"

She laughed with surprise in her voice. "Seeing as we Calverts are all hicks from Bardill's Ridge, I guess they might. We'll ask Gran."

"I didn't mean it that way." He didn't have to tell her, but he wanted no more misunderstandings. "James Kendall might set up something special for them."

"We could ask Olivia."

His ex-boss's daughter and Zach's wife. "Oh, yeah. I always forget she was part of the life you used to lead."

"Any chance that life is over?"

He glanced over his shoulder. "What do you mean?" The shadows beneath her eyes made him feel guilty.

"Can't you find another line of work?"

"No." He wanted to give her anything and everything, but she couldn't ask the impossible. "Would you give up your work if something happened to a patient?"

"I might not have a choice." Distrust invaded her gaze. "You do, and I guess you're making it."

"Sophie…" How could he make her understand? Why should he have to explain that his work was important? "Make sense. Think about your grandparents, your gran's attitude toward her job."

"Wait." She gave the chair an extra shove. "I don't want to argue today. I don't want to compromise. I just want to be glad you're alive."

He almost dialed the agency and quit on the spot. Fortunately he'd skidded across the road in front of Union Station on his cell phone, and it hadn't survived.

CHAPTER ELEVEN

"I FELT IT."

Ian's excitement drew Sophie from the comfort of being cradled in his good arm. Late afternoon brought watery sunlight through the living-room windows to the sleeper sofa she'd made up before she'd left for Knoxville.

"You felt what?" She scrubbed at her face, trying to wake up. She hadn't meant to sleep. Ian had simply asked her to lie down beside him.

"The baby. My hand was on your stomach, and I felt the baby move." He flattened his palm over the bulge that seemed to expand hourly. "At least I think I did. You don't have gas?"

"No." She pulled back, appalled, but he only laughed at her.

"I felt the baby," he said.

"Keep accusing me of embarrassing bodily functions, and you won't be feeling anything again."

He closed his mouth on a wide grin. "I'm starving."

"That's an acceptable physical need." She shifted,

careful not to hurt him as she braced herself on one elbow. "I can't believe we fell asleep."

"We were both exhausted." He kissed her lightly, continuing to grope her stomach to make the baby move. "Got anything in the fridge?"

"I can't remember." Her life had taken on a before-Ian-was-hurt quality that seemed to put a year between last night and this morning.

"Where's your mom? I forgot all about her."

"I begged Molly to let her stay at the B and B, and then I told her she had to go."

He clearly struggled with another urge to laugh. "You *made* her leave?" He fingered strands of her hair away from her cheekbone. "She's the only person who gets away with pushing you around."

"No one pushes me." She smiled. "At least that's what I tell myself. Let me see about food. You're liable to starve before you heal. You're the better cook."

"I can tell you what to do."

"I should be able to rustle up something." She understood surprisingly little about kitchens. That would have to change if she was going to provide a child with a nutritious diet. She padded to the kitchen on bare feet, a pair of flannel pajama pants flapping at her ankles. "Do you want coffee?"

"I'm dying for ice water."

"Coming up."

She got the water and sipped some as she opened the fridge. "Oh, score."

"What did you find?"

"Someone's brought staples." She peeled tin foil off the edge of a baking dish. "Mmm, ham. The real stuff, you know? Not that canned ham people up north like so much." She broke off a chunk and nibbled. "Yum. You want a sandwich?" She checked the next bowl. "And potato salad. Ian?"

"They both sound great to me."

She started taking the fixings out of the fridge. "I should drive you down to see Dr. Fedderson tomorrow."

"Why?"

"He'll be taking care of you, unless you know of some other doctor?" She peered through the kitchen doorway.

"Fedderson's fine. Your father tells me he'll make a good doctor for the baby, though I thought I'd schedule a physical myself before he's born." Ian faced her stoically, ready to be scoffed at. "Just to make sure he's thorough. I meant, why should I see him tomorrow? I'm supposed to have the ankle checked in two weeks. I dislocated my shoulder, but it's fine now that they popped it back. A little sore..." He smiled as she flinched. "What?"

"I had to put a shoulder back once in my ER rotation. I'd rather dig ditches."

"Imagine how the patient felt." He held out his hand. "How's the water coming?"

"Sorry." She carried the glass to him, taking another sip on the way. "Have you talked to Adam?"

"From the hospital. I broke my cell phone, and I hadn't memorized your grandfather's phone number, so I asked Adam to get it for me."

She nodded. "Did you talk to him about quitting?"

He drank his water, watching her without expression. Afterward he took his time about wiping the excess moisture off his lip. "Why would I?"

Because he had a wife and child who needed him alive? Why weren't she and the baby enough reason to leave such a dangerous job? "What happened in D.C.?"

"The guy I was supposed to walk to the meet had set up his own meeting. His buddy was supposed to grab the CD and run." He half shook his head. "I got in their way."

"You almost got yourself killed for a CD?"

"I reacted, Sophie. I wasn't even sure my guy was bad when I went after the CD. No wonder they cooked up that story about unreliable fire walls."

"We don't need to discuss fire walls." She sat on the edge of the uncomfortable bed, ignoring a metal rail that bit into the back of her thigh.

"We can't talk about my job, either. You want me to quit, and I'm not ready to give it up." With six stitches in his arm and four more on his thigh, cuts and bruises all over his face and neck and his ankle in a dark-blue cast, he looked more like a victim than an action hero. He narrowed his eyes as if reading her mind. "I know I look bad, but this is the only job I've ever had. I don't know any other work."

"I understand all that." She smoothed her hand along his beard-roughened chin. "But I thought you might be dead when Grandpa first came to see me."

She'd begged him with reason, but her trembling voice affected him more. He pulled her close, but then hissed with pain. She tried to move away.

"No, don't go," he said. "You were my last thought, Sophie. I don't intend to die. I won't make any more stupid mistakes. Any other CDs can go wherever they want after this."

He splayed his fingers against her cheek, holding her close to him. She caught his wrist and clung. "It's not enough," she said.

"It's what I can offer right now."

"I don't like honesty anymore. Lie to me."

His laugh ruffled her hair. "I'm not lying. I only have to learn a lesson the hard way once. That's why I know I won't be dancing with any more cars. I just learned they're tougher than I am."

"You can't put yourself in my shoes?"

"Not yet." He let her straighten. "I wouldn't ask this kind of sacrifice from you, Sophie."

She had a feeling they looked at their jobs differently. She considered herself lucky she could help people. He had something to prove. Maybe he was proving he still had a life apart from their marriage by clinging to the promise of another assignment that would take him away.

"I need to call Gran," she said. "They'll be worried about you, and I have to find out about a patient I left with her."

Two weeks later, Ian was sick to death of being waited on from his makeshift bed on the sofa. Each morning Sophie changed the bed back into a couch. He suspected she did it to give him a more manly stage to sprawl from, and he was grateful, but he was more than ready to take care of himself.

Her family helped. Her dad set up a mini-workshop in the living room, so Ian could help build the baby's crib. Ethan, who was using the hand lathes and old-fashioned tools that had built furniture in these mountains since Revolutionary times, was generous with his knowledge. Ian realized how lucky he was to learn from a master—how lucky his child would be to have this hand-hewn crib to pass down to his own family.

After Ethan left each day, Nita showed up with DVDs, videos and some sort of ready-made dinner that she tucked in the fridge to be warmed up later. She did laundry, swept up the sawdust that escaped Ethan's dust sheets, and generally made the house more habitable before Sophie came home.

Late on a Friday, Ian and Nita were sharing a beer and a tape of a boxing match Ian hadn't seen when an unfamiliar car spewed gravel in the driveway. Nita stood, twisting toward the wide window.

"Is that Sophie?"

"No." Ian hauled himself to his feet—one foot and the cast—and leaned over the back of the couch.

A tall man rose from the driver's seat. His black jacket had to be too warm. He peeled it off to reveal a perfectly pressed white shirt that still looked too hot for July. On the other side of the car, a woman got out. Her dark hair barely moved in the mountain air. She surveyed the cabin with a mixture of surprise and shock that made Ian laugh.

"My parents," he said.

Nita veered her gaze toward him. "You don't sound pleased."

"Wary."

"Your poor mom and dad. I already know how they feel."

He liked Nita. She'd gone out of her way to help Sophie while he was out of commission, and he didn't know that many women who were so happy to share boxing commentary. But she put equal effort into maintaining the blind spot that kept her from understanding Sophie's guarded affection.

She turned to him, as if she suddenly noticed his silence.

"What?" she asked.

"Nothing." He nodded toward his parents, picking their cautious way to the front door. "Would you mind letting them in?"

"Glad to."

She greeted Alex and Rachel Ridley with an enthusiasm that made Ian laugh. She'd startled them enough in today's getup of retro sixties lime-green. She looked hardly ten years older than Sophie, whereas his parents had settled contentedly into re-spectable middle age.

After the introductions, Nita brought them into the living room. "We were just having a beer." She pointed to the bottle she'd abandoned on the coffee table. "Want one?"

"No, thank you." His mom eyed the bottle as she would a poisonous snake. "Alex?"

"Do you have any Scotch?"

Ian waited. Neither of them had pried their eyes off Nita to look at him yet.

"I'll look in the kitchen," she said. "Scotch, Ian?"

"No, thanks." Then he realized she was asking if they had any. "Oh—I think there's a bottle in the cabinet above the fridge." He met his father's re-lieved expression with a touch of resentment. His dad had not been pleased when Ian had told them about the baby in his call from the hospital. "Sophie thought we should child-proof from the start."

"Oh, the baby," his mother said in a faint tone.

"What are you doing here?" Ian saw no reason to waste time with pleasantries. His accident was less urgent than his and Sophie's wedding had been. They should have come for that.

"Son." Ignoring his aggressive tone as much as the question, Rachel lifted careful arms around his shoulders. "I don't want to hurt you. Are you all right?"

"It was hard to find you," his dad said. "I had to use the GPS in the car."

"I'm fine."

"We thought we should meet Sophie before the baby comes." His mom backed away, eyeing his father as if prompting him to take his turn at showing affection.

Alex stepped up, offering his hand. "Glad to see you on your feet, son."

"You didn't have to come now."

"I had a meeting in New York, anyway." Though retired, he still sat on several company boards. "We thought we could work in some time in Tennessee."

"Thanks." He didn't want the explanation after all. Ian took his spot on the couch again and wished he'd knocked back that Scotch himself. "How's Ireland? Sit down. Mom, do you want to take off your jacket?"

"I'm fine. Though it's a bit warmer here than I'm used to."

"Ireland's great, son. You should come over after the baby. I'll plan a few rounds for us."

"Sophie would love that," he said dryly. He could just see her celebrating such a visit. She'd borrow his father's clubs, maybe play a few rounds on his head.

"What's all that?" His mother pointed to the dust-sheeted crib-under-production.

"Sophie's dad is making a crib for the baby. He's building it here so I can help."

"And your wife doesn't mind this mess in her living room?" His mother turned Sophie's possible understanding into a flaw.

"She's making do," he said. "I keep asking why you came."

"You were hit by a car, son. Naturally, we want to see for ourselves that you're all right." His mom leaned over the coffee table to pat his knee, and then she finally sat on the love seat, suggesting with a look that his father possess himself of the cushion beside her.

"I'd rather you'd come to the wedding."

"It was such short notice." Alex peered around the room, tugging at his collar. Nita was taking too long with the Scotch.

"How much longer until the baby comes, darling?"

"About nine weeks, Mom."

"Do you know if you're having a boy or a girl?"

"We didn't want to know."

Nita finally appeared in the doorway with a dose of Scotch in a glass. "It would make things easier for us, wouldn't it? We'd know what colors to buy. Although I've been thinking, Ian, we may have to get the family started on your nursery. Sophie doesn't seem to have time with work and you won't be climbing those stairs or painting from stepladders for a while." She turned to his mom, sitting empty-handed. "Rachel, I'd love to bring you something. You must be thirsty after your drive. Or maybe you'd like to freshen up?"

His mother lifted a hand to her salt-and-pepper hair with a swift glance at Nita's more youthful color. "I think I'm fine." She sent Ian a somewhat desperate glance. "When will Sophie be home? We made reservations at a bed-and-breakfast in town, and I'm not sure we'll be able to find it if we wait until dark."

"Are you staying at the Dogwood?" Nita looked pleased. "I'd be happy to lead you down when I go." She leaned forward confidingly. "I was staying here, but after Ian's injury, my daughter just threw me out."

She added a laugh, and Ian believed she was joking, but his mother turned to him again, horribly confused. She faced Nita once more. "Is your daughter very like you?"

"Mom." Ian found himself on his feet again. Nita simply eyed the other woman as if she'd lost her mind. "I think you and Dad should go back to town for the night. Sophie's driving me in tomorrow to have my ankle checked, and we can meet you for a meal. Or something."

"I didn't mean…" Rachel didn't finish. What point would there be in saying she hadn't meant she hoped Sophie was an improvement on her mother?

Nita sipped her beer, a smirk on her face as if she couldn't believe the newcomers' manners. Ian had to agree with her. She might occasionally be clueless, but you knew where you stood with her.

The sad truth was he knew where he stood with his parents, too. Back of the line, on probation. At his age it shouldn't matter, but it was the last place he wanted Sophie to join him. He'd protect her from them, anyway.

"YOU SHOULD COME into the treatment room with me," Ian said as they waited for Dr. Fedderson to check his ankle. "You can talk to him about the clinic."

Sophie hadn't talked to anyone else about it since her grandmother had been so upset about the idea. "I don't think so."

"Why?" He kept his voice low, as if trying to keep her plans out of the Bardill's Ridge public domain—but the children pushing wooden cars around a track inlaid in the coffee table were probably louder than he was, anyway.

"Gran and I have dropped the subject. I don't want to make things bad again."

"When is she going to start cutting her hours at the baby farm?"

"I don't know that, either."

He nudged her with his elbow on the blue-padded chair arm. "I've never seen you scared before."

She moved her arm, resisting his teasing. "You've never seen my grandparents at each other's throats. If I thought I'd managed to break them up, too…"

"You didn't break your parents up. Sophie, you're not that powerful."

He probably meant to comfort her, but she hated the flavor of condescension in his reassurance. "Suddenly you're the family psychologist?" Dr. Fedderson's receptionist opened the door from the waiting room and called for Danny Sutton. Sophie nodded at the little boy and his mom. "Besides, do you want to look like them? Me going along to make sure you understand your treatment?"

"I don't care how I look, and I may not be a psychologist, but your parents' marriage was in trouble if your mom was having an affair on the kitchen table." Someone had spilled the story. Probably her mom in an effort to justify herself. He sat up straighter. "I don't like to believe Nita would do something like that."

"Because she's your new best friend." Sophie lifted her feet off the floor and then tapped her heels on the carpet. Her house had become a boy's club, with her mother as the honorary girl. Even Zach had started dropping by to sand down crib parts and join in the sports commentary. "Beer and boxing. Who knew you'd have so much in common?"

"You're a bitter woman."

His teasing finally made her laugh. "I just don't understand why you get along with her so well when she drives me crazy by the time I'm home fifteen minutes."

"You're still upset with each other. She wants you to love her like you did before the table incident."

"I can't. You'd think acceptance would be enough."

He caught her hand, and his was comforting. "Would it be enough for you?"

She stared at their linked fingers. Her kind of acceptance would be a slap in the face from their child. But then again, she didn't plan to make the same mistakes her mom had. She'd certainly avoid making her mother's choices. "It wouldn't be enough."

"So give her a chance."

His tone didn't exactly plead, but he was trying to heal the rift between her mother and herself.

"I'm glad you like her, Ian, but I can't forget the way things were because you want me to."

"You don't like me meddling."

"It's a Calvert trait." She shook her head. "You're fitting in here better than I am. You've started a social club at our house, and I'm trying to break up the strongest marriage I've ever known."

His smile, a hint of understanding, a tang of hurt feelings, made her sorry for being so flippant.

"You don't want my help." He looked tense.

"I'm not trying to say you don't have a right." Although it was her instinctive response. "I'll take care of it on my own. You all want to be friends, and you have no history with them—other than getting me pregnant—which you've already made up for. I'm still the outsider."

"That's in your head, Sophie. They love you unconditionally. I wish you could see that, because most people would give a whole lot for the kind of affection you don't even recognize."

"Don't analyze me, Ian." Regret gave way to irritation. Her life seemed to be spinning out of her grasp. At night she clung to him. During the day, she worked while he played around with her family. He couldn't know how long she'd resisted coming back here—and how much her grandmother's anger over the clinic idea had hurt. He couldn't know she was feeling shut out as everyone gathered him close.

And if she wasn't careful she'd start driving her husband away from her because of her own sense of loneliness. She tugged at his arm.

"Ian?"

"Hmm?"

"I didn't mean to be abrupt, that 'don't analyze me' thing. I'm just—"

"Tired?" he said.

She hated admitting weakness. "A little. Because I'm dancing around Gran at work."

"Take time off. She'd love to have the place to herself, and you could use a break. Maybe I could close the clubhouse at our place for a day or two?"

She sighed. "It sounds like such a good idea except Grandpa would probably divorce Gran on the off chance she's making me want to quit working with her."

"Maybe it's time you told her to leave. You were able to say it to your mother."

"Because of you," she said with a blush. Why was she embarrassed? He had a right to know she'd wanted to be alone with him. "I can't throw Gran out of the place she built."

"I can see that."

The receptionist came back. "Ian Ridley?"

He looked down at Sophie. She hesitated only a moment. And then she helped him to his feet, though he shook off her assistance.

"You can hand me the crutches." He glanced quickly around the room to see if anyone had noticed she thought him infirm. "But you can't treat me as if I'm an invalid."

Sophie nodded, all empathy. He closed his eyes, muttered a "sorry" in an apology that matched hers and started toward the waiting receptionist. Sophie followed, grinning only when his back was firmly turned. He thought *she* insisted on being too independent?

DINNER AT THE DOGWOOD with Ian's parents resembled an interrogation. Only Molly and Aunt Eliza, taking turns at serving courses and offering support made the meal with Alex and Rachel Ridley bearable.

That and Aunt Eliza's cooking. Sophie spooned apple crisp into her mouth. Thank God it was almost over.

"Tired?" Ian rubbed the small of her back with his fist as he asked.

Nodding, she closed her eyes, all but purring. At twenty-nine, she'd expected to sail through pregnancy. She understood the reasons for all the little aches and pains. They weren't supposed to bother her, but Ian unerringly managed to find and relieve the one ache that continued to nag at her. She put it down to so much time on her feet each day. Remembering his parents, she pulled away.

"Thanks," she said. "Busy day at the office."

"You must get tired of babies." Rachel, in a designer suit and anxious expression, made Sophie ridiculously defensive of Ian. His mother seemed to have no more maternal instinct than Nita.

"Why would I get tired of them?" Sophie asked.

"Around you all day, pregnant women, talk of babies. Worrying about babies. And of course..." Rachel pointed to Sophie's stomach, where the newest Ridley performed a lazy roll that made Sophie smile.

"I hardly ever get to see them since I came down here. I'm more concerned with the moms, and really, knowing what's at stake makes me a little bit of a hypochondriac. Who knew?"

"What do you mean?" Alex pulled a cigar from the pocket inside his jacket, inhaled its length and then must have seen Sophie's look of distress at the thought of telling him she didn't want the smoke anywhere near her baby's oxygen supply.

"Dad," Ian said, waving his father off.

"Sorry." Alex put it back in his pocket. "But how are you a hypochondriac, Sophie?"

"The morning sickness, for one. I'm almost thirty two weeks along. It should be over, but I'm keeping the cracker company in business on the off chance saltines will eventually ease the problem. And apart from feeling queasy all the time, every little twinge—the ultrasound—I couldn't wait to have it done."

"Ian said you didn't know the baby's sex, but you must have seen…" Rachel frowned, possibly at the thought of a daughter-in-law who'd be a drain on her son.

"I didn't look." She glanced at her husband, who seemed the most unperturbed of the three of them. "We agreed we wouldn't find out, so I looked away from the screen." It had been one of the hardest things she'd ever made herself do.

"How much longer will your mother be in town?" Alex then summoned Molly with an imperial gesture. Sophie watched her cousin carefully. Molly, resistant to any authority, seemed to consider her response with a swift glance at the bowl of floating candles on the sideboard at her hip.

"My mom." Sophie braced herself in anticipation of a flying candle, but Molly met her gaze and soft-ened, smoothing her sleeves over her wrists as she started toward their table. Sophie straightened in relief. "Mom's going back to D.C. on Sunday after-noon."

"She's been here a while, hasn't she? I had the impression you'd grown close to her, Ian."

Sophie turned to him. Why would his mother think that? Had her mom done something to make Rachel feel left out? "What happened with my mom?"

"Nothing." He looked at Molly. "We have an unusual request. Port for my mother and brandy for my father?"

"Not that unusual. We aren't rubes here, Ian. I'll be right back."

She flounced away, and Sophie continued to feel as if she were in the eye of a bad storm. "How much longer can you stay, Mrs. Ridley? I've hardly seen you both."

"We had originally hoped to stay a week or so, but—" She flicked a quick glance at her husband. "We've had an invitation from Nashville, and when the governor beckons..."

"You understand, Ian?" Alex asked his son.

The undercurrents blew as fast and hard as the look on Ian's face. "I understand perfectly, Dad." He looked up, sprawling in his chair. "But here's something you and Mom should consider. I'm your only son. I hardly know you. You refused to come to our wedding and meet my wife." He curled his hand around the nape of Sophie's neck, making her shiver. Then he slid his hand, in a fist, back under the table as if he didn't trust himself. "Now you don't find the company here to your liking so you've accepted a better invite.''

"Ian!'' his mother said in shock.

"No, Mom, this is long overdue. You won't expose my child to your ideas or your disapproval. Before you and Dad come back, you'll think about what you want with me and with my family. You'll promise me you can behave with a modicum of good manners that won't embarrass me in front of Sophie's family. Or you just won't come back.''

"If that's your choice, son.'' His father sounded as arrogant as Ian.

Sophie stared at him, her heart aching for the pain in his voice.

"It's not my choice, Dad. I'm not making a speech. I'm asking you and Mom to be a part of my child's—no—of my life. I want you to fit your visits to the governor around seeing my family.''

"Ian.'' His mom gave Sophie an accusing look. "I think you're letting these people influence you.''

"I could do worse.''

Beneath the table, Sophie reached for Ian's hand. He threaded his fingers through hers. She smiled to offer him comfort.

They were going to have to be the responsible adult figures in their daughter's life. Reasonable grandparents appeared to be out of the question.

CHAPTER TWELVE

AT SEVEN-THIRTY, Seth stopped watching his empty driveway and dialed Tom Fedderson's number. He did it out of spite. He'd probably regret it later, but for now, it seemed like the only way to strike a blow at Greta's oblivious self-absorption.

"Dr. Fedderson."

"Tom? Seth Calvert, here. Have I interrupted your dinner?"

"No, Seth. Good to hear from you. What's up? You're not sick?"

"Couldn't be healthier." He rubbed his chest reflexively. It hurt because he was so angry he could hardly breathe. "I'm calling on my granddaughter's behalf. You remember Sophie?"

"I just saw Sophie. I put her husband in a walking cast."

"Good. Maybe she spoke to you already. She seemed reluctant to broach the subject, so I thought I'd see how you felt about it."

"What are we talking about, Seth? Sophie talked to me about her practice in D.C. and what I needed her to do for Ian."

"She didn't mention opening a clinic here?"

"A clinic?" To Seth's surprise, Tom sounded more interested than shocked. "Sophie's thinking about working here in town? What does Greta say about that?"

A moment's guilt slowed Seth, but he glossed over it. "She's actually concerned you would feel Sophie was trying to poach business."

"I wonder how she'd feel about possibly pooling our resources. When I heard she was coming to help Greta, I thought maybe it was time I looked for help, too."

A normal human being, who saw slowing down as an opportunity rather than a punishment. "I'll have Sophie get in touch with you, then. Sounds as if you may be able to help each other out."

"Thanks, Seth. I'm going to think about this, so I'll have a serious answer if she's serious about making the change."

Seth closed his eyes as his heart beat a military tattoo. He'd put the clinic in motion. Greta would have to deal with it. She'd be only too willing to deal with him, too. "Talk to you later, Tom."

He hung up the phone. At least he'd have his wife's undivided attention.

THE MORNING AFTER their disappointing dinner with his parents, Ian used his brand-new walking cast to make his way outside the cabin and soak in the fresh mountain sun. Behind him lay baby clothes, the half-finished crib and so many stacks of diapers he and Sophie'd be wearing them in their eighties if they somehow managed to stay together.

All spoils of Calvert visits.

With his coffee mug almost to his lips he lifted his head, and the bluest sky he'd ever seen bit into his soul. Wind pushed the tall pines back and forth, an ocean surge on dry land. Wildflowers waved to and fro. Teenage girls in the meadow near his and Sophie's borrowed cottage were laughing as if they hadn't a care in the world.

Life seemed to throb in the air. Small plants, eager for life, poked out of the ground. Honeysuckle now covered the ravine and climbed over new ground each day with its spreading skirt of branches that emitted short bursts of heavy scent.

And coming from the spa, more female voices. Three pregnant women marched along the walking path in front of the cabin, barely noticing him as they discussed aching backs and varicose veins. By the time they reached the cars, one of the women had gone on to say it was all worth it each time she heard her unborn child's heartbeat.

He stared after them. The past two weeks had passed in a dream. Sophie and he, sharing a bed and careful lovemaking because of her pregnancy and his cast and stitches. He'd been grateful she wanted to lie next to him. He'd needed her bountiful passion, the certainty that they were together.

But today, this mountain and all the life bursting

into being on it, a man who didn't know what kind of father he'd make could get scared.

Scared? That piece of self-knowledge exploded out of nowhere.

He dropped his mug, and coffee splashed on his feet and the wooden porch. The mug hit the big toe on his good foot. He swore.

He hadn't been afraid since the day he'd decided no one would ever bully him again. He'd searched for circumstances in which to prove he was brave.

Behind him, the screen door squeaked open. He turned unsteadily. Sophie looked up, wearing his T-shirt again. She still worked too hard. Even first thing in the morning, dark circles bloomed beneath her eyes.

"What?" she asked.

Feeling foolish, he stopped holding his breath. "Come here."

Her eyes questioned him. He curved his hands around her shoulders, noting the seeming frailty of her bones. Slowly he leaned down, waiting for her to pull away. She didn't.

Her mouth opened as he touched her lips with his. She slid her arms around him, tentatively at first, as if feeling her way. He pushed his fingers into the hair at her nape and deepened the kiss.

Despite the nights they'd spent together, he remained unsure. Holding her out here among the life on her mountain, he questioned whether her need matched his. Her answer came loud and clear in her hungry response, in the desperate angle of her head and the deep breath she gasped as she pulled back.

"Where have you been?" She blushed. "You've been…different since the accident. More careful."

"Not ever." He grimaced. "I realized how easily I might have lost you and our baby. I'm glad to be alive. Thankful to have you with me. Suddenly I can walk again, and I came out here…"

She turned, pulling his arms around her. His hands met on her belly, on his baby.

"What did you see?" She made him think she was trying to see her home through his eyes.

"Life. New grass and flowers and women who are soon going to have their children and even those kids." He pointed. "Laughing—when they face more responsibility than they should have dreamed of at their age."

"The blessing of being that age. They're able to stop thinking about it once in a while."

He tucked her against his side. "Sophie, are you happy?"

She didn't answer right away. Finally she turned her head, lifting her face to his. "I am. My baby is healthy. You didn't die and I've had you alive and loving in my arms every night since you flew over that car."

He would have picked her up and carried her to their uncomfortable steel-braced bed, but he didn't think he could lift her anymore. She looked serious as she traced his chin with her fingertips.

"I like having the right to touch you."

He kissed her index finger, sucking the tip between his lips, but her distracted expression unsettled him. "Something's still wrong."

"Tom Fedderson just called. He asked if I'd be willing to meet in his office."

"You talked to him, after all?"

"No. He said he's been anxious to speak to me since my grandfather called him."

"Seth approached him about the clinic?"

Anxiety sharpened her gaze. "Why would he do that, knowing how Gran feels?" She sank against him. "What have I done to my family?"

It was no use reminding her she wasn't responsible for her grandparents. She seemed to think she'd started a chain of catastrophic events. "Explain to Fedderson. Frankly, I think you're working too hard already, but talk to him. Find out what he wants out of the idea and keep your options open if you want to back out."

She stepped away to rest her bottom on the porch rail. "I wonder if I can if he's willing."

Ian lifted both brows. "Do you know what you're saying?"

"Do you mean Gran? I won't do it if we can't convince her, and as for us, I won't take on more than I can handle. But if Dr. Fedderson's willing, we could bring something useful to this town. We'd just have to make it work with our current commitments."

"You could drive your grandmother insane."

Staring at the girls, still shrieking and laughing in the meadow, Sophie nodded. "I've been able to turn to her for help since I was small. I have to make sure she can depend on me now."

Ian agreed. "And if she's against it, the town might be, anyway, Sophie. You know how people are around here. They may think the baby farm wasn't good enough for you, so you had to make more for yourself. We're creating a family here. You don't want to be the lady doctor who ran roughshod over Dr. Fedderson."

"Or over Gran. I'll talk to him first. Maybe by the time I have to bring it up with her, she'll see the greater good."

"Even if she does, Sophie, I'm against you taking on more work."

To his utter amazement, she smiled instead of throwing up a barricade. "Grandpa told me Dr. Fedderson suggested pooling our time so no one would be overburdened."

Owing her some understanding in return, he opened the cabin door. "Why don't I drive you?"

"With that cast?" Her grin teased. "You can walk, but I don't see you driving. Why don't you finish the homework Dad left you on the crib, and I'll be back before you know it? I'll even try to find something for dinner that I can't destroy."

"I'll do dinner." Unwilling to terrify her, he kept

his appreciation of their sudden collaborative efforts to himself. But he hoped she'd get used to it.

DR. FEDDERSON HAD SHOWN her into his office where two cups of coffee waited on a tray with a sugar bowl and a jug of cream. Sophie smiled at the homey offering. She would never have thought of such amenities in her own office.

"Help yourself," he said. "I thought we should talk in person."

"I can't drink coffee right now, but thank you." She patted her stomach and he nodded.

"I forgot. Let me see if I can find some orange juice."

"Don't bother." She sat in the chair across from his. On a Saturday morning the unnatural silence of an empty medical office rang in her ears. "I'm fine, and I don't want to be away from home too long. Even with the new cast, Ian has a hard time getting around outside our house."

"He was lucky. A guy who slides across a moving vehicle often has worse injuries."

She shuddered. Variations of those moments had played through her sleep every night since it had happened. "We were both lucky." She crossed her legs in a pointed effort to change the subject. "As a matter of fact, Ian was the one who suggested the clinic in the first place."

"I think it's a good idea, and I know your grandmother has delivered some babies up at the resort over the years. She used to have privileges at the hospital in town.''

"She still has them, but most of our clients only come for a vacation. They don't stay to deliver.''

"And you miss that part of your practice?''

"I miss it,'' she said. "But I also think we could bring something to the town with an OB.''

"I agree with you, and I'm ready to start pulling back in my own practice.'' He tipped cream into one of the coffee mugs. "Since I spoke to Seth, I've called the OBs in Danton and Spillforth.'' He named two nearby towns. "They'd be interested in sharing resources, as well. We could split up time in the clinic. I know a couple more G.P.s who'd also be willing to put in some hours here. I assume we're talking about a new building?''

"Unless I can find a suitable existing structure in town.'' She studied his faded wallpaper and somewhat tatty curtains. "You don't want to keep this office?''

"My lease expires next year. That's one of the reasons I've been rethinking my options.'' He sipped his coffee. "Would you be willing to work with so many other physicians?''

"The closer I am to delivering, the more I think I might find someone to help me up at The Mom's Place. I can't imagine working these hours when we have a baby at home.'' The moment she confessed it, she wished she'd waited. Ian should have been the first to hear that thought spoken aloud.

"I've always wondered how Greta managed."

Sophie wasn't sure how pleased Gran would be with her granddaughter's changing priorities, but she knew the secret behind Greta Calvert's success. "She's strong and she's always wanted to help."

"Maybe she'd be willing to do some time here, too—if your grandfather doesn't put up too much fuss about it." As she tried not to look stunned that everyone knew their family's business, Dr. Fedderson seemed to reach his own decision. "You and I agree. We should arrange a meeting with the other people I've spoken to. First thing we should cover is the amount of time we're all looking to contribute, and then if we have a viable idea, we should discuss the financial aspects."

"Thanks, Dr. Fedderson." Sophie stood. "You've already gone farther with this idea than I had." He didn't have her grandmother to fear. She shook his hand. "If you want to fax me a list of names and numbers, I'll make some of the calls?"

"No need at all. They're my friends. I'll let you know when we have a time and meeting place."

"Thanks." She hovered, feeling as if she was betraying her gran. "I appreciate your receptiveness."

He nodded. "It sounds like a solution many of us would find acceptable."

Sophie shook Dr. Fedderson's hand and left his office. Gran lingered in her head, disapproving, disappointed. Sophie considered asking Dr. Fedderson not to mention their meeting, but she kept going toward her car. She wasn't the stealthy type as a rule, and she had to explain to Gran, anyway.

Sophie stared up at the ridge above town. Green and verdant, full of mysterious life that seemed to whisper in the swaying trees of summer, Bardill's Ridge was like another parent to her. More reliable than her mother in the continuity of the changing seasons, as welcoming and unchanging as her father's love. Bardill's Ridge wasn't just a refuge anymore. It had become home, and she wouldn't do anything to ruin it.

SOPHIE WAITED FOR Dr. Fedderson to call her before talking to her grandmother. She didn't want to bring up her meeting with him until they knew if the other physicians in the area wanted to go forward. Worse than that, she felt guilty, and she didn't know how to tell her grandmother she'd met with Tom Fedderson without having to explain her grandfather's role in making the appointment.

Every time the phone rang while she was at work, she jumped, thinking it was the doctor. On the other hand, this was just the sort of project that could use Gran's touch. Greta Calvert had cared for the women in these mountains for more than fifty years.

A couple of weeks after her meeting, Sophie was reviewing nutrition with the younger girls in a conference room when one of the receptionists came to the door. Sophie dropped her foam-filled cheese-and-bread cutouts.

"Phone call for you, Dr. Ridley. Olivia Kendall. She says it's urgent."

She tried to swallow her own tongue. Suppose Olivia, editor of a news magazine, had gotten hold of the proposed clinic idea. Since she'd moved to town, Olivia had made fund-raising a priority for the baby farm, and any other organization Greta mentioned to her.

Unable to speak, Sophie nodded and then cleared her throat as she looked at the teenagers. "I'll be right back."

The girls were already chatting to one another. She left the room, wondering if she could have been as self-possessed at their ages. They'd all decided to have their babies on their own, but she'd chosen to marry her baby's father, and she was twenty-nine. As if she'd needed Ian to make her daughter's life complete.

Maybe she did. Maybe he made her life complete. She'd gotten used to hearing him in the house. She enjoyed his humming as he shaved each morning. How did a man hum and shave at the same time? One day, if she ever felt comfortable enough to leave their bed and watch from close range, she'd ask him.

She picked up the phone, and Olivia started talking.

"I know this is unacceptable. I shouldn't have interrupted you, but I have a favor to ask."

"Sure." Zach had been Sophie's surrogate brother through childhood. That made Olivia a sister. "What can I do?'' As long as she didn't want information on the clinic.

"You can't even tell your grandmother. I want Zach to be the first to know if it's true, and Gran wouldn't be able to hold it in.''

"You're pregnant." Sophie turned, making sure no one was near enough to hear what she'd just said.

"I'd like a test. I've done the home ones.''

"They're reliable.''

"I know, but I want a real test from a real doctor.''

Sophie dropped her voice. They ran the tests up here, but Gran could easily stumble on it. "You know about Dr. Fedderson's office?''

"You don't want me?" Olivia sounded uncertain. "It's just I've always had female doctors. Dr. Fedderson might be great, but I'd feel more comfortable with you.''

Sophie owed Zach a few favors even if Gran caught her starting her own clinic out of The Mom's Place. "Sure. Come on up tonight if you want.''

"When does Greta usually leave?''

"Around six." The only good thing about their confrontation at the Train Depot Café was that Gran hardly ever wanted to gab after work anymore. Whether she was spending more time with Grandpa or less with Sophie, she went home at a more appropriate hour.

"Do you mind waiting for me until six-thirty? Just to make sure she's gone? My father's in town, and he and Beth will look after Evan for me.''

She and Zach had built a guest house for her dad
on Zach's farm. Olivia said it made his extended visits bearable. James Kendall claimed he had to visit
to make sure her magazine, part of his "empire,"
ran smoothly, but they'd all noticed how quickly he
cut his business short to see Aunt Beth when he came
to town.

"I'll be here," Sophie said.

"Thanks. I'm so glad you took my call."

Sophie laughed. Olivia normally handled herself
with the confidence of someone who was a tycoon's
daughter and the managing editor of an important
news magazine. "Me, too." Sophie cupped the receiver. "Congratulations, just in case."

"Thanks. I hope the tests are right."

Tests? The phone clicked before Sophie could ask
how many Olivia had taken.

That evening, Gran asked Sophie to meet her in
her office at six-fifteen. She could hardly refuse.

Gran was hard faced when Sophie took her chair
across the wide desk. But her eyes were soft and
wounded.

"I've heard a rumor."

"The clinic?" She braced herself against the chair.
She refused to lie.

"Tom Fedderson's asking about available prop-
erties in town. I guess he's in league with you?"

Sophie crossed her legs and arms, no doubt looking as guilty as she felt. "I don't want to hurt you,
but I thought I should talk to him to see if the idea

might work. He wants to slow down, and he thinks a few other doctors nearby might want to share their time, as well. You could work there too, Gran, once in a while. When you're bored with your leisure.''

Rage blew up in Gran's eyes, startling Sophie, but almost as quickly, her control took over. "No, thanks. If there were a place for me, you'd have told me the first time it came up. I wouldn't have had to confront you after you'd gone against my wishes.''

"I'm not. Tell me to stop and I will.'' Sophie's cell phone rang. She pulled it out of her pocket, read Olivia's number on the digital face and dropped it back in, unanswered.

"You already knew I didn't approve. Still, you approached Tom.''

She refused to betray her grandfather. "You have to see we could do some good.''

"I see. I just don't like your methods, and I'm hurt after all we've been through together. At the very least, you should have told me working up here wouldn't be enough for you.''

"I didn't know how much I'd miss the actual deliveries.'' Her phone rang again. She ignored it. "I'm used to seeing my patients from conception to handing the newborn over to the pediatrician.''

"So working here was a mistake?''

"No.'' Sophie's alacrity was sincere. "I'm glad I came home.'' She couldn't see herself living anywhere else now. "But I'm sorry you and I are arguing about work. This should be our best time together." She stood to circle the desk and put her arm around her grandmother. "I'm serious about you taking a shift. You'd be great. Everyone knows you. They trust you."

"Everyone except you. This clinic isn't a done deal. You have to pass it by the town first, and people here vote with their pocketbooks. You'll know you've failed when you can't afford to open the doors one morning."

Sophie had no answer. She'd never seen such arrogance in her grandmother before. She couldn't begin to explain it, but she felt responsible. "Gran, I'm sorry."

A knock at the door interrupted them. Greta stood, avoiding Sophie as she crossed the room. Sophie saw Olivia hovering behind one of the patrons.

"Oh, no." She stared at Sophie. "You promised to keep quiet."

"I didn't say anything. We had a late meeting."

"Say anything about what?" Greta studied her newest granddaughter closely. She claimed she could sense a pregnancy from a hundred yards, and experience usually proved her correct. "Oh." She turned to Sophie, the disappointment in her eyes as sharp as any lethal weapon. "I see. Your first patient."

CHAPTER THIRTEEN

"I CAN'T EXPLAIN my behavior, Seth." Tearfully Greta lifted her head from her husband's shoulder. "Maybe you're right. Maybe I'm jealous because Sophie's at the beginning of her career and I'm at the end of mine and she's starting something new without me." She searched his pockets for a handkerchief but couldn't find one. He reached across her for a tissue from a box on the nightstand. He'd found her crying on their bed. "Thank God I can count on you."

"I wish you needed me for more than reassurance, Greta. You know you're a vital woman. You have as much energy as our great-grandchildren. You're intelligent. You have fifty years of medical history in this area. You don't have to look at retirement from the baby farm as a death sentence."

"It's not a baby farm." Still, he sounded encouraging for the first time since he'd started all this crazy retirement talk. "But thank you for seeing me through rose-colored glasses."

"You know what I mean. You have a lot to offer

the community. You just don't have to work fourteen hours every day."

She blew her nose and then straightened to look him in the eye. "You wouldn't mind if I found something else to do?"

"I want more of your time and attention, but I'm not asking you to barricade yourself in this house with me."

She sniffed. "I never said that, Seth, but we've both been busy all our adult lives. You still visit the courthouse. You write for several different law journals. You haven't put your work life behind you."

"I'd work a lot less if I had you to come home to. I'd like to travel. I'd like to take Evan and Lily and Sophie's new baby for ice cream when she's a toddler. Don't you want to spend time with me and our family, Greta?"

"I do." She straightened his collar, fingering the smudge of her mascara on the material. "But, honestly, I wanted to work with Sophie. I've dreamed of sharing The Mom's Place with her since the day she told me she wanted to be a doctor, too. Now, because she's finally come home, I have to quit, and she's expanding."

"And I'm the one who's making you quit." Instead of looking guilty for forcing her into retirement, he looked annoyed that she minded so much. But he lifted his shoulders, regaining his patience. "I know it's hard, and if you tell me you can't quit now, I'll try to understand, but I want my wife with me."

She stared into his eyes. Offering to let her continue working had drained all the blood from his face. He'd asked her to stop for years. She'd agreed on their anniversary last fall. She'd made a promise to this man who'd stood by her for fifty-five years. She owed him her best effort. "I'll start phasing out." She kissed him, and the excitement of their youth still rushed her pulse. That never changed. "Maybe you and I could talk about ways for me to go on helping our neighbors. Even with the clinic. They'll need some sort of guidance. Sophie said it's going to be a multi-community project."

"They'd be foolish not to use you when you've been around for most of the births on this mountain in the past fifty years. And you've kept your eye on the other health issues that have affected us up here. They'll need you, Greta. You're not ready for a pasture." He pulled her close, fitting her head beneath his chin.

As her cheek rested against his chest, she smiled. No matter what he said about their lack of time together, this was a memory ingrained in her body—her head beneath his chin, his chest against her cheek, his breathing, deep and even.

"Greta, I have to tell you something. I can't let you blame Sophie."

She pushed away from him instantly. "Blame Sophie? I don't understand."

He took a deep breath, and his confession erupted from him. "She didn't call Tom Fedderson. I arranged their meeting. Anyway, I suggested he meet her to discuss the opportunity.''

Greta stared at him, stunned into silence. But not for long. "Why would you do that?''

He begged her for forgiveness with his eyes, then looked away.

"You could only have one reason.''

He didn't have to answer. She scooted away, feeling the scratch of the cotton bedding beneath her palms. "You wanted to get back at me because I wasn't moving fast enough, and you knew I was upset about Sophie and Ian's idea.''

Seth lifted his head as if it were on a spring. "I did, but that passed quickly. Tom was so grateful I saw the clinic as a good idea. He and the other doctors in the area want a central location. They're all willing to do hours. This is the county seat. I didn't pursue it to hurt you, Greta.''

"You started it to hurt me.'' She didn't know this white-faced ghost of her husband, and she hardly knew what she was doing as she strode across their bedroom. She found the closet door in her hand and yanked it open.

"Greta?''

Almost without thinking, she pulled an overnight bag off a tall shelf.

"Come back here and talk to me,'' he said without following her.

He couldn't be bothered, and that suited her fine. She tossed clothes into the bag. When she came out,

Seth was leaning on her dressing table, holding his chest as if it hurt.

She hoped his pain matched hers. She couldn't share this roof with him tonight. "I'm going to Sophie's." She decided as she spoke. "I owe her an apology, and I think I'll ask her to put me up until I can stand coming home to a man who's not only betrayed me, but let me blame our granddaughter."

"Greta, you have to see how desperate I am."

"You crossed a line."

Early in their marriage, there had been a few times that no one else knew about when she'd felt overstressed and she'd needed time to herself. She'd found a hotel room and taken a break from school and family and later from work. Those days had inspired her to open The Mom's Place.

She'd needed a break from her life back then, but she'd never dreamed she'd need a break from the husband whose place was at her side, not working against her.

THE THIRD EVENING Greta was with them, Ian almost called Seth to ask him to beg his wife to come home. She and Sophie talked shop from the moment they left the baby farm until the moment they returned. After two hours and forty-five minutes of watching Sophie wrestle her uncomfortable kitchen chair for a position that didn't exacerbate the nearly constant ache in her back muscles, he decided to take a more direct approach.

Sophie took one of her many bathroom breaks and Ian looked up from his newspaper. Greta glanced at him from the files and notes spread across the table. He'd grown to love Sophie's gran, but her distracted smile annoyed him.

"Greta." He waited for her to focus.

"Hmm?"

"You're too much work for Sophie."

In silence, she stared as if he'd spoken a language she didn't understand. Probably true. "What are you talking about?"

"You've been with us three nights. You and Sophie pore over notes from work all day and plans for work for the next year. It's time you made up with your husband and let my wife rest up for having our baby."

"Ian." Sophie, shocked, stood in the doorway, bracing her hand on the lintel. "This isn't your call."

"I disagree." He matched the steel in her tone. "You and the baby are my family. You're due in just over two weeks. You should be taking better care of yourself." He didn't add that Greta should have taken better care of her, as well, if Sophie wasn't capable of turning off her grandmother's work ethic.

Sophie pushed away from the door, looking for trouble. "I'm fine. The baby is fine."

"Wait." Greta began to gather papers. "Ian's right. I don't know what I was thinking."

"Where are you going, Gran? You should call Grandpa."

"I called him. He didn't want to talk." She swallowed, her throat working. "He said maybe I shouldn't come home if we're going to split up, anyway."

"Split up?" Sophie crossed the room at a run, leading with her belly. "What are you saying? You forgave me. Forgive him. This is all my fault, anyway."

"Not this time." Greta gathered herself. "Not ever. It wasn't your fault with Nita and Ethan, and nothing is your fault now."

"Then talk to Grandpa."

Greta glanced at Ian as if he were an intruder. He didn't point out that Greta hadn't so much forgiven Sophie's interest in the clinic as both women had decided to ignore it. The truth would just start a bigger fight, and his wife needed sleep.

"Come upstairs with me, Sophie, and leave your gran to the phone."

Sophie looked annoyed. Teamwork went out the window every time he suggested she take things easier. The closer her time came, the more she suspected any such suggestion of being a ploy to take over her life. He shook his head. You'd think a doctor who understood the effects of pregnancy hormones could control her mood. Fortunately he found Sophie's temper charming, because of the reasons for it.

"All right," she said at last. "Good night, Gran." Leaning over the back of Greta's chair, she kissed her gran's hair.

Greta looped both arms around Sophie. "Night, honey. You have to learn to tell me to shut up and let you get on with your own life."

"You're a huge part of my life. I'm just glad you were willing to be friends with me again."

"Am I that difficult?"

"No—but Grandpa isn't, either. He loves you. I don't care what he says."

"I can't stand him doing things just to hurt me— and that's why he called Tom Fedderson."

"Tell him, Gran. But maybe it's time you faced the truth. He wants you to be home more, and you're going to have to arrange that with him."

"I can't stop cold turkey. Maybe I should tell him that."

"That's a much better idea than breaking up after fifty-five years." Turning with tears in her eyes, she joined Ian. "Ready?"

He pushed her hair away from her face, his awareness of her beleaguered body making him gentle. He wished she could be as wise about her own actions as she was with Greta. "Come on."

At the stairs, he maneuvered her in front of him and put his hands on her hips.

"I can make it on my own." But for once she didn't sound as if she really minded his assistance.

"I like helping," he said.

At their room, she reached behind him to shut the door and close her grandmother out. He pulled her into his arms, leaning to make room for her stomach.

"You make me crazy when you take charge," she said.

"Crazy in a good way?" He smiled, refusing to argue, no matter how badly she wanted a fight.

"Not really." She caught his face in her hands. Finally, as he leaned down to kiss her, she smiled back, and he loved the curve of her lips beneath his.

"I can't believe you still want this now."

"You're carrying my child." He ran his hand over her belly, amazed as always by its tautness. "*This* is all my fault."

She laughed and he kissed her again, needing her. He kissed her cheek and then her throat. She slid her hands into his hair, holding him close. After all these months, she still didn't admit it with words, but she needed him, too.

She let him go to grab the hem of his T-shirt and push it up his chest. Helping her, he tossed it behind himself. She was already kissing his chest, her mouth finding his heartbeat with unerring accuracy that sent it thumping at an unsettling speed. She turned her head and captured his nipple. His eyes closed as sensation rocked him.

"The bed, Sophie."

"Always a bed with you."

"Greta would be shocked if we tried some new spot downstairs."

"And I'd probably overbalance if we start testing the furniture."

He managed to undress her on their way across

the floor. She peeled the comforter back and they met on the cool sheets. Her hungry mouth made him forget he longed for the days when they could lie skin to skin, neck to toe. She turned in his arms and he found a way to please them both. The urgent sounds she made, tensing against his chest, pulled him with her.

"Ian." She turned her head. Her mouth caught his chin. He kissed her, moving mindlessly, seeking only intimacy that had once terrified him, always eluded him. These nights had lulled him into trusting Sophie. She didn't talk of love. She might not want to hear of love, either.

But holding her was nearly enough. Teasing her, knowing just how to touch her to prolong her pleasure, he realized he'd become a husband. Sophie mattered most to him.

The knowledge spun his head, lent their lovemaking new tenderness. "Sophie." Guiding her hips with his hands, he nuzzled the nape of her neck. She stretched, pressing herself into his body, until suddenly she strained, sighing with joy that made him laugh. She made him happy.

After a few moments, she rolled over, searching his gaze with hers. "You didn't—"

"No," he said, his tone husky.

Her smile was provocatively wicked. "Good." She kissed him, opening his mouth with hers. He followed where she led.

ONE NIGHT ABOUT A WEEK after her grandparents reached their unsteady truce, Greta gave Sophie a ride to the courthouse. All the physicians who'd discussed the clinic had arranged a town meeting. The people of Bardill's Ridge generally had an opinion, and Sophie was more than ready to listen, but Ian had made her promise to take a ride from Gran.

After her grandmother had agreed to start pulling back by one day a week at the baby farm, Sophie had seen the value of compromise. She was trying to listen to Ian's concerns.

He hadn't trusted the weather after eight days and nights of summer storms, so he planned to meet her at the courthouse after he came back from a supply run to Knoxville with her father. He didn't want her to drive back up the soggy ridge alone in the dark.

Dr. Fedderson had warned Sophie not to expect much from this first meeting. He'd heard rumblings during his appointments. Folks who thought a new clinic might bring strangers to town; others who suspected Sophie was at the bottom of the whole discussion, and she couldn't be trusted to stay.

He was right. About the third time she took a direct question about her intentions, she began to worry she was making a mistake.

"The clinic is supposed to help you, Mrs. Caldwell." She scanned the crowd, burying her fist in her aching back. "All of you. And your families. Apart from the fact I wouldn't start something this important to the community without a commitment to stay,

I'll be contributing part of my savings to this project." She glanced down. "You can see I have good reason to make sure my savings work for my own family."

At that moment, Ian, finally free of any cast, opened the door at the back of the room. Across the sea of bodies, she felt their connection in his warm smile. He took a seat while she fielded more doubts.

Dr. Fedderson stepped in. "Even if Dr. Calvert—I mean, Ridley—decided to leave, we'd still have the full complement of physicians."

"Yes," Mrs. Caldwell said, "but my daughter visits an OB near Knoxville. The drive takes her forever, but she has a relationship with her doctor. What if she switched to this new office and then Sophie ups and goes again?"

"I didn't up and go before, Mrs. Caldwell. I was in college, and then I had a practice." She glanced at Ian. His rueful grin induced a smile.

"Look at me when I'm talking to you, Sophie."

She met Mrs. Caldwell's annoyed gaze.

"You could leave again anytime, and then my girl might be high and dry with a little one on the way."

"No." She nodded at Ian. "My husband and I are making our home here from now on. We want our daughter—or son—to grow up among family and friends. I don't know how to make you believe me, Mrs. Caldwell. All I can say is that we plan to stay."

And that should be good enough. How could she

commit more strongly? Beside her, Gran patted her hand.

"Lucinda, I understand your concern, but I wouldn't have asked Sophie to join me at The Mom's Place if I didn't believe she meant to stay." She took a deep breath. "I've been as reluctant as you, Lucinda, but I'm here tonight to find out if I'm just resistant to change. Give these people a chance."

The meeting went on and they eventually covered the buildings they'd considered renting so far, the plans they'd made to share duty at the clinic and the full range of services they'd be able to offer.

"Won't you be working here, too, Dr. Calvert?" another woman asked.

Dr. Fedderson spoke up. "At least consider giving us some time when you stop working at the baby— The Mom's Place."

Greta laughed, and Sophie witnessed her first truly relaxed smile in weeks. "I've promised to discuss any future commitments with my husband, but there's nothing I'd like better."

Relief drained Sophie's last store of energy. She was grateful when talk finally began to dwindle. She lingered after they adjourned to help calm any left-over fears, but she reached for Ian's hand as he approached her. Without speaking, he massaged the small of her back, finally excusing them both with the not-so-tactful observation that she looked exhausted.

Outside in the gusting wind she slid her hand into the crook of his elbow. "Did you hear Gran?"

"You think she and Seth are all better?"

"I won't be surprised if she stretches her working hours again because she can't seem to help herself. But she must be trying." She rubbed her own back as they walked. "Thanks for meeting me. I'm too tired to drive home."

"Let's start before the rain washes out the roads. I've heard we might even be in for a tornado tonight."

"You sound worried."

He laughed as if he'd never heard of such a possibility. "No, but I haven't been in a tornado. Have you?"

"They've touched down around here, but not on a house I lived in."

"So don't talk big until you know how you'd react."

"Fine." She lifted his hand and draped his arm around her shoulders. "You're the toughest guy I know."

"You're just saying that."

"Yeah."

"But I appreciate it."

"Are you hungry?"

"Let's pick up something from the café."

She drowsed in the car while Ian ordered and picked up their takeout. When he came back, his hands full of brown bags and delicious smells, she leaned across the console to kiss his cheek.

He turned and deepened the kiss, smiling with passion in his eyes as she sank back. She studied him, aware of his body, of his wanting her. She'd become a wife over the past few months, and she wasn't sure when it had finally happened or how.

She didn't mind, as long as Ian didn't try to manage too much of her life. A ride here, a word with her grandmother there. It could be upsetting, but it wasn't as if she couldn't warn him to back off.

While rain drummed on the roof she closed her eyes. "Wake me when we're home."

"Have you considered starting maternity leave?"

She opened her eyes. "I go along feeling happy and then you say something like that, and I wonder if you realize how having someone try to manage my life alarms me."

He smiled, only half-amused. "I wonder how to make you realize you're responsible for more than yourself from here on."

She could have been annoyed without guilt if he'd just sounded angry with her, but his concern was correct. He'd made a lot of effort to be with her. He loved his child. With each day, he was more and more a member of the Calvert clan. A guy deserved combat pay for that endeavor alone.

She made light of his anxiety, too tired to go deeper. "Carrying a baby who thinks she's training for the high jump, how can I forget I'm about to be a mom? But I won't schedule any more after-work meetings till after she's born.''

She wasn't entirely asleep during the rest of the drive. Thunder and wind buffeted the car. Lightning bolted, turning night into brief flashes of day in the dark woods. She braced herself between the console and the door handle as Ian tried to choose the more shallow ruts in their rain-soaked driveway.

He resisted her attempt to help him carry in their dinner. In the kitchen she set the table while he unpacked the brown bags.

''We have a message,'' he said from his vantage closer to the telephone.

''I hope it's no one at the baby farm.''

''You'll call Greta if it is.''

She let that pass. ''Could you play it?''

He hit the button. A man's voice spoke Ian's name and waited. Then started again. ''It's me, Adam. I have another job for you. Shouldn't take you more than a week. Call me, buddy.''

Sophie turned. ''In this one area, I'd like you to take care of me.''

Ian frowned. This was his sore point. ''What do you mean?''

''Tell him you won't take any more assignments.''

He froze in a cessation of all movement. ''I can't do that, Soph.''

He'd begun to use her father's pet name for her. She liked it. ''You think I don't take care of myself, but I'm not doing anything dangerous.''

258 THE BRIDE RAN AWAY

"I don't, either."

At her incredulous expression, he dared to grin. "I take calculated risks. But it's my job. I can't just quit. I'm part of this family—and I contribute to our income."

He had contributed his fair share, despite working only once since they'd been married. His bank account must be taking quite a hit.

"Find some other work." She refused to phrase it in an appeal. He tended to demand, rather than request when he thought her actions didn't benefit their family. Maybe he'd understand a similar approach.

Harsh lines drew his mouth tight. "I've worked in protection all my adult life. I can't quit because you're scared."

"I was more than just scared." Admitting the depth of her fear for him took more courage than leaping in front of a speeding car, herself. "Please don't make me feel like that again."

His expression softened. "We don't have to talk about it now. Let's wait until after you have the baby. I'll turn down anything Adam offers until then, anyway."

Putting off this conversation hadn't helped before. "We have to settle this, Ian. It's important."

"You're tired and hungry. Your back's obviously tense, and you feel bad. Let's drop it for tonight."

"I can't. I somehow persuaded myself all this time while we weren't discussing your job that you wouldn't be doing it anymore. Now I need to know."

"I can't quit." He came around the table, turning her as he pulled her toward him. Apparently assuming an argument made no difference to her addiction to his back rubs, he began to knead the aching muscles. "How about a compromise?"

"I don't think you can offer one that will work." But he knew just where to stroke to ease the pain.

"I've thought about opening an agency of my own. I couldn't stop taking dangerous assignments right away, but eventually I could hire employees to take those jobs for me."

"You make me feel bad for the faceless guys who'd be in harm's way."

"No one takes this work because he's scared." The words were glib, but his tone was gentle.

"And when are you going to hire these people who I hope won't have spouses and children to put first?"

"Not now. I can't afford it yet—and I can't turn myself into an accountant or something safe enough for you overnight."

"I see you're trying to be patient." Though the accountant jab felt a bit like a challenge. "But I'm not just thinking of myself." And the abject fear that had nearly broken her when her grandfather had said Ian was hurt.

He turned her to face him. "I want to be around to watch my son grow up, too."

She stared, mesmerized by the sometimes hard,

always expressive face she'd grown to care for without even realizing how vital Ian had become to her.

She pulled away slightly. She'd survived their affair because she'd known exactly what she'd wanted from the relationship. She hadn't expected him to stay in continuous touch or bring flowers, or even to explain his time away from her. Needing him now made her feel less in control.

A sudden gust of wind and rain at the windows gave her an excuse to look away from him. He took her hands.

''What are you thinking when you look as if you don't trust me, Sophie?''

She couldn't trust herself. Ever since the day her innocent question about her mother's playmate had destroyed her family, she'd steel-plated her emotions, measuring her involvement with any man to avoid letting him hurt her. Ian had somehow eroded her defenses, but she was the one who'd made herself vulnerable.

Feeling as if she'd cheated him because she couldn't quite believe in forever, she gripped his hands. He'd done all he could to prove his commitment. She was the one who kept thinking their marriage might be temporary. He deserved better. ''I promise I'm trying to trust you.''

His laugh was more a breath leavened with bemused acceptance. When he pulled her close, she wrapped tight arms around him.

"I'll take what you can give," he said against her hair.

She blinked hard to hold back tears. She couldn't be that generous. She needed to know beyond the shadow of a doubt that she couldn't lose anything. That she couldn't lose him.

CHAPTER FOURTEEN

IT WAS ONLY LATER, as she lay awake staring at the rain-slashed windows and Ian slept beside her that Sophie realized he'd put off making any promise she could accept about his job.

Sighing, she eased onto her left side, withholding a groan as the muscles in her back seized up. Maybe Ian was right. Staying out of his work life might be a good character lesson for her. Wanting so much control, feeling a frantic need to stop him from doing something that meant so much to him, disturbed her.

Even to her, the feeling wasn't rational.

Rain buffeted the house. She edged closer to Ian, taking comfort in his warmth. The past week had brought fallen trees and mudslides. She'd missed a morning at work, waiting for the county to chop a fallen tree into small enough pieces to move them off the road.

"Are you okay?" Ian asked sleepily, his breath hot on her throat.

"Fine." She was restless, but she tried to lie quietly so he could sleep. When his breathing became even again, she slid from beneath his arm and crawled out of bed.

At the window she could hardly make out anything except the branch that scraped lightly at the window. She flexed her back. This pregnancy had already made her a better doctor to her patients. She'd learned a deeper understanding of their aches and pains.

The baby performed a quick tap dance beneath her ribs, and Sophie smiled, flattening her hand over her tight, rippling skin. The baby had been quieter than usual today. Sophie was ready to hold her daughter in her arms.

She turned, staring into the black room in the direction of the bed. Sleep didn't look likely. It was pointless to lie beside Ian trying not to wake him. She felt her way across the room, snatching her robe off the bed as she went.

In the hall she switched on the light and pulled on her robe, stopping as a Braxton-Hicks contraction crept from her back to her belly, surprisingly strong for false labor. Descending the stairs had become a ponderous process over the past few weeks. She gripped the banister with one hand and pressed her other palm to the wall.

She turned on a favorite movie in the living room and wallowed on the couch, trying to find a comfortable position. As the wind and rain pounded the house and the power wavered, another Braxton-Hicks caught her breath.

She traced her stomach with her fingertips. These contractions weren't supposed to hurt that much. She'd never make light of them again.

"Are you all right?" Ian, behind her, must have wakened when she'd tried to sneak out of the room.

She struggled onto her side. In a T-shirt and sweatpants, he rubbed at his head as if trying to make himself alert.

"I couldn't sleep. You don't have to get up."

"I'm serious. Are you okay?"

His concern and his sleepy mess endeared him to her. "What's up with you?"

He finally stopped scrubbing at his hair. "I'm good at my job because I usually notice when things are different. You've been different tonight."

"Maybe it's all this rain. A week of storms and struggling over bad roads just to go to work would make anyone tense."

He looked dissatisfied. "Okay. You want some coffee?"

She'd really love some coffee, but she started to say no.

"I'll make decaf," he said.

"I'll bear your firstborn child."

"Keep it up and I'll start thinking I want a second-born."

"Don't threaten me, Ian Ridley." Another Braxton-Hicks hit as he entered the kitchen. Sophie frowned, but this one didn't seem as intense. She expected that and she sank into the cushions.

Ian swore from the kitchen as glass rattled on the counter.

"Did you break it?" she asked.

"I caught it." He leaned around the door brandishing the glass carafe. His glance narrowed on her. "What's wrong?"

"Nothing." That last contraction, though not as intense—maybe—didn't seem to be passing off as quickly.

"Are you sick? Something hurt?" He looked suspicious and a little bit afraid. She laughed. The only person she knew who enjoyed being in charge more than she did was Ian.

"I can't get comfortable." No need to send him into a panic.

"I'll get you a pillow and a blanket when I finish here." He went back to the coffee. "Listen to the wind. Does this happen every year?"

"Usually tornadoes come in the spring, not August." She shivered as a new gust rattled windowpanes. "I hope we keep the roof."

"Sophie, I've been thinking we might want to look at buying our own place."

It made sense if they were going to make their marriage work. If they were about to become a family. "Yeah," she said, not sure why she suddenly couldn't breathe. "Maybe we should."

"You don't like the idea?"

At least he'd stayed in the kitchen. Lying to his face would have been difficult. "It's a good idea."

Had she been playing house all this time? The idea of signing a mortgage with Ian carried a terrifying feeling of forever. She'd promised "till death do us part," and she'd done her best to mean it since he'd come to Bardill's Ridge, but buying a house with a man…a thirty-year mortgage…

"You're reluctant."

She hesitated long enough for another contraction to travel from her back to her belly. She glanced at the clock on the mantel.

"You know," she said, spacing the words because she wanted him to understand her lack of enthusiasm as well as she could, "my grandparents have always been close. You don't know how they were before. They argued, but they made up, often with embarrassing zest." And they were in love. They hadn't married because it was the right thing to do. They hadn't agreed to stay together because of a baby.

"Yeah? What are you saying?" Ian asked when she didn't go on.

"They've been together fifty-five years, and yet she left him, and you had to force her to go home."

"You have to be blunt with me, Sophie."

"What's ever certain, Ian?" She looked toward the kitchen as he came to the door. "What's safe when it comes to a thirty-year-or-more commitment?"

"Safe? I don't understand." He came into the room, his gaze hard. "It's too late to back out now."

She planted her feet on the cool wood floor. "I

don't want to back out.'' She just wanted certainty. The promise of a whole life with the same man. And the kind of love Ian had never mentioned.

"When you talk about Greta and commitment, you make me nervous. You're too much like her, and she's had her marriage all her own way. What do you want?''

Another contraction started with a pull that made the others innocuous. She looked at the clock. "For one thing, I want to be having false labor.''

"What?''

"I think it's real, though.''

"Soph?'' He crossed the room, ending up in front of her on his knees. "Why didn't you tell me? How long has this been—you're a doctor.''

"But I've never been in labor before. It rarely goes this swiftly in theory. The contractions seem to be about four and a half minutes apart.''

"Call Dr. Sims, and let's go to the hospital.''

"In this weather?'' She breathed again as the pain finally eased. "I don't think we have time, Ian.''

He closed his hands on her thighs. "We don't have time?'' He squeezed so hard she tried to lever his fingers open. "Sorry.'' He stood, grabbing the coat he'd thrown across the sofa earlier. She had a wild thought that he might be leaving. To her relief, he dug his cell phone out of the pocket.

"Call an ambulance and my gran and the doctor.''

He'd clearly memorized Dr. Sims's number because, after a few moments, he all but yelled into the phone. "My wife's in labor. Call us." And he hung up.

"I don't think he knows your voice, Ian."

"God." He hit redial and left complete information. "The man doesn't even have an answering service. This place needs the clinic to drag the twenty-first century up the ridge."

"911."

"I am." His hands shook so hard it took three tries to dial the three-digit number.

Another contraction clutched her. She hadn't bothered with birthing classes. How on earth could she need them? Or so she'd thought. But she forgot what she told her patients and she fought the pain that had mounted far too quickly.

"Hurry." She bleated the word between gasped breaths. "And call Gran. Then get clean towels and some twine. Old, but clean bedding."

"Can Greta get here before the baby?" He turned to the phone. "My wife's in labor. Ian Ridley, up at The Mom's Place?" He waited a moment, scowling fiercely. "What are you talking about? Get a helicopter. Do something."

"What?" Sophie tried to stand, but he came to her and eased her back onto the sofa. Just as well. Walking tended to speed up labor, the last thing she needed.

"They can't send anyone. Both ambulances are with vehicle accidents on washed-out roads. Can't someone from The Mom's Place come?"

"I'm the medical person on call. You can try for the duty nurse, but I doubt she'll have an easier time getting here than anyone else.

He called anyway, but his brow knotted as he spoke, and when he hung up he looked helpless. "She agrees with you. The roads are bad, but she's going to try to come."

Sophie didn't panic. She kind of knew already, because she might not be an expert at labor from this side of the doctor's office, but the symptoms were clear. She'd caught a few rapid deliveries in her career. They were going to have to do this on their own.

"Try Gran." Another contraction had her gritting her teeth. "She'll come if she has to climb the ridge in her bare feet."

He dropped the phone and yanked her into his arms, but his wretched expression frightened her. "This is perfect," he said. "You couldn't be happier. You're in charge. You know what to do, and you're going to instruct me step-by-step. Just the way you started our marriage."

Considering she'd like to tear something apart to take her mind off the creature struggling to be free of her body, she wasn't that happy. But he was right about one thing. She liked calling the shots, and maybe she couldn't change. All this time when he'd tried to take care of her, when he'd collected her family—building what she'd called his little club in their house—when he'd tossed her grandmother out, she hadn't actually minded that he was being high-handed with her family. She'd hated him thinking he had the right to decide what she needed. She didn't want any other human being to have control in her life.

She couldn't defend it and she wouldn't waste the strength arguing now. "Call Gran." As he dialed, she sank against the couch. A sudden burst of water between her legs spilled to the floor. Ian didn't seem to care that he was getting wet.

"How long have you been in labor, Sophie? I can't believe you didn't feel I had a right to know."

"We don't have time to chat. Can't you tell it's going fast? I think the backache I've had for two days was early labor."

He swore and they both heard a voice through the phone. She couldn't tell what Gran was saying as he clamped the phone to his ear, but Ian clearly didn't have to explain.

"Thanks," he said. "I'll get everything." He flipped the phone shut. "She knew."

"She knows the roads are bad, and I'm only a week from my due date." She grabbed at the phone. "Call back and tell her I'm going to deliver before she gets here."

He looked as if he'd like to escape, but then he steeled himself and dialed back. "Seth, it's me. Tell Greta Sophie's going to deliver before you can get here."

"I don't want Grandpa to see me like this." She

pushed sweat off her forehead with her palm. "This isn't a spectator event."

"Yeah," Ian said to her. To her grandfather, he added, "Hurry."

He shut the phone again, and he was already on his feet. "Should I get Greta back so she can talk me through it? Are you going to be able to speak?"

"You've read all the books I had for nervous parents." Panic depleted her ability to be tactful. "You know what's going to happen."

"I know what happened to the people in those books. I've forgotten everything, now that I'm about to do the delivery myself."

Fear suddenly squeezed her throat. Things could go wrong. Her baby... She refused to consider what might happen. "If I start to bleed or I pass out, you need to find someone else, but everyone we need is coming."

He didn't bother to answer before he ran up the stairs. Seconds later he flew back down with clean sheets and clean clothing for her. From the pile against his chest, he drew out a plastic-covered ball of twine. "I don't even know why I had this, but I never could find a place to put it after I unpacked it."

"We're not going to cut the cord, but—" She broke off to breathe through the worst pain yet. Suddenly he was calm, but she felt scared. "Aren't you concerned?"

"About a lot of things." He dropped the bedding

on the end of the couch and helped her to her feet. "Why don't you change out of those wet pajamas?"

"What are you worried about?"

He met her eyes. His looked defensive. "That you've lied to me. You kept everything you really felt inside. You wanted me to commit, but you didn't. You don't give anyone else a right to really know who you are, Sophie."

"I'm the girl who ruined my parents' marriage. I'm the woman who takes after my grandmother when it comes to sharing. I give my all to a job, but I measure parts of myself into relationships. And I don't ever want someone else to be the one with the final say, the one who either saves my life or loses it, when a crisis—" she spread her legs, indicating her wet lap and the floor "—like this comes." She gritted her teeth. The truth hurt more than the worst contraction. "I might be too much trouble to be worth it."

"You might be out of your mind." Before today, he would have smiled to make the accusation a joke, but he meant it. "Until you trust someone to want to stay, you're never going to be happy."

The next contraction nearly doubled her over. Ian caught her and held on until the pain subsided, and then he helped her to the bathroom.

"Sit." He dropped the toilet lid and eased her onto it and then handed her the clean pajamas.

"A gown would be better. Or one of your shirts." Maybe he wouldn't want her ruining his shirt.

"I should have thought. Don't get up. Shout if you need me. I'm going to get everything ready, and then I'll come back for you."

"I can walk."

"Sophie." He paused at the door. "You have to listen to me now. I'm angry. You've run me like your own personal family drama all these months. You didn't even bother to tell me you were on the verge of giving birth to our child. *Our* child." He caught himself, clearly feeling a brawl right now would be insensitive. "Just shut up and let me handle this one thing. Tell me what to do, but don't risk falling and hurting yourself or my son because you aren't safe if you aren't in control."

"I'm getting sick of the snap diagnoses, Dr. Ian." She gasped as another pain hit.

Ian left her, but his footsteps pounding up the stairs to their room comforted her. And they comforted her again as he made his way back at lightning speed. He opened the door to hand her one of his T-shirts and a pair of socks.

"I read that your body goes through temperature changes."

She was hot as hell right now. He shut the door behind himself as he went back to the living room and she managed to work her pajamas off. She'd barely pulled Ian's shirt over her head when he opened the door again.

He looked away, as if he wasn't supposed to see her naked, and she realized he was serious about his resentment. This wasn't going to be a tiff they could resolve with a chat.

The next contraction included a painful pulling sensation that ended with an urge to push. "Ian!"

He helped her to stand.

"We don't have much time," she said.

He hoisted her off her feet, undoubtedly drowning in adrenaline. Seconds later, the bumpy couch met her back. She lifted her knees, and Ian got between them.

"Can you see her head?"

"I see something dark. Hair?"

She nodded, barely able to speak. "Any blood? Anything dark in the fluid?"

"A little blood. Nothing in the fluid."

"You just have to catch her. If her hands are over her face or caught, ease her out as gently as—" She groaned in agony. Good God. She should be the one catching the baby. What kind of life was it when a woman had to depend on someone else at a time like this? "And make sure you don't hurt her."

"Sophie, concentrate on your part of the process."

"Process?" She ended with a bone-shaking groan as she braced her feet against his thighs and pushed. She prayed the baby was still positioned normally. If she got stuck pushing here for hours on end, they could be in trouble, but she didn't dare tell Ian.

She sagged for a moment. He stroked her legs. He didn't speak, but his touch calmed her. She'd whipped all the way through transition in record time. The next contraction began, and she pushed with all her might. Five more burning, tortuous attempts, and she found the most exquisite relief as the baby's head and shoulders passed out of her body.

"Sophie." Ian's voice held no more anger. He simply leaned down and lifted their blue, wet, beautiful child. "She's not crying. What do I—"

Before he could finish, their infant daughter let out a war whoop that probably rang down the Great Smoky Mountains. Sophie looked at Ian, laughing through tears. He wiped the baby and then wrapped her in a clean white towel and passed her to Sophie.

Sophie eased the towel open for a quick examination. Her baby girl was perfect. Furiously screaming, tiny hands and feet already changing to pink, quivering with rage.

"Is she okay?" Ian asked.

"Absolutely. Look at her eyes. I think she can see." Between screams the baby seemed to be taking a survey of her clearly unsatisfactory surroundings.

"You know she can't. You're the doctor." But he sounded pleased.

Sophie cuddled her daughter close, trying to give her back the warmth she'd just lost.

"Are you all right?" Ian asked.

Sophie looked at him, distracted but touched by his soft tone. "Fine. I still have to deliver the placenta, and that's going to be messy, but from the cramps I'm having, it's coming. Are you all right with blood?"

It was the wrong question. Anger came back into his eyes. "I'll take care of it."

"I'm sorry." She looked from the baby, slowly moving her mouth in a pantomime of hunger, to him. Her whole life felt different than it had just an hour ago. This child who already had Sophie's heart in her hands, belonged to Ian, too. "Thank you."

His expression changed, but Sophie couldn't read it. He looked like a stranger. How could he turn into a stranger now? "You were right." He cupped their baby's head. "She's a girl."

"She has your dark hair." Sophie already loved the strands that stood up half an inch on all sides of her daughter's skull.

"She does." He smiled, but his eyes looked hollow.

Sophie wished she were different. She wished she could have kept her secret fears to herself just a little longer. "Are you okay?"

He lifted both brows as if he could hardly believe she had the guts to ask. "We'll have to talk, but I don't want to now."

Emptiness in his eyes predicted her worst fears had come true. She'd managed to push him away from her. She didn't want the details. She hugged her baby as close as she could get her. "You'll want to tie the cord when it stops pulsing." She caught his hand. "And could you call the nurse back? We can wait for Gran now, and I'd rather someone stayed on duty at the baby farm."

"Relax," he said. "I'll take care of everything."

She had a feeling he said it to prove a point, but he looked at their daughter with such love, Sophie didn't care what else he might be thinking.

GRETA STILL HADN'T shown up by the time Ian had Sophie and the baby clean enough for company. On the one hand, he'd just as soon she lost her way. He wanted his family to himself, maybe for the first and last time ever.

Yet, no matter how normally Sophie kept assuring him everything had gone, he needed Greta to second her opinion. Funny, but he'd realized how deeply he loved his wife at almost the exact moment he realized that she liked control better than a husband, that she trusted herself and her decisions more than she trusted the future they'd promised each other.

Impatient with her and with himself, Ian had enough of sitting on the edge of the bed. If this was the last night he'd lie with Sophie, he'd have these hours.

Without asking what she thought, he curved himself around her and the baby, soaking up the sweet aroma of his wife's hair, the tender softness of his child's skin. He slid his hand beneath Sophie's on the baby's backside.

"We never thought of names," Sophie said.

"I liked Stephen."

"I like Chloe."

He scrutinized their baby's face, falling in love. "It suits her."

"If only everything between us was that easy. Ian, you're not going anywhere, are you?"

At the naked plea in her eyes, he was tempted to resign himself to what she could give. Not much.

"Not tonight," he said.

"But?"

"I can't pretend I don't care." He cared more. He couldn't live with her, love her and be her puppet. "I want the promises we both made. I was serious, and I thought you were, too." He laughed, totally unamused. "You got yourself the perfect revenge for that wedding mistake I made."

"I didn't want revenge."

"Shh." He kissed her hair on the pretext of quieting her. His body ached with loss already. "Greta and Seth will be here soon."

"I wish tonight could just go on."

It couldn't. It wouldn't be enough, though it had brought him almost everything he wanted most. He leaned over Sophie to kiss his daughter, now clearly rooting for her mother's breast. He admired Chloe's demanding blue eyes. No Calvert green for his girl.

CHAPTER FIFTEEN

SOPHIE AND CHLOE SPENT a night in the hospital to make sure both were okay. The next morning, Sophie'd lost all sense of dignity and begged Ian not to leave her, but he moved down to Aunt Eliza's B and B the day she and Chloe came home from the hospital. He needed distance. If he was acting out his own vendetta this time, it worked. A dad should help bring his child home, and the house felt empty without him.

"This place sure is quiet," Gran said as Ethan carried in their things. "I'm used to seeing half the family over here."

Inside, Sophie also saw empty spaces where Ian always dropped his keys on the console table behind the couch, on the mantel where he left whatever book he was reading. He often abandoned a coffee cup in the living room.

"I still can't believe Ian didn't want to see Chloe home on her first day." Surprised disapproval colored Ethan's tone.

Sophie stiffened. Ian most likely had wanted to be with Chloe. She was the one who'd put him off. "I don't know how anyone could have seen her home on her first day more than he did." Though she felt guilty for not even understanding how much trust and commitment she'd withheld from him, temper made her gripe. "Although I thought family mattered to him."

"It must, or he would have gone…" Greta straightened in the middle of pounding a sofa cushion into the exact configuration she judged most comfortable. "Where does he live?"

"Here." She knew Gran meant where had he lived before, but his place was here now. They could have worked on being together. He'd made changes. She was no less mature. But maybe he didn't want her to change. Maybe he also only gave a person one chance to tell an extended hurtful lie. He didn't even trust her to change, and she couldn't blame him. She'd been the same.

She couldn't help being terrified that the people she loved best would desert her. And in the end, he had.

She had to be honest—she'd given him a shove. But if she had it to do over again, she'd sign the first thirty-year mortgage she could find on the dotted line. If that was what it took to make him happy.

Only that wasn't right, either, to keep on pretending she really felt the kind of trust that had always eluded her, just to make him happy.

As her dad came down the stairs, Sophie worked her way onto the cushions Greta had pummeled.

Chloe stretched and moaned in her sleep, but settled into Sophie's arms. "I half expected to find Mom here when we drove up, Dad."

He scooped a brass pineapple off the mantel and began to fiddle with it. "I'd like to talk to you about Nita." He glanced at Greta. "Alone for a minute, Mother?"

"Oh." She seemed surprised.

"Mother," Ethan said again when she didn't move.

She stirred. "I'll make lunch."

"What's wrong, Dad?" Sophie made room for him beside her.

"About your mom—you know I've spent a lot of time here with her and Ian while you were working."

"She was only here for two weeks." Dread filled Sophie's mouth with a bitter taste.

"You don't want us to get along?"

"I don't want you to get hurt." Didn't he remember what had ended their marriage?

"I know her now. She knows me. She wants to make up for how she was with you. And with me."

"How do you know? I mean, she was polite to Ian's parents even though they don't seem to know what they want with him, and she tried to be a mom to me, but she's still got those empty spots in her character where normal maternal instincts are supposed to be."

"Knowing that, neither of us can get hurt again," her dad said. His earnest look softened Sophie's heart. "She did try to fill in for Ian's parents, and she thinks she and I can try to make him feel as if he has parents of his own, until they see what a good son they have."

"I should have known why she's been calling so often since she went back," Sophie said. "And why she's been so careful." Nita had said nothing hurtful in any of those phone calls.

"She wanted to be here when you came home. She's on the level, Sophie."

"For now."

"So put her on probation."

She felt queasy as she snaked a hand from beneath Chloe to clutch her dad's arm. "Are you going to marry her again?"

He bumped his head against the back of the couch. "I'm seeing how I feel about her."

"Oh." That relieved her mind a little. "I could do that, too. Now that I have Chloe... I mean, I won't let Mom hurt her, but I'd like them to know each other—I think."

He leaned forward, eyeing her carefully. "Then I can invite her back down here to see the baby?"

"Okay—but she stays here. Not with you."

He laughed so loudly Chloe jumped. "Are you insane, little girl? She and I will decide that for ourselves."

"I just don't want you confused." And even she could see the charm in her mother's perfect grooming. To a man who'd never dated anyone since the day he'd told his wife she had to leave. "Have you missed her, Dad?"

"More since you came home." He looked embarrassed. "I asked you to work with Ian on being married, but maybe watching you two, your mother and I have discovered we should have tried to fix our problems rather than pruning them out of our lives."

"Okay, Dad. You want to call her now?" She pointed at the phone.

"No." He kissed first Chloe and then Sophie. "I'll call from home. I need to get back and put the last coat of wax on my granddaughter's crib. Can I bring it by tomorrow?"

"Whenever you like." She reached for him and kissed his cheek again. "You're a smart guy."

"I don't know. You and Ian aren't working together now." He peered toward the kitchen. "You got everything, Mom?"

"I'm not happy about it," she said without appearing, "but I heard."

"Good—I won't have to fill in the rest of the family." He chucked Chloe's chin with exquisite tenderness. "You might consider, Sophie, how this baby will like growing up without her father if you don't straighten out your own mess."

"Thanks, Dad." She could hardly force Ian to come home.

"But mind my own business? I probably won't." He leaned around the kitchen door. "See you later, Mother."

Sophie couldn't make out Gran's answer, but it made Ethan laugh again. He paused for one more kiss on Sophie's temple.

"You did a great job with Chloe. She's the best treat this family's had in years."

"You'll be saying that again when Olivia's baby comes."

"I think I'm going to stay partial to our girl. I'll bring the crib in the morning."

As soon as the door shut behind him, Gran strode into the room. "I guess we may have to get used to Nita being around here again."

Sophie nodded, still uncertain about dealing with her mother, but positive family mattered more to her than ever. "And where's Grandpa? Why didn't he come with you today?"

"He says we'll end up talking work, so he didn't consider coming was worth his while."

Sophie grimaced. "Not worth his while?"

"He's annoyed with me again." Greta bent over the bag that held Sophie and Chloe's clothing from the hospital. "Let me wash these for you." She looked up when Sophie didn't speak. "I may have worked a few extra hours last night."

Impatiently Sophie stared at her grandmother. "Why? You didn't need to. That place runs fine without us at night."

"I'm trying to do what your grandfather wants, but you all have to give me room. We had a new teenager check in, and she needed extra attention.

Plus, a patron who's visited through each of her four pregnancies joined me for dinner. I had to look over her kids' pictures. I have a stake in those boys of hers, and she's still trying for a girl." Greta started to the laundry room with her handful of clothing but turned back. "Honey, do you plan to sleep down here? I can make the couch into a bed for you."

Sophie was tempted, reluctant to sleep alone in the bed she'd shared with Ian. But she'd have to get used to it sometime. "We'll go up later. I've been in bed for over twenty-four hours." Sitting wasn't entirely comfortable, but it made a nice change. "Gran, you did promise Grandpa. I know I shouldn't be one to talk, but don't throw him away."

"I've planned a special dinner for us tonight, and I promise to grovel, and I'll leave half an hour early every day for the rest of the week."

Sophie didn't answer and she didn't believe.

"I promise." Gran held the clothing to her chest. "Are you thirsty? You need to keep your liquids up while you're nursing."

"I'm fine."

"Well, lunch will be ready soon. I expect you to eat it." She disappeared, and Sophie swung her legs up on the couch, tucking Chloe into the crook of her elbow.

What a strange day—her parents trying to get back together, her gran and grandpa still arguing, and she'd managed to alienate her own husband. She brushed Chloe's stand-on-end hair down a bit.

Sweet little girl. Didn't even know her daddy had deserted them.

Sophie lifted her head, staring through the windows at the cloudy late-summer sky. Ian wouldn't stay in Bardill's Ridge.

Her dad had been right. If she and Ian didn't do something, Chloe faced a two-home childhood, commuting between here and wherever Ian happened to land. It wouldn't be much fun. Sophie had loathed choosing between parents when she had extra time off from school, feeling as guilty for her choices as her parents had felt for making her pick.

Gran returned, sporting a glass of ice water. "You should drink whenever you have a quiet moment."

"Thanks."

"I'll be just a few minutes with lunch."

"You don't have to finish it." Sophie stared after the woman who'd been her mentor, the woman who simply couldn't sit still. "Why don't you go start that surprise dinner for Grandpa?"

"I will. We have plenty of time."

It was like looking in a mirror that showed only truth. "You're fooling yourself." Sophie nearly bit her own tongue in shock. Hadn't Ian accused her of the same thing? And he'd been right. Gran had been her mentor in good things like work ethic and caring for people and love of family, but she'd also mentored her in taking what she wanted from a relationship and still maintaining a prudent distance.

"I was pretending I had a handle on retiring before, but your grandfather and I've faced our troubles." A touch of acid sharpened Gran's tone. "We've negotiated a work schedule for me that I'm trying to stick to, and your grandfather will understand my occasional backslide."

Sophie straightened. A man shouldn't have to accept a return to such bad habits. "Gran?"

"Hmm?"

"Can you help me up?" She could probably manage if she put Chloe down, but suddenly she wanted to ask for help. She had to fix the problems she'd made before it was too late.

Gran swept into the room. "Are you all right?"

"Fine, but I suggest you go home and explain you love Grandpa more than your job, more than anything else that matters to you. And while you're at it, tell him you'll only work at the baby farm three days a week."

"Huh?" Too shocked even to complain about the "baby farm," Gran helped Sophie stand, but she also brushed the back of her hand over Sophie's forehead, briskly checking for a temperature.

"*Now,* Gran, because maybe we don't get that many second chances, and I'm thinking you must be on way more than your fair share of chances with Grandpa."

"I have a good marriage."

Sophie shuddered. She possessed that same kind of arrogance. "I can't force you, but except for the work part, that's exactly what I'm saying to Ian.

What the hell do I care if I'm safe if I'm also alone? If I've forced Chloe's father out of her life because I'm afraid he'll leave me? I made him leave and he didn't even want to.''

"Ian doesn't want to leave. He's clearly miserable.''

Sophie eased out of her grandmother's hands. ''So is Grandpa. I'm learning my lesson now, Gran. Imagine how much more it would hurt to assume you weren't your husband's priority for fifty-five years.''

''Seth is my priority. I told you, we've sorted out our problems.''

''And he'll wait for you to get around to him? Okay.'' Sophie reached for the diaper bag with her free hand. ''Will you drive me to Aunt Eliza's?''

''Sure.''

Though they were intelligent women, they both had to refer to the instructions the hospital had given them for seating Chloe securely in her car seat. They didn't talk as they drove through sprinkling rain. Sophie blankly sought words that would convince Ian. Gran seemed intent on deterring all further offers of advice. In the back, Chloe slept on, possibly even comforted by the constant bumping over rutted roads.

As they passed the square, Sophie suspected she might be hyperventilating. She covered her mouth and forced herself to count respirations.

''Want me to look after Chloe for you?'' Greta offered.

"No, thanks. I'm low enough to use her against him."

"You aren't going to have to use anything. If you love your husband and you want to be with him, Ian will stay. He loves you, too."

Sophie stared at her confident grandmother, who'd proved fallible today for the first time in Sophie's life. "I hope you're right."

After they parked, Sophie took Chloe, and Gran waved her toward the B and B. "Go ahead. I'll wait, just in case."

"No, I don't want you to wait. But if you can get that seat out, you could bring it in. Ian's going to have to drive us home and then walk out if he wants to leave us." She'd suddenly found her fight.

AUNT ELIZA LOOKED UP from the desk, sweeping salt-and-pepper hair off her surprised face. "Sophie, I was planning to bring you some dinner tonight."

"Thanks, Aunt Eliza, but I've come to settle my marriage."

"Good idea. I thought about refusing the man accommodation so he'd have to go home and talk some sense into you, but he's in room four."

"How'd you know I was the one who needed sense talked into me?"

"I love you, dear, but I know you run to keep someone from running out on you first, and Ian came all the way down here for you. If he wasn't serious, he would have accepted your decision to leave him then.''

''I should have talked to you a long time ago.''

''You've never taken advice until you want to hear it. Look at the decisions you already made without our input. You got pregnant and married without thinking you needed family.''

''That's not entirely true, but I'll explain later.''

''Shall I watch Chloe for you?''

''No, thanks.'' Balancing Chloe in her arms, Sophie climbed the stairs and wished her aunt and uncle would install an elevator for women who'd given birth within the past forty-eight hours. She walked to the door to room four, and pounded on the wooden panels.

Ian opened it and then backed up. ''I thought you were a pizza.''

''It's hardly past noon and you're ordering a pizza?'' She walked past him without waiting to be invited. ''Lucky for me, I guess, or you might not have opened the door.''

''I would have opened the door. What's wrong?'' He peered over her shoulder at their daughter sleeping on her shoulder. ''She's all right.''

''You want to hold her?''

He took Chloe in his arms. She looked incredibly small against his black T-shirt. Sophie dropped the diaper bag on the floor and eased into the nearest armchair.

''Can we talk, Ian?''

"What's the point?" he asked with eyes only for their baby.

"We're a family."

He looked up. "That's not good enough."

She flinched, but the time had come to stop being a coward. "I love you."

He might not have heard. It certainly didn't seem to count. He sat on the bed, cradling Chloe, but his expression didn't change at all.

"I want you in my home, in my bed, in my daughter's life. I want to consult you before I make dinner." She was babbling as she forced herself back to her feet. "I want to consult you before we decide where Chloe will go to school."

"She'll only have one choice down here."

Sophie saw an opening and rushed through. "I'll go wherever you want to go."

Ian shook his head, his expression carefully bland. "I don't believe you. What makes this time different?"

"You matter to me." She pushed between his knees, curving her hand against Chloe's cheek. "More than anyone else. I love you."

"So I should take a chance on you?"

"Yes." She pressed her other palm to his cheek and he lifted his head. "Because you love me."

"Do I? Or did we marry because of Chloe?"

"I don't care why we got married. What happens from today is what matters to me."

He frowned. "The past few months mean quite a bit to me."

"I should have noticed I was balancing between annoyance and panic, but I didn't see it until I was in labor and I had to depend on you." She grimaced as pain flitted through his eyes. "I would have felt the same if I had to trust anyone with my life, but no one else would have mattered the way you do. I don't want to hurt you."

"And I don't want you to stay married to me because you're a kind woman."

"I'm not all that kind lately."

Finally, the corners of his mouth twitched. "I noticed."

She caressed his cheek again, loving the familiar stubble. "I do love you. I don't like seeing the empty places in my life where you're supposed to be."

"That's pretty talk, but it doesn't convince me."

Her heart began to thud. "I don't want to lose you."

"I'm not sure we ever had each other, Sophie."

"You had me. That's why I was so afraid." She felt undressed. "Remember when you said I'd never be happy until I trusted someone not to leave me?"

"I did trust you." He looked down at Chloe again. "And I do love you. That's why pretending isn't good enough anymore." He faced her, acceptance in his eyes. "And I'd rather bounce off another speeding car than admit any of this."

She believed him. "I'm not pretending, but I guess

you have to decide to trust me.'' She sat beside him.
''Or not.'' Bracing one hand on his thigh, she leaned
across him to look at Chloe. ''I'll tell you this—when
you said you couldn't stay after she was born, I knew
I wanted you to. Picture me leaving, and tell me how
you feel.''

''What really changed your mind, Sophie?''

She didn't think he'd be surprised. ''I talked to
Gran.''

He laughed, and Chloe jumped, but he hugged her
closer, as natural with her as if he'd had daughters
all his life. ''Greta's a bad influence on you.''

''Just in this one aspect.'' She felt alone, holding onto him while he held their daughter so close
she might be part of his body, instead of Sophie's
after all this time. ''I'm worried about Gran and
Grandpa.''

''So am I.''

''But I didn't want to repeat her mistakes, so I told
her she should go home and beg him to forgive her,
after she brought me to you so I could do the same.''

''You're begging?''

She loved his smiling face so much she wanted to
kiss him. She prayed she wasn't too late. That he
wouldn't be content to make a friendship out of the
marriage she'd taken for granted. ''I would beg if it
would change your mind.''

''I don't want you to beg. I just want you to believe in me the way I believed in you.''

"I do." She twisted her hands together. "You delivered our baby. You stuck by me."

"I wanted to run."

"I meant you stuck by me when I made impossible demands on you." She hoped her quiet tone expressed an apology, but then she smiled. "Any sane human being who's never delivered a baby wants to run when he's the only nontrained medical help available."

"What about my job, Sophie?"

The old panic punched her right in the stomach, but she was smart enough to learn from her mistakes. Eventually. "You know how I feel, but I'll stand by your decision."

He clearly doubted her sincerity.

"I didn't pass the test?" She didn't know how else to prove she could share the reins in their marriage.

He hesitated, but then Chloe made a noise that drew both their gazes. Sophie was already going through her mental checklist—diaper, sustenance, rattly toys that Chloe didn't even seem to notice yet.

"I don't think either of us has room to pass or fail the other on any test." Ian smoothed Chloe's forehead as she settled down again. "But you knew it was a test, and you didn't argue."

Hope flickered, but she understood his attachment to their child already, and Chloe had distracted them just in time to add her input to the argument. "I don't want you to stay because of the baby. And I can't promise I'll always be able to keep my mouth shut if you feel like testing me.''

"I love you, Sophie. I guess I've learned most of your weaknesses.''

Tears filled her eyes and the back of her throat. "Unconditional love. It's my favorite kind.''

He laughed, but gently, to avoid disturbing Chloe. "Kiss me and convince me you mean it.''

An easy test this time. She took his mouth with the possessiveness of a wife who loved deeply and knew she was loved in return. When she retreated, shaking, Ian cupped the back of her head and kissed her again, a sweet sampling of her lips.

"It is different.'' Wonder filled her husband's voice.

She laughed, putting her arms around both him and Chloe. "That's because we don't have anything left between us except our baby girl.''

EPILOGUE

AT A MONTH OLD, Chloe had stopped almost sleeping around the clock. She awoke from her nap with a yelp and Sophie scooted from behind the kitchen table where she and Gran were sorting résumés.

"I'll get her," Nita called, ensconced with a book in front of the blaring television.

"Got her." Ian had been going over blueprints with Ethan and Seth in the far corner of the living room. He and Sophie were building a home of their own.

He bounded up the stairs, and Ethan and Seth brought the blueprints to the kitchen counter where they poured mugs of the coffee Ian always had brewing.

"Have you found OBs you could share the baby farm with?" Grandpa asked.

"I like several." Sophie pushed her stack toward Gran. "What do you think?"

"I'll arrange interviews." She faced her husband. "But this is my legacy we're talking about. I know Sophie wants more time with Chloe, but I have to be sure…"

"Greta." Grandpa only said her name, but it came out as a warning, and she gave in.

"I'll interview them."

"And you won't mark the best off your list beforehand?"

Gran looked frustrated. "Sophie wouldn't let me."

"You got that right." Sophie's priorities hadn't wavered since the day Ian had come home again.

"Look, honey, what do you think of Ian's office?" Sophie's dad pushed the blueprint in front of her, pointing with a finger whose nail had recently had a too-close encounter with a piece of sandpaper.

"Across the hall from the nursery? He'll never get any peace."

"That's the point," Ian said from the kitchen door, holding Chloe, who gnawed on his pinkie as she searched for her food source. "I get to spend more time at home with Chloe than you do, but I still have to work. All the better if she has her stuff close at hand while I'm in my office."

"What about when she's sleeping?"

He shook his head. "I want her close. She'll probably evict me to the basement when she's a teenager." He jolted forward as Nita eased him through the doorway so she could join them, looping her arm though Ethan's. Her ex-husband smiled.

Sophie tried for a look that didn't scream her anxiety for her father—even as she longed to believe her parents could truly love each other. Everyone else spoke at once about nothing in particular, all trying to pretend it was easy to trust Nita again.

"I think our child will be used to sleeping through a lot of noise," Ian said.

"He's talking about our family." Nita gazed into Ethan's eyes with real affection.

Sophie nearly choked.

"I like all your racket," Ian said. "I always wanted a big, noisy family. You're a dream come true." At a collective "Awww," he added, "for my daughter."

The Calverts present laughed at him, but he didn't seem to care. He passed the baby to Sophie, and Chloe shrieked with delight, already opening her mouth like a little fish. Sophie reached for the hem of her shirt, but then stopped to eye her family.

"I could use a little privacy."

The others headed for the door, and Ian made his way between them to join her. Sophie beamed at him. She loved the quiet times they shared, talking together while Sophie nursed. They had so much to say these days, with no secrets dividing them. He took the chair next to her and pulled her against his side where all the warmth in the world surrounded her.

Ethan turned back at the door. "That 'dream come true' crack, Ian."

They both looked up.

Ethan laughed. "I've always admired your gumption, son."

Ian kissed the top of Sophie's head. "I needed gumption to take this wife."

Sophie decided to let him get away with that. She loved him after all.

Koomera Crossing

Welcome to Koomera Crossing,
a town hidden deep in the Australian Outback.
Let renowned romance novelist Margaret Way
take you there. Let her introduce you to
the people of Koomera Crossing.
Let her tell you their secrets....

Watch for

Home to Eden,

available from Harlequin Superromance
in February 2004.

And don't miss the other Koomera Crossing books:

Sarah's Baby
(Harlequin Superromance #1111, February 2003)

Runaway Wife
(Harlequin Romance, October 2003)

Outback Bridegroom
(Harlequin Romance, November 2003)

Outback Surrender
(Harlequin Romance, December 2003)

Visit us at www.eHarlequin.com

HSRKOOM

If you enjoyed what you just read,
then we've got an offer you can't resist!

Take 2 bestselling
love stories FREE!
Plus get a FREE surprise gift!

Clip this page and mail it to Harlequin Reader Service®

IN U.S.A.	IN CANADA
3010 Walden Ave.	P.O. Box 609
P.O. Box 1867	Fort Erie, Ontario
Buffalo, N.Y. 14240-1867	L2A 5X3

YES! Please send me 2 free Harlequin Superromance® novels and my free surprise gift. After receiving them, if I don't wish to receive anymore, I can return the shipping statement marked cancel. If I don't cancel, I will receive 6 brand-new novels every month, before they're available in stores. In the U.S.A., bill me at the bargain price of $4.47 plus 25¢ shipping and handling per book and applicable sales tax, if any*. In Canada, bill me at the bargain price of $4.99 plus 25¢ shipping and handling per book and applicable taxes**. That's the complete price, and a savings of at least 10% off the cover prices—what a great deal! I understand that accepting the 2 free books and gift places me under no obligation ever to buy any books. I can always return a shipment and cancel at any time. Even if I never buy another book from Harlequin, the 2 free books and gift are mine to keep forever.

135 HDN DNT3
336 HDN DNT4

Name	(PLEASE PRINT)	
Address	Apt.#	
City	State/Prov.	Zip/Postal Code

* Terms and prices subject to change without notice. Sales tax applicable in N.Y.
** Canadian residents will be charged applicable provincial taxes and GST.
  All orders subject to approval. Offer limited to one per household and not valid to current Harlequin Superromance® subscribers.
  ® is a registered trademark of Harlequin Enterprises Limited.

SUP02   ©1998 Harlequin Enterprises Limited

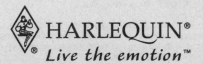

COMING NEXT MONTH

#1170 LEAVING ENCHANTMENT • C.J. Carmichael
The Birth Place
Nolan McKinnon is shocked when he's named his niece's guardian. He knows nothing about taking care of a little girl—especially an orphan—but he still would've bet he knew more than Kim Sherman. Kim's a newcomer to Enchantment—one who seems determined not to get involved with anyone. But Nolan can't refuse help, even if it comes from a woman with secrets in her past....

#1171 FOR THE CHILDREN • Tara Taylor Quinn
Twins
Valerie Simms is a juvenile court judge who spends her days helping troubled kids—including her own fatherless twin boys. Through her sons she meets Kirk Chandler, a man who's given up a successful corporate career and dedicated himself to helping the children in his Phoenix community. Valerie and Kirk not only share a commitment to protecting children, they share a deep attraction—and a personal connection that shocks them both.

#1172 MAN IN A MILLION • Muriel Jensen
Men of Maple Hill
Paris O'Hara is determined to avoid the efforts of the town's matchmakers. She's got more important things to worry about—like who her father really is. But paramedic Randy Sandford is determined to show her that the past is not nearly as important as the future.

#1173 THE ROAD TO ECHO POINT • Carrie Weaver
Vi Davis has places to go, people to meet and things to do—and the most important thing of all is getting a promotion. So she's not pleased when a little accident forces her to take time out of her schedule to care for an elderly stranger. She never would have guessed that staying with Daisy Smith and meeting her gorgeous son, Ian, is *exactly* the thing to do.

A great new story from a brand-new author!

#1174 A WOMAN LIKE ANNIE • Inglath Cooper
Hometown U.S.A.
Mayor Annie McCabe cherishes Macon's Point, the town that's become home to her and her son, and she's ready to fight to save it. And that means convincing Jack Corbin to keep Corbin Manufacturing, the town's main employer, in business. Will she be able to make Jack see the true value of his hometown...and its mayor?

#1175 THE FULL STORY • Dawn Stewardson
Risk Control International
Keep Your Client Alive is the mandate of Risk Control International. And RCI operative Dan O'Neill takes his job very seriously. Unfortunately, keeping his foolhardy client safe is a real challenge. And the last thing Dan needs is the distraction of a very attractive—and very nosy—reporter named Micky Westover.